*To Kim —
God bless you!*

GAELA'S GARDENS

☙ ☙ ☙

by
Debbonnaire Kovacs

Debbonnaire

GAELA'S GARDENS
Copyright 2012 by
Debbonnaire Kovacs
Cover Art copyright 2012 by
Debbonnaire Kovacs

All rights reserved, including the right to reproduce this book or portions thereof in any form or by any means, electronic or mechanical, including photocopying, recording, or by any information storage and retrieval system, without permission in writing from the author. All inquiries should be addressed to debbonnaire@debbonnaire.com

This book is a work of fiction. Names, characters, locations, and incidents are products of the author's imagination. Any resemblance to actual events or places or persons, living or dead, is coincidental.

Please visit my website at www.debbonnaire.com
Follow me on Facebook and Twitter @debbonnaire
LinkedIn @Debbonnaire Kovacs

Printed in the USA
ISBN-13: 978-1480123755
ISBN-10: 1480123757

It was worse than she'd thought.. . .

Gaela found Caine down by the lake throwing rocks into the muddy water.

"You were wrong," he said. "It matters what you've done."

"I never said it didn't matter what you'd done."

" 'I don't care what you've done.' That's what you said."

"I said there is forgiveness and healing, no matter what you've done. It certainly *matters* what you've done, both to yourself and to other people."

"For murder?"

He said it so baldly that for a second she didn't get it. Then a chill started in her belly and spread. "Yes."

He gave a scornful laugh and turned away to pick up another stone. "You little saints. That's what you're taught to say. Everybody's all forgiven, and everything's all daisies, *no matter what*. It's hogwash." He threw a stone so hard she thought he was trying to hit the other side of the lake. *Oh, God, what do I say now?*

Thank you!

Every word of this book passed through the eagle eyes and diverse brains of the Killbuck Valley Writers' Guild. Thanks so much, guys! I couldn't have done it without you! And thanks to my brother, author Levi Montgomery, for holding my hand through the publishing process.

The legal matters later in the book benefitted from the expertise of attorney Garrett Roach. And you should know, dear reader, it would have been worse without him! He said, "You can have this and this happen. Or you can have this and *this* happen. You can't have this and this *and this* happen!" And he made sure it wasn't too far outside the realm of legality as well as probability.

Thanks always to:

my grandmother, who told me stories,

my mother, who helped me learn to tell stories,

my brothers and sisters and later my children, who listened to my stories,

and my beloved husband, who created a safe space, not just for stories but for all of life. I love you all.

And most of all, thank you to God and my gardens, for keeping me well-watered and thriving throughout the cycle of seasons.

"The Lord will guide you continually, watering your life when you are dry and keeping you healthy, too. You will be like a well-watered garden, like an ever-flowing spring." Isaiah 58:11, NLT

*This book is dedicated to
the beloved memory of
my mother, Corienne Hay,
and my husband,
my Gypsy Prince Zoltan,
Leslie Kovacs*

*I cannot possibly express
my gratitude and my grief.
See you in The Garden,
one of these days.*

Chapter One

Gaela Clancy was transplanting flowering crabapple slips when she saw the man. He was just standing there, staring at her. Her heart gave an erratic thump and she looked quickly back down at her work.

As head caretaker at a public garden estate, Gaela was certainly used to being watched at her work. But it was still early in the year, and there weren't many visitors to Eden's Gate yet. She told herself that was why he had startled her. It was just the unexpectedness of it.

Ragged, dirty clothes didn't necessarily mean he was an evil person, for pete's sake. Maybe he was poor. And lots of guys had long, dark hair and beards. Resolutely shutting out the memory that stuttered through her pulses, Gaela gritted her teeth and concentrated on smoothing the mulch just so. She was reacting ridiculously. He was just a guy. He liked to watch her work. People always liked to watch you work. Methodically, she planted three more baby trees, breathing in the comforting smells of damp earth and compost. Maybe he was gone now.

When she looked at the stranger again, he looked away too quickly, gazing out over the lake as if he were meditating on its quiet beauty. She looked at it herself, sparkling and dimpling in the sunshine. Cheery drifts of gold and lavender crocus spread a quilt of color under an early flowering cherry and dappled the stretch of greening lawn that led down to the shore. But when she looked back at the man for a second, she somehow knew he wasn't even seeing the landscape.

Gaela turned determinedly to the last transplant. The sooner she finished here, the sooner she could move on to another chore, farther away from the unnerving stranger.

଼ଷ ଼ଷ ଼ଷ

Brown. Curly brown hair, matching golden-brown skin, even a well-worn brown coverall. It was enough to make a man believe in pixies again. Watching as the young woman deftly transferred dead-looking sticks from a plastic bucket of water into rich black soil, Caine wished he dared move closer to see if her eyes were brown, too. Her strong, tanned hands caressed each twig as if it were her child, spreading its roots carefully in a hole she dug with a trowel, then holding it upright with one hand while refilling the hole with the other. She pressed down the dirt and snuggled blankets of mulch around each tall bare twig. For one shaken instant, the gesture transplanted Caine back to his own barely remembered babyhood. He turned away abruptly, shaking his head to dislodge the sharp hook of unwanted memory. The lake drew his eye, but didn't calm him. A stiff March breeze whipped up a froth of waves, just like the constant churning in his gut. A scattering of water birds flew up from the water, shrieking noisily, as if he spooked them just by watching.

He looked back at the woman. Her eyes slid toward him, and Caine realized he'd spooked her, too. Story of his life. Scaring innocent women just by existing. He ought to go away and leave her alone. He would. In a minute.

Shifting his feet, Caine looked toward at the lake, doing his best to appear ordinary and nonthreatening. The sign in town--a new sign since he had been here last, though he had to admit that had been years ago--proclaimed that "the fifty-seven acres of Eden's Gate offer beauty for the eye, and peace for the weary soul." On a whim, and not without a sneer for the name, he had taken them up on their offer, but he hadn't found any peace yet.

Truth be told, there wasn't much "beauty for the eye" to be had in March, either, even though this winter had been short and mild. He had seen patches of shivering crocus, clumps of green blades knifing through the smothering dirt and leaves, and a few white-blossomed trees with birds already squabbling in them. Everything else was pretty much still winter-dead. Like himself. He kicked a stone in the graveled path. How long could winter's claws keep their grip? How many more years? He might as well leave.

As he turned away from the uneasy heaving of the lake, a movement caught his eye and he looked toward the young gardener again. She was standing, bending this way and that to stretch her back, then bending to pick up her tools. Her hair, a cloud of short, loose curls, caught gleams of gold from the sun. Caine watched her, mesmerized by her grace and tiny size. Even from this distance, he could guess that she wouldn't reach his shoulder. Maybe she really was a pixie. The woman lifted her bucket and tools to a wheeled cart, then walked quickly away, pushing the cart.

An irrational spurt of panic threatened to rouse the old, never-quite-banished sense of abandonment. Keeping her in sight, Caine followed the young woman to another bed, where she took a rake and began scraping dead leaves out of the edges of some shrubbery. Stopping at a safe distance, he watched. He had been wrong. One thing here brought him a measure of peace. Watching the garden pixie. He wouldn't speak to her. He would just watch. Why should that frighten her? He leaned against a tree, trying for a nonchalant pose. If she looked at him again, he would gaze calmly out on the landscape. It was a public garden, after all.

ଔ   ଔ   ଔ

Gaela concentrated assiduously on raking old oak leaves out from under the dwarf spreading yew. She would not look behind her like some nervous heroine of a cheap TV thriller. Of course that guy hadn't followed her. He wasn't a stalker, he was just a garden visitor. She carefully gathered the last of the leaves and scooped them into a large back plastic bag. They would go to the compost bins hidden decorously behind the largest garden sheds. Maybe she would go and take them there right now, although she had intended to fork this bed over, in preparation for the johnny-jump-ups she meant to put in it. Blowing her tangled hair out of her eyes and peering sideways at him, she saw the man. He *had* followed her. He was still watching her intently.

Gaela looked at her hands. They were starting to shake. Stupid! It had been years since a man had spooked her like this. She'd thought she was over it. She pushed at her hair again and tried to distract herself with the thought that it needed cut. It was too curly to allow it to get past collar length. She ought to make an appointment . . . the distraction wasn't working. Escape was her only option. But she couldn't let it look like escape.

Hanging the bag of leaves from the hook at the end of her cart, Gaela marched matter-of-factly in the direction of the sheds. After she had gone a short distance, she looked to her left as if checking out the budding dogwoods along the edge of the woods and peeked behind her again. He was following her! Gaela picked up her pace, fighting not to break into a run. Anger warred with the old fear she had sworn never to feel again. Eden was her sanctuary. For six years she had felt completely safe and at home here. Now she was longing to sprint for the big house and lock herself in.

Gaela stopped suddenly. Deliberately she stoked the anger and ignored the fear. These were *her* gardens. They belonged to her much more fully than to their legal owners, who seldom even came home anymore. She was an adult, not a terrified fourteen-year-old, and nobody was going to make her frightened or ashamed ever again. Lifting her chin and squaring her shoulders, she transferred her death grip from the cart to the handle of a sturdy shovel, turned around, and opened her mouth to challenge her pursuer.

Mouth still open, she looked around. He was gone.

"There now, see how stupid that was?" she chided herself, not quite out loud, but in a defiant whisper. "You got all upset over -" Gaela let out a yelp as heavy footsteps ran up behind her. She whirled, trying to wrestle the shovel from its rack, but only succeeding in nearly knocking down a whole tray of hand tools.

"Whoa! Hey, what's the matter, chief?" Ted Waite, one of her assistant gardeners, grabbed the cart, which was in imminent danger of tipping, and pushed the tool tray back into place.

Gaela clutched at her chest, feeling her heart race painfully. "Oh, Ted! Oh, my word!" she gulped breathlessly. Ted, just Ted, she told herself. Blond, clean-cut, football-star-looking Ted. No beard, no long hair, no dirty... well, dirty... but then so was she... *Stop it!* "You scared me to death!" she accused.

"So I see!" Ted's gaze took in her white knuckles, still clamped around the shovel. "I'm sorry. Didn't you hear me coming?" His blue eyes moved to her face and narrowed in concern.

Reining in her galloping nerves, Gaela tried for a laugh. "No--yes--I guess I did, actually, but you know me--just daydreaming!"

All she needed was for Ted to go all over-protective on her again. He was always nagging her to keep her cell phone on, and of course she would, later when the busy season was upon them and the crew needed to be in constant contact. But during the slower seasons, Gaela relished her solitude. Angry all over again at the strange man who had broken the peace of that solitude, she irrationally found herself turning that anger on Ted. Why did men either have to menace her or spend their time trying to take care of her? Not for the first time, she wished she were six or eight inches taller.

She let go of the shovel, hoping he didn't see the difficulty she had with that simple action, and grabbed the cart handles again, but Ted's large hand easily prevented any forward movement. "What happened, Gaela?"

"Come on, Ted, I was just taking this stuff to the compost bins."

"Something terrified you, Gaela. You want to tell me what's going on?"

Did she *want* to tell him she had been scared out of her mind by a passerby who stopped to watch her work, as did every other visitor to the estate? Did she then want to explain *why* she was terrified because a black-haired man's path happened to take the same direction as hers for a hundred yards? Not in this lifetime!

"Nothing happened, and you aren't my daddy, Ted." Gaela hoped she sounded sufficiently quelling. Gathering up her most straightforward expression, the one she hoped would cover any remaining trace of nerves, not to mention any deceit, she gazed innocently into his narrowed eyes. "I was somewhere out in la-la land, and you startled me. Sorry to make such a production of it. If I need a bodyguard, I'll be sure to give you first consideration. However, what I need is a gardener. Did you finish tilling that new bed by the drive?"

Ted stared at her a minute longer, then sighed and let go of the cart. "Sorry, chief, ma'am, I guess I got carried away again. I actually came to ask you something. I wish you kept that cell phone on!"

"All right, all right, I'll try to remember. What did you want to ask me?"

Ted rubbed his head. "I have no idea. You knocked it straight out of my brain. Are you sure you're all ri—" Her eyes must have flashed visibly, because he did an about-face in mid-sentence. "No, fine, never mind. What did I—oh, yeah, I did finish that bed, and I had an idea that we could extend it in a curve along the bend up to the first rhododendrons. Come and see, and let me know what you think. There's still gas in the tiller, and the day's young."

He grinned, and Gaela smiled back, relieved. "Sure, just let me get rid of this stuff."

She continued on the path to the sheds, and Ted walked along with her. "Here, let me." He reached for the cart and she let him take it. Her heartbeat was only now returning to normal.

As irritating as Ted could be, she was glad to have him on her staff. He was big, for one thing, a handy characteristic for a gardener. More than that, he was almost as "green" at heart as Gaela herself was, and he often had creative landscaping ideas. Besides, Ted was . . . well, Ted was Ted. Kind of cute, definitely endearing, and if there *had* been any kind of real danger, instead of precisely nothing but her own stupid, erratic brain fevers, she'd be awfully glad to have him at her back. At her back? Not likely! He'd throw her behind him as fast as any TV superhero. She grinned to herself.

"Ted?"

"Hmm?"

"I guess I overreacted. Sorry about that."

He smiled at her, and she had to admit that smile did something to her insides. Not that she would let him know it under threat of torture and death!

They dropped off the garden cart at the work shed and passed the big house, headed for the new bed by the drive into Eden's Gate.

"Here we are," said Ted, as they reached the spot where the big tiller waited silently at the edge of a sweep of freshly tilled soil. "What I'd like to do is extend the bed in a curving line over to that bank of Fortune's rhododendrons. They're great for a month or so in spring, but after that it gets kind of dark and gloomy there, don't you think? I've been wondering for a while what would like acid soil, bloom most of the summer, and complement the foliage of the rhodies. What do you say to flax and white lilies, with a carpet of lungwort in front?"

Gaela forgot her worries. "Cool!" Ted's quirky eye for gardening was one of his best assets. She'd never seen lilies and flax together, but as soon as he mentioned them, they seemed so perfect for each other that she wondered why not. And the blue purple of the lungwort would be wonderful in front of the purple rhododendrons. The bloom time would be short, but lungwort foliage would remain attractive all summer. "This is one of your best ideas yet, Ted!"

She left him happily wrestling the monster tiller and decided to check on her other workers. Never mind that they all knew perfectly well what they were doing and didn't need checking on. Gaela wasn't as enamored of the idea of working alone today as she usually was.

Besides herself, there were four people who worked year-round at the estate. Randy Bowman and Chuck Knowles, the groundskeepers, were cleaning up the woods from the last of the winter storms. Maybe they could use a hand. She went on up the drive to the woods on the other side of the parking lot.

A long trill of whistling and warbling told her the wrens were back, and she shaded her eyes with her hands and tried to find them in the bare tree branches. She couldn't see them, but their cheerful singing began to relax her.

As she rounded the stone restroom building and went toward the signs marking the trail heads, distant yelling replaced the birdsong. Gaela grinned. Not far up the Forest Lake Trail, she came within sight of Randy, short, bowlegged, and round, staggering in the general direction of the riding mower and trailer, under a load of brush bigger than himself. His vociferous complaints were easily audible from a hundred yards away.

"Can't you at least pick up the blasted thing? You could have got it before you loaded up, couldn't you? Howdy *doody*, this stuff is heavy! And prickly? My neck'll be as raw as hamburger!"

Chuck, long and narrow in every dimension, strode silently along with a chain saw in one hand and an even bigger pile of brush balanced on the other shoulder, held there apparently effortlessly with one bony hand. Gaela's grin widened as she came nearer. Apparently Randy's ubiquitous cowboy hat had parted company with his head and Chuck was as unresponsive to demands that he retrieve it as he was to any and all of his partner's generic complaints.

"Consarn it, Chuck, if you can't pick it up on the way by, you at least better not step on it with those big gunboats of yours!" Randy dumped his load of brush into the trailer with a sigh of relief and turned to rescue his hat. "Gaela! Come to crack the whip, have you?"

"Came to catch a glimpse of that bald head of yours. I thought that hat had grown to your head by now."

Randy grabbed the hat and crammed it on to his head, yanking out a spotted handkerchief with the other hand to wipe his sweating brow. "Hot enough for March, ain't it?"

"Only because you're working hard. Need a hand?" Gaela watched Chuck drop his brush into the trailer and shove it around to make room for the chain saw, still without speaking.

"Nope, I reckon there's just about enough work for one hardworking man and one lazy bum." Randy winked at her. "If you worked, too, old Chuck, here, wouldn't do anything at all!"

Chuck ignored this byplay and started the tractor, galvanizing Randy into action. "Oh, no, you don't, you horse thief. That's my bronco!" Randy sprinted for the tractor, shoved Chuck aside, and climbed on. Chuck shrugged and climbed aboard the pile of brush, long legs dangling over the tailgate. Gaela thought she saw a glimmer of a smile on his lined face, but couldn't be sure.

Clearly, she wasn't needed here. Turning away, she decided to see what Lillian was doing in the greenhouse.

Lillian Blumfeld, greenhouse expert and bonsai enthusiast, was usually good for a "chinwag", as she herself expressed it. Today, however, she was apparently involved in some complicated procedure concerning her tiny trees. Gaela found her bent over a work table in the warm, moist greenhouse, an empty dish in front of her, dirt everywhere, and an uprooted tree about six inches tall in her hands.

"What are you doing?" Gaela leaned past Lillian's elbow to watch. Bonsai was a fairly new endeavor at Eden, and she knew little about it.

"Root pruning," mumbled Lillian, cutting back tiny, threadlike roots with nail scissors. Almost as tall and bony as Chuck, she was hunched over in a position that Gaela suspected would give her a backache, if not a permanent hump. She watched silently as Lillian carefully pruned the roots, eased the tree and its soil back into its pot, and watered it.

"There you are, little guy."

Did Lillian even remember Gaela was there?

The older woman reached to pick up another bonsai. Turning back, she started visibly and pushed wiry, graying hair behind her ear, leaving a streak of dirt on her cheek. "Oh! Gaela!" Guess that answered that question. "Did you need something?"

"Uh, no, nothing. Just came to see what you were doing."

Lillian bent to the new tree, crooning to it. Gaela smiled and left. Might as well give it up and get back to her own neglected work.

She had almost managed to forget the strange man of the morning when she saw him again. This time she was perched precariously on the top of a six-foot step-ladder, with one foot braced against the trunk of the storm-damaged ornamental cherry she was pruning. Her first glimpse of the ragged black head near a stand of hollies almost made her fall off. She prudently brought both feet to the ladder and descended two steps to the rung labeled, "To Prevent Injury, Do Not Climb Higher Than This Step." Gaela was usually strict about safety procedures. There was only one broken branch she couldn't reach, and she hated to ask Ted. But if he saw her teetering on the ladder's top, he would forget who was boss again and scold her like the mother hen he insisted he was not.

Her mental babble never succeeded in distracting her. Gaela peered through the lacy branches of the cherry toward the hollies. There he was. Still just standing there, looking at her. What was it about him that frightened her, anyway? She looked over her shoulder, gauging the distance to the drive. She could hear the distant roar of the tiller, which meant Ted would not hear her if she screamed. She should have gone to her cottage to get that dratted phone. Of course, he probably wouldn't hear that over the tiller, either.

The stranger just stood there, gazing around with his hands in his pockets. Gaela looked back up to where the last branch was half cut through. She couldn't leave it like that. With exaggerated care, she climbed to the top of the ladder again. It was nearly lunchtime. She would finish this job, put her tools away, and retreat to her private cottage. He would never find her there. Not if she took a roundabout route and made sure he wasn't following. And then, by the time she had finished lunch, surely he would have gone back to wherever he came from.

Placing her right foot cautiously on the trunk, she reached for the branch with her pruning loppers. They needed sharpening. She should have been able to finish this the first time. The not-very-firm platform under her left foot shook suddenly. Gaela gasped and looked down.

The stranger's grimy, black-nailed hands had a firm grip on her ladder.

Chapter Two

"Go ahead, I've got you," said the man, gripping the ladder securely.

Gaela gaped at him. Close up, he looked younger than she'd thought, but no less alarming.

"Go ahead," he repeated. "You really shouldn't stand on the top of the ladder like that, you know," he added conversationally.

Gaela looked back toward the drive again. The tiller still roared. With one mighty squeeze of the lopper's long handles, she chopped the branch in two. Now what? Climb down into this guy's arms? She risked another glance downward.

"Brown," the man remarked, with apparent satisfaction.

"What?" She hadn't meant to speak to him.

"Your eyes. I was hoping they were."

Gaela's heart stuttered. He was crazy! Well, she was armed, at least. He'd find out, small or not, she wasn't to be reckoned with. She backed down two steps then looked at him again, clutching her loppers. Twice in one day, a man read danger in her eyes. The tentative half-smile that had begun to show through the matted beard disappeared and he seemed to hunch in on himself a little. Then he backed off. "I guess you can handle it from here," he said, and turned and walked away.

Gaela stared after him. She couldn't seem to move. Finally, when he had almost passed the hollies, she climbed the rest of the way down. "Th-thanks," she called, but not very loudly. He probably couldn't hear her. Or had he nodded slightly just before he disappeared around the trees?

Gaela discovered her hands were shaking. She broke her cardinal rule and left her tools where they lay on the ground. Still clutching the loppers, watching for any sign of the crazy man, she made tracks for home.

By the time she reached the garden sheds, she was running. Dashing around the sheds, behind the row of compost bins, and through the low-hanging branches of mature white pines, Gaela slid into a narrow path even the other gardeners didn't use. She barely noticed the tangy evergreen scent she loved so much, and didn't stop to listen to the chuckle of the tiny creek as she bounded across the little arched bridge and into her own private hideaway. Breathing hard, she dropped to the step leading to her front porch.

Safe!

As her breathing slowed, the chirping and warbling interrupted by her precipitous arrival slowly started up again. Gaela watched some chickadees flit around her dormant old roses and empty bird bath, ran her fingers through the damp curls on her forehead and gave a great, shuddering sigh of relief.

She couldn't really explain why she felt so secure at her cottage. Anyone who tried could find this place. It was no secret, after all, and the path was only unused by courtesy. But surely that weird, unkempt man would never come here. Breathing slowly, trying to calm her shivers, Gaela concentrated on her surroundings.

Six years ago, when the Sullivans had hired her as their full-time caretaker so they could travel, they had let her live in this tiny cottage as part of her pay. It had once been a guest cottage, and boasted a setting Gaela thought was truly straight out of paradise. In her small clearing between lake, woods, and creek, there was no hint of the big house and its extensive gardens. Given free reign ("It's your home, dear, do as you like!") she had put her heart and soul into a small, sunny garden, as well as brightening shady nooks with wildflowers and benches. Gaela's Garden of Eden, that's what it was. She felt her heart returning to normal.

She could almost laugh at her morning. Pretty eventful for March! That bearded visitor was probably harmless, after all, otherwise why would he have held her ladder? Poor man, he must have thought she was the one who was crazy! She hoped he had heard her thanks, half-hearted though they had been. But she also hoped he was gone when she went back to work.

Feeling a little chilly, she went inside to fix a sandwich in her miniature kitchenette. It boasted a tiny table that could seat two people, but after casting her customary grateful glance at the pink African Violets on the windowsill, Gaela took her sandwich and milk across the living room to the bay window. This was the cottage's one claim to elegance, jutting proudly out on the south side so that it was always sunny. Sitting in her window seat, surrounded with hanging plants and embroidered pillows, Gaela had views of shimmering water with forest beyond it, her sundial and stone-flagged side garden, and the creek with its bridge and path to the woods. When you weren't outside, this was the place to be.

"Thank you, Earthmaker," she murmured, "for the food, for the sunshine, for the bits of Eden you give us to draw our hearts to you. Thank you for the best job anyone ever had, and for your endless love."

It was a familiar litany, especially in the spring, when Gaela's "real life" began again. She loved the privacy and quiet of winter, but not the lack of playing with dirt and growing things. Winters were only bearable if she could still get out every day, at least for a little while. She was deeply thankful the winters here in southern Ohio were not like the ones in upstate New York, where she had grown up. A good snowstorm could be great fun, but not one that lasted six months.

Gaela did enjoy going home with her big family for Thanksgiving or Christmas sometimes. But while she didn't exactly like to thank the Lord for the fact that they were far away, she was glad of it, nevertheless!

"And God bless Mom and Dad and all my siblings," she added scrupulously, then paused. A picture of that young man rose unexpectedly in her mind. "God bless him, too," she added dubiously. "I suppose he really needs blessed more than any of us, doesn't he? Just, please, if you wouldn't mind, bless him somewhere else! He gives me the creeps!"

When she finished her lunch, taking a little longer about it than usual, Gaela started toward the path in the woods, then hesitated. Sighing, she went back inside and found her phone. Fortunately, it still had half a charge. Shoving it into one of the pockets of her coverall, she went back to work.

The first thing was to get those tools put away. Now that she had some perspective on the situation, Gaela was ashamed of herself for leaving them in the first place. What was the matter with her today, anyway? The stranger had offered no danger or insult whatsoever. He had even offered a helping hand. Still, she kept a weather eye out for him, and was relieved not to see him anywhere. She decided to go and see what Ted was up to. The tiller no longer roared from the new bed at the drive. Arriving there, she felt her usual sense of deep satisfaction at the sight and smell of a brown swath of freshly turned soil. The big tiller was definitely worth its weight in gold, which was about what it had cost. Gaela knelt and picked up a handful of soil, running it through her fingers.

"What do you think, chief?"

She was proud to discover that she hardly flinched when she heard Ted's voice behind her. "I think it's a good thing you're here to run that monster," she said cheerfully, getting up and swiping her hands on her filthy coverall. "It would run away with me."

Ted grinned. "Nah, it's pretty mannerly. Besides, I thought you could handle anything."

Seeing movement from the corner of her eye, Gaela turned quickly and saw a family with a couple of small children and a stroller. When she turned back, Ted was regarding her with a strange gleam in his eyes. "Jumpy today, aren't you?" he observed.

"Jumpy? What makes you say that?" Rats, she thought she had moved quite smoothly. She watched a small brother chase his even smaller sister and drag her screeching back to Dad.

"Gaela?"

Maybe she ought to tell him. On the other hand, the guy would probably never come back, and Ted was unreasonable enough without reason. Give him any hint that she might really need looking after, and he would become impossible.

"I was thinking," she said blandly, "we already have lilies started in the greenhouse, and we can ask Lillian about lungwort. We could go ahead and plant some of it right away."

Ted raised his brows. "Don't you think it would be better to wait and till it again in a week or two? Don't forget it's a new bed. The grass would come back like gangbusters."

Gaela hoped she didn't look as red as she felt. "Well, of course. What I meant was, couldn't we go and pick out some stuff? Like, uh, I thought petunias would add some summer color, just behind the short edging. And, um, we could plant some seeds. In flats. To start, you know." Did she sound as half-baked as she felt?

She must, because Ted was looking at her more suspiciously than ever. "Sure, why not?" he said, and they fell into step in the direction of the greenhouse. Gaela tried not to look around too much. He was entirely too sharp-eyed. She gave herself a mental shake. Whether or not she told Ted the truth, she might as well not lie to herself. The real truth was, she wanted to work near Ted today.

They soon lost themselves in the joys of choosing which plants would go into the new bed when it was ready. Lilian got involved too, and Gaela forgot all about her strange follower in arguing the merits of snow-in-summer versus sweet alyssum for edging.

"Not instead of lungwort — with it! The snow-in-summer would add white, and would last all summer."

"But it doesn't smell as nice as sweet alyssum."

"Well, then, how about all three?"

By the time they had the new bed all planted, at least in their heads, Gaela had recovered her equilibrium. But once they'd planted flats of all three edging plants, counted out the right number of lilies, and ordered flax seed, there was nothing else to do. Lillian was clearly itching to get back to fussing over her tiny tree babies. Gaela figured Ted would really get suspicious if she tagged after him to clean up the tiller and put it away for the day.

In the end, she went in the big house and locked the door behind her. Here, she would be safe, for sure. Not only from odd garden visitors, but from long-buried memories as well.

෪ ෫ ෪

Memories were likely to drive him the rest of the way over the brink on which he'd teetered for a decade.

The hands he watched planting things should have been wearing flowered cotton gloves.

Birdsong segued into a girl's lilting laughter.

The waves of the lake lapped at the side of a boat which had long ago crumbled into well-deserved oblivion.

Sun on the water brought tears to his eyes and unheard screams to his ears. Caine clamped shaking hands over them and stumbled away from the lake toward a large rocky outcropping at the edge of the woods.

The rock—who was sitting at the top of the rock? No one. It was no one. His fevered imagination. He crashed through the woods until he ran out of breath.

He found a cottage, slumbering in sunshine, covered with vines heavy with roses whose perfume would cast a spell on you and make you sleep for a hundred years. But it wasn't summer. There were no roses.

Caine ran on.

There was a brick wall. A wall could be a prison or a shelter. Which was this one?

When he found a hidden area of heavy shrubbery, Caine crawled in between the prickly shrubs and the cold brick and curled up into as small a space as possible. He was past master at sleeping anywhere, anytime he got the chance. He bent one arm under his head and the other over his ear and slept.

A cottage, slumbering in sunshine, vines heavy with fat roses. An old woman, face wreathed in smiles, body made soft for hugging.

"The flowers smell so nice, Nonny."

"They're magic roses, to lure a prince to sleep."

"Will I sleep for a hundred years?"

A rich chuckle. "No, my little prince. Nonny will wake you at three o'clock. You wouldn't want to miss your snack, would you?"

So he slept on Nonny's lap, but she lied. He did sleep for a hundred years, and when he awoke, everyone was dead and the world was dark and loud and the roses were black and shriveled --

Caine awoke with a gasp, jerking upright and hitting his head on the bricks behind him. Memories were bad, but dreams were worse. How could you combat dreams?

There was only one way. Don't sleep.

He pulled himself to his feet and put his hands on top of the wall. He could see a quiet road, nearly deserted. It was late afternoon, almost evening. He should leave now. He braced himself and started to climb over the wall.

No. He couldn't go yet. She was still here, the garden pixie. He had to see her one more time. Just so he could have one unblighted memory to take away when he left.

Caine walked out of the woods and across the lawns between the house and the lake. He walked slowly, nonchalantly, like any garden visitor. Two men came out of the woods on the other side of the house with a garden tractor pulling a trailer of brush, and Caine angled in a direction that would avoid them. Where was she?

His eye caught movement at the side of the big house. There! Going inside and closing the door.

Too late. He couldn't see her now.

Shoulders slumped, Caine went back into the woods.

ぴ　　　　ぴ　　　　ぴ

Doing her weekly checkup on each of the fifteen rooms, Gaela decided it was almost time to hire the cleaning service again. The Sullivans had not been heard from lately, but they usually did show up for a week or two in spring. They'd likely be here sometime in April. Better start getting ready for the tempest.

It was nearly sundown when she was startled by a knock at the door. "Chief? You in there?"

Gaela had been going over some plans in her small office, and hadn't realized how late it was. She hurried to the door. "Ted! Good thing you rescued me! I was so deep in paperwork I would have been there all night! Going home?"

"It's about that time," Ted agreed. "Everybody else is gone. Randy said to tell you they're finished cleaning up the east woods trails." He glanced at the door. "I've never known you to lock the house when you were in it before.

Dare I congratulate you on your caution, or will you bite my head off?"

Gaela let the barb pass. "You may congratulate me. Maybe your wisdom is finally rubbing off on me." She dug the key out of her pocket and locked the door, setting the security alarm. She could straighten the papers tomorrow. She wanted to get to the cottage before dark.

"About time," said Ted. "Just think of all my wisdom you've been exposed to in the last year, and never taken in at all." He looked aggrieved, and Gaela laughed at him.

"Nobody could handle that much wisdom!"

Ted gave her a sideways look. "I don't suppose you'd let me walk you home, too?"

"What? *All* the way home, from *here*? It must be all of two hundred yards!"

"You never know," maintained Ted.

"Never know what? When I may need a big, strong man to save me?" The truth was, she would really like to take him up on it this time, but Ted was much too easily encouraged, and she wasn't sure how encouraged she wanted him to be. "You did your security sweep, didn't you?"

"Yeah, right, on my trusty golf cart. I always have thought it was ridiculous for people as rich as the Sullivans to have no security to speak of!"

"I know, I know." She'd better deflect this homily before it got started. She'd heard it enough times already. "You just saw me set the alarm on the house. Besides that, there is a wall—" She overrode his scornful opinion of Eden's security alarm and four-foot wall by the simple expedient of continuing to speak as if she couldn't hear him— "and a gate, and no visitors to speak of today, and nothing's ever happened yet, and here's your truck, good-bye, see you tomorrow!"

Gaela waved and turned toward the garden sheds, leaving Ted standing by his pickup scowling. He would stand there until she was out of sight, she knew. She didn't admit even to herself that she was glad of it. In fact, once she was out of sight, she started sprinting, with the general goal of getting in her door before he was out of earshot, just in case. It was really stupid—that guy was long gone. Just the same, Gaela was glad she didn't hear the truck start until she was over the little arched bridge.

That was when she froze. There, in the spot by the end of the bridge where it was almost always muddy, was a boot print. A big boot print, much too large to be hers. In slow motion, Gaela squatted and put her hand in the print, then even more slowly, stood again. Paralyzed, she listened to the sound of Ted's pickup, dying away in the distance.

Chapter Three

"Dear God, please God, don't let me just have been the world's most stupid idiot!" Probably the world's most stupid prayer, actually, since what was done was done. Gaela's eyes darted frantically around, looking for anything unusual in the rapidly darkening woods. Nothing. Suddenly unfrozen, she flew for her front door, then jerked to a halt again. What if he was inside? Oh, why hadn't she agreed to let Ted see her home? Or given in and gotten a dog, another of his perennially repeated suggestions? The little house was dark and silent, seemingly innocent. She reached for the door knob as if she was moving through molasses, and flung it open with a shout. "Who's in here?"

Still silent.

Gaela groped for the light switch. Her stiff lips were still stumbling over inarticulate prayers. She saw the pruning loppers on the table by the door—so that's where she'd abandoned them!—and picked them up. Systematically, she moved through the cottage. There wasn't much to check. Just the living room, kitchenette, bedroom, and miniature bathroom. Nobody. She even looked under her bed, laughing a little hysterically as she pulled up the eyelet dust ruffle. Obviously there was no one in her house. Probably there had been no one here at all. She had been so spooked she had imagined the size of her own boot print to be twice what it was.

It was Ted, with his everlasting worry. She had never been scared here at Eden before. Never! She was not a scared kind of person. And she'd always been a loner, in the best sense of the word, one who loved her own company, and loved solitude. The very idea that she could be in danger here in her beloved gardens made her angry. She slammed the door and locked it, then checked all the windows, pulling curtains closed with jerks that almost tore some of them. Her temper was not improved by the alarming realization that there were tears on her cheeks.

Putting her face in her hands, Gaela prayed for peace and safety. She also, not for the first time, prayed not to remember, although, as always, with a nagging sense that God did not approve of this prayer and answering it was up to her. Well, she could do that. Not remember. It was easy.

Usually.

Methodically, taking solace in comfortable rituals, she lit a fire in the small stone fireplace, put Debussy on the CD player, and set about preparing a light supper. By the time she had finished eating and washed her few dishes, she felt measurably better. The friendly crackle of the flames and the smell of wood smoke were all the company she needed.

An hour of reading, first in Psalms and then a new book on gardening, restored her equilibrium to the point that she could consider bed. But for the first time she could remember, she left the light and the CD player both on. Her next-to-last conscious thought, after seeking sleep for a fruitless hour, was that tomorrow she would get a dog. A big dog.

Her last conscious thought was another inarticulate prayer for the stranger, which went something like, "Help him, Father/Mother God, I think he needs you."

છે છે છે

Crouched under the boughs of a tall pine tree, hearing the shouting and then the slam of the door, Caine struggled with fury. She was afraid of him. After all his attempts to seem normal and ordinary. Well, so she ought to be. As history had shown, women were not safe around him. He laughed mirthlessly. Not that he ever meant to harm anyone. Caine put his head in his hands. Of all the damning phrases, that had to be the worst. *He never meant it!* Or worse yet, *he meant well.*

He raised his head again, peering through the dark branches that surrounded him, and watched the curtains pulled ruthlessly together on every window he could see. He imagined her going around to the windows on the other sides of the little house and doing the same, and laughed again. As if that would keep him out if he wanted to get in.

"Well, I *do* mean well, really I do," he whispered to the pine tree. She was such a pretty little thing. He had kept her from falling off that ladder, hadn't he? A crooked smile came as he relived the fantasy in which she did fall, and he caught her in his arms. "I would never hurt you, not a single hair on your head."

He should just go away and leave her alone. He was glad he had seen her, and glad he had found her little nest. If only he had a den half so cozy. The strains of Debussy floated out through the closed windows, and his eyes closed. "*Afternoon of a Faun.*" If she knew what that piece of music was about, would she still like it? Still, it was a peaceful thing, no doubt about it.

Inside his eyes, Caine saw again her little brown hands on the transplants. If anyone had ever treated him as she treated her plants . . . Memory poked at him, and he clenched his teeth and concentrated on the clarinet until he could almost feel the smooth weight of the woodwind in his own hands, the cool stops under his fingers.

When her light went out, he got up stiffly and stepped out from under his tree. Stretching until his back popped, he walked around breathing the fragrance of her evergreens and of the wood smoke, with a twisted smile for the screams if she were to discover him here. Then he went away, stopping at the edge of the bridge to rub out the telltale boot print she had seen. For a long minute he stood at the top of the arched bridge, looking back one last time at the cottage sitting so peacefully in its moonlit garden, a curl of smoke still rising lazily from its stone chimney. He took that sight, those smells, and the singing of the brook with him when he left.

ଔ ଔ ଔ

It rained late that night, and Gaela couldn't find any sign of a big boot print by her bridge. During the stormy days that followed, she never saw the stranger. Gradually, she began to believe that he was really gone. There wasn't much gardening to do, aside from putting straw between her hedge transplants and on the new bed, so neither would be washed away. She finished her paperwork in the big house and worked with Lillian on bedding plants being started in the greenhouse. She sat by her fire and cross-stitched Celtic knotwork on a new pillow for her window seat. She even gratified Ted by accepting one of his dinner invitations, not to mention carrying her phone faithfully.

She didn't get a dog. It would be an awful lot of work. And it would dig in her beds, and chase rabbits, and besides, if it was big enough to deter prowlers, it would scare off the visitors. Or bite somebody, and she'd be sued. Or worse yet, the Sullivans would be sued. He was gone. It was over.

Now if only she could stop looking over her shoulder.

After several stormy days and then several cloudy days, the sun came back. The gardeners were out in force, and Randy thought maybe it was time for the first mowing of the season. Gaela laughed at his eagerness. The staff at Eden maintained loudly and often that the reason for Randy's bowed legs was his constant riding--of a lawnmower. In fact, the loving relationship between him and his "bronco" was the subject of endless jokes at Eden.

Chuck, jokes and banter flowing around him like ripples around a rock, checked over his topiary for new growth. He might be silent as one of the yews, but the man had the touch of a genius with topiary.

Lillian opened a vent or two in the greenhouse, and Gaela and Ted started planting the new bed. They placed hardy white lilies helter-skelter throughout the bed in front of the greening rhododendrons, then scattered flax seed abundantly in between. It was not yet late enough to put out the edging plants, but the bed looked better already. Gaela stood back and tried to imagine the white trumpets lifting their heads above a sea of little blue stars.

"It'll be great," Ted prophesied.

"Heavenly!" she agreed.

More visitors began to wander in, and Gaela started answering gardening questions and pointing the way to the public restrooms situated at the end of the parking lot behind a screen of arbor vitae.

She was on her knees planting sweet peas beside a trellis when she heard a scream and jumped up, her heart in her mouth.

"Joey!" a woman was calling. "Joey, where are you?" Her voice was rising to a panicked level.

Lost child. Gaela grabbed her phone, glad she had it. It was a little early in the season for this sort of thing. But before she could give the alarm, she saw Chuck walking toward the mother from the direction of the lake, with something squirming under his arm. She ran to join them, stuffing the phone back in the belt holster she'd begun wearing.

"Oh, Joey!" gasped the woman, rushing to grab her child from Chuck. "Thank you, sir!"

"Found 'im by the water. 'Nother two seconds, he'd a gone in," growled Chuck. "Keep ahold on him, now." And he turned and went his way.

Gaela skidded to a stop, breathless. The woman turned to her. "I only turned my back for one second!"

"Yes, ma'am, that's all it takes. I'm glad he's safe." Gaela watched for clues to tell her if this was one of those women who'd need to be told the lake was dangerous, and to hold on to her kid, or if it was just one of those things that happen even to the most responsible mothers

"Thank you so much!" The woman's eyes were wide with relief and leftover fear. She was visibly tempted to shake the child, but hugged him instead, and Gaela hid her sigh of relief. "Joey, you scared Mommy to death! I told you to stay right here with me. Now, you have to ride in the stroller."

Joey began to wail, but his mother strapped him in firmly. Good. One of the responsible ones, then. Gaela gave her a sympathetic smile. "Over to the right, beyond that trellis you can see," she pointed, and the woman followed her pointing finger, "there is a topiary garden. I'll bet Joey would like to see bushes and trees shaped like animals!"

The young mother gave her a grateful smile. "Did you hear that, Joey? Trees shaped like animals!" Joey's wails abated, and the woman held out her hand to Gaela. "Thank you again. And will you thank that man for me? He might have saved Joey's life!"

"I'll thank him. Chuck doesn't talk much, but he's quick!"

The woman turned her stroller toward the topiary garden, and Gaela went back to her interrupted sweet peas. She remembered less pleasant scenes. Once, she'd even had to call the police hotline and report abuse. She had been too cowardly to give her name, and had always felt guilty about that. Thank heaven it had never happened again.

Gaela stood, stretched, and collected her gear, then turned her head suddenly. Hadn't she seen something? She scanned the area. Nothing. Must have been her overactive imagination. She climbed into the golf cart and pushed the gas. The vehicle grunted and shuddered. Both the Eden's Gate golf carts were cantankerous; that was why Gaela usually preferred her own feet.

There! It was that strange man, ducking into the vine-covered pergola. She was sure it had been the same one.

Through the still-leafless vines, she could just make out the same shaggy head of black hair, even the same ragged jeans, or so it seemed. This time he had a backpack. Was he homeless? Why was he back here?

Gaela stomped the pedal a time or two, and the cart lurched into motion. He could come back all he wanted. It was a public garden. Just so long as he didn't come to stare at her. And just so long—a chilling thought hit her. What if he had been living here? What if he had been hiding all this time? It would be easy enough to do. She drove as quickly as the wheezing cart could manage to the garden sheds and went inside. No one was there.

Coming out, she ran smack into Ted's solid chest. He grabbed her as she reeled backward. "Easy! Where are you going in such a hurry?" Laughter lit his eyes only for a second, then disappeared in concern. "What's the matter?"

Time to tell the truth. "Listen, I should have told you--there's a man-"

Ted's eyes darkened, and Gaela could almost have laughed. It settled her a little. "I'm sorry, I'm being rather incoherent about this. Remember that day a couple of weeks ago when you thought I was scared about something?"

"Right before the storms? Yes, I remember. What about it?"

"You were right, I was scared." He opened his mouth, and she rushed to add, "And I didn't want to tell you because you get so overbearing!" His mouth shut abruptly. "That's better. Now listen, and don't go off the deep end. This--guy showed up that day. Pretty scruffy-looking, with long black hair and beard. He didn't do a thing but watch me, but he made me nervous. He even seemed to be following me. That's why I jumped and squeaked when you came up behind me. I was just spooked, that's all." Ted was listening obediently, but his jaw looked grim, and Gaela couldn't bring herself to tell him about the ladder. And what about that might-have-been boot print? No, too impossibly silly. "Anyway," she said lamely, "he's back. And the thing is, he's carrying a backpack. I can't help wondering if he's been camping out in the woods, or something."

"Where did you see him?"

"What are you going to do?"

Ted's trademark grin lightened his forbidding face for a second. "Kill him, of course, what do you think? Idiot," he added fondly. "Where did you see him?"

Gaela still wasn't sure she wasn't signing the stranger's death warrant. "By the pergola. Now remember," she called after his departing back, "he didn't *do* anything!" Oh, drat, why had she told him? She could have waited to see if the man would hang around and stare at her again. "It's a public garden," she repeated her credo aloud. It didn't help.

Lillian showed up at her shoulder. "Who didn't do anything?"

"Oh, some guy. He stood around and stared at me a couple weeks ago, and now he's back."

"Is that all?"

"That's all."

"You shouldn't have told our boy Buck Rogers, then." Lillian shook her head morosely, as if the stranger's demise was a foregone conclusion.

Gaela shrugged defensively. "Well, he just gives me the creeps!"

"Oh, well, that's different, then!" Lillian brightened.

"No, you're right, I shouldn't have told. I don't know why I did. Gaela, the self-sufficient, the stand-on-her-own-two-feet, the one-woman island. I don't know what's the matter with me. I think I'm going crazy."

"Maybe he put a spell on you," suggested Lillian, brightening further at this tantalizing possibility.

"Oh, Lillian, for heaven's sake!"

Lillian patted her arm. "Seriously, dear, you should always follow your instincts. If this man gives you the creeps just by looking at you, then you don't want to risk further contact. Better safe than sorry."

"So I should just let Buck Rogers chop off his head?"

"No, no, he won't do that. Just rough him up a little," said Lillian with unbecoming relish.

"Oh, go pot petunias, or whatever it is you're doing, you old ghoul," said Gaela, and Lillian laughed and went away, characteristically shoving salt-and-pepper hair behind her ear.

Gaela was pretty sure there was something she was supposed to be doing, too, but she couldn't think what. She couldn't think, period. Why, oh, why did this stranger have such a strong effect on her? She wandered away from the sheds, thinking. Instincts, Lillian had said. Trust your instincts. Gaela wasn't sure that was so wise. A tiny worry sprouted somewhere way down deep inside her. A worry she didn't want to think about, let alone identify.

She discovered she was nearing old Mrs. Sullivan's "Secret Garden," one of Gaela's favorites on the whole estate. Quickening her step, she decided to check out the rock garden inside the Secret Garden's northern inner wall. Facing south, that was the most sheltered and the warmest spot on the estate, and she hadn't even thought about it lately. With sun, then rain, then sun again, there just might be real action beginning there. Garden action, the kind Gaela knew about. Weeds to pull. Something!

Gaela hurried purposefully down the mossy stone walk between gnarled yew trees over a hundred years old. The lowest branches had been clipped bare so that there was room to walk on the winding path. Children who had been to Eden's Gate before headed unerringly for this path. Hanging among the trailing ivy on the wall was a big key on a rusty chain. The key opened the wooden gate, which creaked invitingly.

Inside, it was a different world. Noises seemed to come from far away, and the air was richer and moister.

Outsiders never knew that was because of the hidden soaker hoses which would keep this garden from turning into a barren desert in the dry summers. Deciduous trees had also been strategically placed both inside and outside the walls to give shade in the hot months. But this time of year, to Gaela's way of thinking, was the perfect time for the Secret Garden. She was tempted to take the key off its chain, as only she could do, and keep it with her. But it was, after all, "I know," she answered herself aloud, "a public garden!" Then she laughed, but restlessly. The catch phrase had made her think of the stranger again. Had Ted found him by now? Had he been thoroughly embarrassed by being accused of harassing a gardener by watching her work? Everybody else watched her work.

After glancing desultorily at the rock garden inside the south-facing wall, she wandered over to sit in the covered swing. "He didn't do a thing," she murmured.

"Then why are you afraid of me?"

Gaela nearly fell out of the swing in shock. The stranger sat on a fallen log not far away. His voice had a soft sound, like honey.

"I'm not afraid of you!" she blurted. Now why had she said that? "I don't know if I'm afraid of you," she amended. "Should I be?"

His dark eyes looked her up and down, then through, she thought. She could feel her insides quiver. He could probably see that, too. White teeth gleamed momentarily through the tangle of beard. "Probably," he admitted darkly. "If you want to run away, I'll wait right here."

She should. She would. She would do that very thing. She would run and find Ted. Her hands were locked to the edge of the swing. "Why?"

"Why what? Why should you be afraid? Why should you run away? Why will I wait?"

"Why do you watch me?"

He looked down then. She felt immediate relief, as if his eyes on her were dangerous in themselves. "I like to watch you." When he looked up again, Gaela tensed. "Aren't I allowed to watch you work? It's a public garden." Again the flash of teeth. "I heard you say so, just a minute ago."

"Yes, but-" What could she say? Was he responsible for her reaction to his watching? Something about his hunched shoulders made him seem vulnerable, lost. Watching his restless hands, she realized that, under their dirt, they were long-fingered and artistic. She stiffened against the tug at her heart and went on the offensive. "Were you at my house?"

He hesitated, and she saw wariness in his eyes. "Yes," he admitted. Then vulnerability disappeared behind a hard wall as he grinned more mockingly than before. "Why didn't you ask me in?"

She didn't answer. She was going to run away now. Right now. She hoped his offer to wait still held. Why was she talking to him, anyway?

"I like Debussy, too," said the man.

Gaela gasped. "You were still there *then*? That late?" Suddenly she was able to stand. "Don't you ever go there again!" she hissed, and then took a breath and did her best to sound professional. "I am the head caretaker here, you know. Eden's Gate is my responsibility, and no one is allowed inside after dark. If I learn you are here again after the gates are closed, I will report you." Professional veneer deserting her, Gaela rushed toward the gate, then stopped and turned back. "And my home is not a public part of the garden at any hour!" At the gate she turned back again. He had not moved. "I prayed for you," she said hoarsely. And fled. His mocking laughter floated after her.

As she stumbled down the uneven yew path, Gaela berated herself. Why had she said that? What a stupid thing to say! So, she prayed for him. She would do it again, too, because he obviously needed it. But she didn't have to announce it to the world!

Her carefully ordered, private, quiet life was falling apart, and it was all because of a chance encounter with some weird guy. Now here she was talking about prayer to him! Gaela didn't talk about such things to her closest friends. Come to think of it, she didn't have any close friends. Only her co-workers. Would Ted count? Or Lillian? *Trust your instincts.*

A truth hit her like a brick wall, nearly blinding her in its intensity.

"Gaela? There you are. Randy, Chuck, and I have looked everywhere, and we can't find him. I think we should call the police."

He's in the Secret Garden. Gaela could almost hear herself saying the words, but they didn't leave her lips. The stranger's haunted dark eyes swam before her. In some inner vision she watched as that small spark of vulnerability was blocked out forever behind the hard walls he put up to protect himself.

And she forced herself to laugh lightly as, for better or worse, she followed her instincts. "The police? And tell them what? That a man came into Eden's Gate and watched me work? It's fine, Ted. I'm sure he's gone. I don't know why I even told you about it, but it's nice of you to worry."

Ted grabbed her arm. "You listen to me. You keep that phone on you, and turned on. And if you see hide or hair of that guy, or anybody else who scares you -"

Gaela laughed again, and patted his hand. "I'll call my hero, right away."

"Don't laugh me off!" said Ted furiously. "Things happen, you know!"

Gaela looked into his face and sobered. "I know. And if I ever need you, I'll call you so fast it will make your head spin. I promise."

She would, too. Just because she didn't want the stranger's arrest on her conscience didn't mean he didn't still give her the creeps.

Gaela locked her little house with great care that night. Then, more earnestly than she had before, she prayed for Caine.

Chapter Four

Gaela lay on her yellow bedspread with her hands locked behind her head and stared at her white ceiling fan, considering the unexpected truth that had hit her earlier. She *wasn't* afraid *of* him. What she felt was more like fear *for* him. There was something she had sensed in him from the beginning, and had seen in his eyes when they met in the Secret Garden, but had only recognized after she left him. Need. An aching, raw, terrifying need. For just a moment, he had seemed only a lost child.

No wonder she had been so panicked by him. She remembered that horrible pit. Hadn't she teetered on its black brink herself? She didn't know what this man sought-- certainly nothing she could provide. But God could fill the black hole. Gaela might not know much about theology, but she knew that much. God and these gardens could heal anything. No one understood that better than she.

Her mind slipped back in time, and for once she didn't stop it.

The year before she came to this place. Or even two years. When had it started? In her teens, even in her childhood? She had never really felt a part of her large, noisy family, though she and they loved each other, in a bewildered sort of way. Maybe there was always something wrong with her. Or not quite right, at least. Anyway, it had culminated in that horrible year she didn't like to think about now.

As she nervously poked through the old photographs in her mind, she found the memories no longer carried the power they once had. They were like frightful nightmares, but small, seen through the wrong end of a telescope.

The stalker. Dark and shaggy, but nothing like the man in the garden. That was clear to her now. Nights of terror. The time she had finally tried to tell her mother. Her mind shied away from that scene.

The night he had caught her.

No. Not that scene, either. She had got away. That was what mattered. She had to cling to that and forget the rest.

She *had* got away. But even after the man was gone, he never left her. He stalked her mind for years, and when she couldn't take it anymore . . .

The aftermath was easier to think about than the events themselves. She remembered shrieking, *"I don't care! There's nothing! Nothing! Let me go!"* Today she could only call up a shadow of the feeling that had so gutted her, like a burned out building. But thinking about it could still chill her with a sense of dread, like that horror in a nightmare where you can't move, and they're coming to get you.

She remembered a white hospital room, and apathy. A kind, young counselor who didn't understand her any more than anyone else did. Pills, and the growing ability to feel pain, to feel relief, to feel. Like needles in a limb that's been asleep. She hadn't liked it at the time. Far better not to feel. Safer.

Little by little, lying on the yellow bedspread, Gaela allowed the memories to take her away to another time.

Someone, she never learned who, brought her a plant for her windowsill. She watched it, and day by day something happened. The plant put out tiny new leaves, like Gaela, and turned its face to the sun, as she did. They forgot to water it, and it began to shrivel, so she got up by herself for the first time and gave it a drink from her water pitcher. She could feel the plant thanking her. It made pink flowers. Gaela was ravished by their beauty and delicacy, challenged by their unsuspected strength.

She found out there was a solarium. She went there, and sat among the plants, listening. They told her there was a Maker, a Toucher, somebody to trust. She told them her pain. She took off their dead leaves and turned them to get evenly sunned. They taught her to pray.

"Let her work in a garden," said the doctor, and sent her home, where everybody treated her like something not quite real, until she began to believe them and the old not-feeling started to come back.

It was a neighbor who rescued her. "There's a couple at my church," she said. "They need somebody to water their plants while they're gone for a week."

That had been the beginning. Gaela learned what peace and quiet were, and that she was happier alone. She began to house-sit, and garden-sit. She didn't know a thing except what the plants told her they needed. But she started reading gardening books, too. And the Bible, watching for anything about gardening and growing things. It was amazing how much she found. She learned that the Creator was the first gardener, and had planted people first in gardens. The entire Bible overflowed with gardening and agricultural imagery. When she read in Romans that creation tells anybody who pays attention that there is a Creator, she almost laughed aloud in glee. That's what the flowers had told her! She also saw that the Creator God was One and plural at the same time, and that this God chose to personify as both Father and Mother, whether it was a mother eagle, a protective "Abba/Daddy," or even a nursing mother. For some reason, this idea drew her, and she began referring to her Maker as "Father/Mother God."

She forgot to take her pills, and found she didn't need them anymore. Perhaps she never had. Perhaps the only thing wrong with her was being in the wrong place, like a rose under a fir tree, or a lady slipper in desert sun. But where would she ever find her right place? She had to find a job, to live on her own. She was twenty, and although her parents assured her she was welcome forever, she needed her own place. She tried to take classes, but the crowds of people still frightened her, and anyway, the "landscaping" they taught was strange, and foreign.

When she read the ad in the back of a gardening magazine, Gaela caught her breath until she actually felt faint. This was it. Her place. She knew it as certainly as she had ever known anything. More certainly. "Caretaker needed for country estate. 57 acres of woods and fields, small gardens, large house. No heavy work, we just want someone to watch the place when we travel and help us with it when we're here. Small cottage and stipend." And the name! *Eden's Gate*. Gaela whispered it over and over in her room. She just had to go there--she had to! But why on earth would they hire her? She knew nothing--*nothing*. Except she had to be there. "Call," whispered a voice in her mind. Was it God, or just her own longings? She had started to think she heard him sometimes.

One of her favorite Bible passages came to her mind: "The Lord will guide you continually, watering your life when you are dry and keeping you healthy, too. You will be like a well-watered garden, like an ever-flowing spring." It was the first time she had the nerve to actually pray *for* something for herself. "Oh, please, oh, please," she whispered, as her shaking fingers dialed the number. Gaela was rather afraid of the telephone under any circumstances, and this call took all the courage she could muster.

An impersonal voice answered. Yes, she could come and be interviewed, but she shouldn't get her hopes up, there were many before her, and they had Degrees. The voice seemed to consider Gaela's lack of a Degree a personal affront.

How had she ever dredged up the fortitude to go to that interview? Did the hand of God pick her up and make her go? She actually bought a bus ticket and told her family she would be gone overnight. This was met with dismay and astonishment, but she told them she was going to stay with a friend she had met in her therapy group, and since she was of age, no one stopped her. They never knew their outcry enabled her to go, just to escape the noise.

She sat rigidly through her interview, whispered timid replies, and was thanked for coming and told she would be contacted if they decided to offer her the job. Outside, nearly in tears, she fled for comfort to the walled garden she could see from the house and wept into the arms of the silver birches she found there. Then she blew her nose, looked around, and began to be enraptured with her surroundings.

"You're the Secret Garden!" she exclaimed with delight. "Oh, I could have made you grow!" She went from one plant to another, confiding her plans for each, weeding a bit here, plucking a dead flower or leaf there, carefully moving a rambling rose cane to a better perch, and stopping in horror when she saw a tiny, wrinkled, old lady and realized she was being observed.

"My dear, you're hired," said the old lady, and Gaela learned she was Mr. Sullivan's mother, her first name was Eden, and she had made this garden when she was young. She bullied her son and daughter-in-law into taking Gaela on a trial basis, and the rest was history. The gardens covered ten times the area they had when Gaela arrived, and three years ago, since they were always the stars of garden shows anywhere in the region, the family had decided to go public. Gaela had been terrified, but now she was the head of a staff of four year-round, and ten more in the summer, and Eden's Gate was the top attraction of the county.

With a deep sigh, Gaela came slowly back to the present. The fan hung above her, still and rather dusty at this time of year. She had allowed herself to look back. It wasn't so bad. Perhaps God was right to refuse to answer her prayer for oblivion. She missed old Mrs. Sullivan, who had died only one year after Gaela had begun to work at

Eden. For the first time it occurred to her that if Mrs. Sullivan were still alive today, it might just be possible to tell her the story. But what would be the point? She knew her old therapist would have said--had said, even then--that she must remember, even talk about it, in order to "deal with it."

Gaela sat up. Deal with it. What was that supposed to mean? It had happened. She had survived. What was there to deal with?

Trying to recall what had sent her down memory lane, she remembered the stranger and realized her instincts might have been faulty. God certainly could heal him. But gardens were another matter. They had been her own salvation, but that might be just the peculiarity of her soul, which often seemed to be as much plant as animal, so to speak. Still, she had learned by now to recognize the Maker's touch with a fair amount of accuracy, and she was sure that was what had sent the man here. Not only that, the stranger seemed drawn back here with some strength. To the garden, Gaela was sure, not to her, as he seemed to think!

Her part was to pray. And she did.

ଓଃ   ଓଃ   ଓଃ

Caine stood in the starlit clearing and gazed at the sleeping cottage. She had warned him off in fine style--he smiled when he remembered the gold fire in her brown eyes--but he had not actually promised he wouldn't come. She didn't understand. It was a compulsion. Something about her. Something about the place.

The little white cottage with its stone chimney and its bay window, the creek and the western branch of the lake, the firs and beeches and maples, somehow it all drew him, called to him. He could put down roots and stop running if he had a place like this. This could be home. Home. A word he had once used and understood, even taken for granted.

The gardens, wrought, no doubt, by the pixie within, made the cottage seem more like heaven than any earthly home. March-silent though they were, buds swelled on waiting branches. There was hope here.

Gaela. Her name was Gaela. He had heard it once, and had then got close enough to read it on her coverall and recognize its curious, Gaelic spelling. Caine whispered it to himself, liking the sound of it, the way it rolled off his tongue. He dropped on one knee to touch a flower he had seen Gaela touch, and held still a moment, waiting, listening . . . for what? For something. The flowers seemed to speak to her. Would they speak to him? Or was he too unfit, too . . . wrong?

Just as he gave it up with a bitter hunch of a shoulder and stood, Caine thought he heard something. Or felt something. The wind? A breeze had sprung up, and he shivered and looked upward to the treetops, which were moving just a little, and seemed to be whispering. His eyes followed the top fir branch to the stars beyond.

Are you up there?

He stared for a minute, his mouth pulled open by the stretch of his neck. That was probably what made his throat hurt suddenly. It was the chilly breeze that brought the tears to his eyes. He lowered his head and rubbed the offending eyes angrily.

Idiotic! This place was making him crazier than he already was! He turned and stamped away, forgetting to be quiet. He tried to laugh at himself, but the sound that croaked out of his throat was horrifyingly like a sob.

He was certain he did *not* hear the gentle whisper on the breeze.

I am here.

༄ ༄ ༄

As March wound to a close, Gaela looked over her shoulder as much as ever, but her lookout for the stranger took on a different feel. She was not as nervous of him, though she still hoped she would not meet him unexpectedly. It worried her when she found what might be another boot print at her place, and she had not told Ted the earlier incident at all. But nervousness for herself seemed to be replacing itself with concern for him. She almost wished she would see him (from a distance) so she could try to gauge if he was all right—if he seemed any more at peace. How she would determine this at a distance she had no idea.

The Sullivans wrote, saying to expect them by the end of April. Gaela hired a local landscape company to help with some of the last winter cleanup and heavy work. She had the drives and paths re-graveled and raked, called the cleaning service to make an appointment for the first week of April, and had a gutter and siding company send a van-load of men to swarm up on the roof of the big house, checking and cleaning gutters and downspouts. They discovered loose slates on the old-fashioned roof, so she had to call in roof repair, too.

Canada geese stormed the lake for their yearly, noisy, messy family reunion.

"Nothin' but trouble," growled Chuck.

But Gaela enjoyed watching them parasail and water ski, liked listening to their gossip and squabbles, and wished she could understand all the news they brought of southern zones. She knew if the flock grew much larger they would have to consider ways and means of control, but so far Eden had been lucky. The flock was small, and seemed to remain about the same from year to year.

New planting was proceeding apace, and Gaela was thinking about doing some hiring of extra hands. She always put that off as long as possible, dreading the invasion of her beloved gardens by clumsy hands and feet, not to mention the invasion of her own peace by the necessity of more stringent bossing. Visitors were bad enough, but at least they mostly stayed on the paths.

She was planting pansies in an isolated corner and frowning over this problem the next time the stranger startled her. This time he walked right up to her and said in his soft voice, "Hi, Gaela."

Gaela jumped. "How do you know my name?" she demanded foolishly. Of course he knew her name. It was embroidered over her pocket for all to see.

The man seemed to see her come to this conclusion, because he only smiled instead of replying. Then he asked, "Why so glum?"

"What?"

"You were frowning just now."

"Oh." Gaela tried to look around unobtrusively for Ted or someone, and the stranger scowled himself and took a sudden step back.

"You know, if I wanted to hurt you, I would have done it long before this!"

Well, how could she know that? Some crazy people, and he was clearly crazy, liked to play with their prey, like a cat. Praying for this man was now so habitual that Gaela sent up a vague request for help, realizing that here was her chance to find out if he was, in fact, more at peace. Maybe the fact that he had accosted her almost like a normal visitor was progress.

"Sometimes I wish this wasn't a public garden," she said, and he turned away abruptly.
"No!" Gaela cried, "You don't understand."

He turned back, still scowling at her, and she hastened to explain. "You asked why I was frowning. That's why. Every year at this time, when I've had the gardens pretty much to myself for months, I regret that the Sullivans ever decided to go public." Carefully matter-of-fact, she knelt and began to work with her pansies again. She could always smack him with a trowel if it became necessary. And she did have her phone.

The man squatted nearby, and she saw his scowl had faded. He looked at her as if he was really interested in what she was saying. "And then?" he prompted.

"Well, then spring and summer and fall arrive, and I'm busy, but happy, and most of the people who come really love the place, and learn something, and . . ." Gaela faltered and looked at the man speculatively. Maybe this was a chance to plant a seed in his mind. "They're a healing place, these gardens. People come sad or lonely, and go away, I don't know . . ."

"All better?" The man gave his mocking laugh, the one that made his face back into the crazy one she feared. "So then when fall ends and the crowds leave again, you miss them?"

Gaela laughed a little. "No, I'm glad to see them go, and have my private world back again." She looked at him sideways, wondering suddenly if she'd said too much. Was she giving him too intimate a glimpse of herself? Worse yet, would he come back this winter? "Not that I'm ever really alone, of course," she added hastily.

She reached for another pansy, and the man's hand was there, holding out the flower to her. She looked at it for a second too long, then took it, being careful not to touch his hand. "Thanks." She set it in its hole, not looking at her companion.

His voice was definitely nearer. "I wish you weren't so afraid of me. Not that I blame you." He stood suddenly, and she flinched, but he was walking away.

Gaela turned her head far enough to watch him go. He stopped and turned, and his eyes caught hers, like a snake hypnotizing its victim. "My name's Caine," he said, and turned away, releasing her. "I've already been cast out of Eden. So put that in your prayers and smoke it!" he flung back over his shoulder. Again, that grating laughter was the last thing she heard. Again, her hands were shaking.

"Well, then, God bless Caine," she said as calmly as she could, and kept planting pansies. "Bring him back to the garden and give him peace and healing as only you can, Lord. Make him see light where there is darkness, and joy where there is pain. Let his face look up to you, as these little pansy faces do." She touched the last one tenderly, and stood, stretching her back. She didn't look nervously around as she left.

Behind her, a ragged man watched her go. Then he came out from behind a screen of budding lilacs and knelt where she had knelt, to touch the pansies.

Chapter Five

April Fool's Day dawned more like a day in May. The sun was brilliant, the flowerbeds at Eden were nearly phosphorescent, and the crowds were jolly. Gaela and her staff were run off their feet, and Gaela knew she had, once again, left hiring too late.

Chuck pulled two enterprising youngsters from the lake and blistered the ears of their parents, and Gaela had to smooth things over.

Gaela caught three big boys trampling the new bed by the drive, in search of a rabbit that had disappeared under the rhododendrons, and blistered their ears herself.

Randy sent out a group text distress call over the phones and when the whole staff converged on him, crowed, "April Fool!" and got *his* ears blistered by everyone at once, especially Ted, who took distress calls very seriously indeed.

Gaela walked into the Secret Garden to check the soaker hoses and caught a couple engaged in amorous exercises that embarrassed her to death, though it didn't seem to upset the couple much.

It was mid-afternoon, and Gaela was sneaking a breather at the edge of the woods down by the lake when she heard music. Light and clear, the sound enchanted her, drawing her to its source as if it wove a spell around her. Through the edge of the woods she stole, along the stony fringe of lake bank, to where she could see the large boulder that jutted out into the water. From here, the music of the water and the woods seemed to blend with the magical sound of the unknown instrument, and Gaela found she was holding her breath. She twisted this way and that, peering through branches of new, green-gold leaves until she could see a figure seated on top of the rock. From her angle, the lowering sun was behind the figure, and she could only make out a vague, dark silhouette. Breathless, she stayed where she was until the music ended, and then sighed with regret.

The figure stood and stretched, raising its arms over its head, then turned toward Gaela to climb down the rock. She almost squeaked her surprise. It was Caine! She stood for another second, before suddenly awakening to the fact that she had now stolen twice the break she had time for, and she'd left the others high and dry on the busiest day so far this year. Turning, she hurried away as quietly as she could.

Gaela was distracted the rest of the afternoon, wondering what kind of instrument Caine had played, and where he had learned, and realizing to her astonishment that she actually wanted to talk to him! How could anyone who played music like that be so dangerous and frightening?

Before sunset, as Randy, Chuck, and Ted were doing the rounds making sure everyone was gone before closing time, Gaela hesitantly opened the gate to the Secret Garden and took a good look around before shutting the soakers off. Nobody there, thank goodness! It was greening very nicely in the shelter of these stone walls. She took a round to check on her favorite friends, thanking them, as she often did, for getting her this job.

When she turned to leave, Caine was there. Gaela jumped, and said in irritation, "I wish you wouldn't sneak up on me like that!"

He grinned at her--almost a regular, normal grin. Or had it always been so, and her own mind had made up all kinds of nonsense about him? Or had the music now blinded her? Oh, good grief, why did she always have to analyze everything to death?

"I heard you play," she said. "What was that?"

"I know. I saw you run away. That, by the way, is why I always sneak up on you."

"I wasn't running way--this time. I was incredibly busy today, as you know if you've been here all day. I had to get back to work. So, what was it?"

"The Last Rose of Summer."

"No, I mean what was the instrument? I don't think I've ever heard it before, and for that matter, it didn't look as if you even had one when you turned to climb down."

Caine grinned again. "I made it by magic!" he said in a sinister tone, reaching behind him and producing a small wind instrument with a flourish.

Gaela grinned back, then came closer. "Is this that dumb plastic thing they made us play in the fourth grade?"

"No, my dear ignoramus, that dumb plastic thing was a fake imitation of this, which is an ancient medieval instrument called a recorder." He played a trill, and she was captivated all over again by the bird-like sound.

"Made of authentic medieval plastic, I presume?" said Gaela drily.

"Very funny. Actually, I have—*had*—a bunch of wooden ones, made out of all kinds of high-brow fruitwood. Purists (as I used to be, I admit) prefer those. But the truth is, a well-made plastic recorder can sound every bit as sweet, never goes out of tune or needs special cleaning or treatment, and is much better suited to my present lifestyle."

"Well, you play it fabulously, believe me!"

Caine's face took on a look Gaela hadn't seen before-- true, honest pleasure, and she felt as if she basked in the reflected glow herself. "Thanks," he said, a little gruffly, as though he were unused to such words.

She realized suddenly that she was having a friendly, ordinary conversation with this man, who still looked like something you'd find in a back alley of a large city. Except his eyes, which she had decided were truly beautiful, close up. When they weren't being angry or mocking or sinister.

"I could teach you," Caine offered. "It's really easy." He held out his recorder as if to offer it to her, and Gaela put her hands behind her back, uncomfortable suddenly.

"Oh, no, I couldn't. I tried music lessons once, and I was all thumbs, believe me."

"That was before, I'll bet," said Caine obscurely, and Gaela looked at him with a spurt of fear, as if he had read her mind and knew her past. "Before you came here," he explained, wrinkling his brow at her curiously. "I've seen you work, remember. Your hands could do this, believe me."

He looked at her hands, which had come back in front of her, apparently of their own volition. Gaela looked at them, too, and was abruptly assailed by--something--even her hands could feel danger in his gaze! She looked around, wishing for escape, but not knowing why.

Caine's face closed again, and he stood back. "I'll still wait, while you run away," he said in a quiet, flat voice. She could have sworn he was disappointed, and she was, too. Or something. She didn't know what she felt, or what to say, but she opened her mouth, hoping some useful phrase would come out. "I'm sorry." No, that wasn't it, but she could tell by his face she'd said it anyway.

A little desperately, Gaela blurted, "Nobody who plays music that beautifully could be the horrible person you seem to think you are!"

He grinned again, not pleasantly this time. "For a praying person, you aren't up on your religion. It was Lucifer, I believe, who made the best music of all."

Now, what was she supposed to reply to that?

"Gaela! Hey, Chief, where are you?"

It was Ted's voice calling from outside the walls, and Gaela looked toward it with relief. "I—I really have to go." Gaela edged away. "And so do you," she added. "It's closing time."

"I'm coming. You go first."

Could she trust him to leave? Hesitantly, she turned away, then stopped at the gate. "I really loved listening to you play," she told him earnestly. Taking a breath for courage, she continued, "I hope to hear you again."

He nodded, but didn't look at her. Gaela hesitated, hating it that their one real conversation would end this way.

"*Gaela!*"

"Coming!" It would never do for Ted to find her here, with this man! With a last apologetic look, Gaela fled.

The next day, Caine seemed to have disappeared again.

Gaela could no longer decide whether she was glad or sorry, but she had plenty of work to distract her. The early weeks of April were always harried ones, if you can be truly harried in a garden, where all work is pleasure. That was "the chief's" opinion, anyway. It wasn't noticeably shared. Most of the staff switched to brown shorts and tan shirts bearing the Eden's Gate logo, and Gaela hired four new hands, the best she could get from the crop that answered her ad.

Jake and Chan were tall and strong, but turned out to be unable to put one foot in front of the other without stepping on it. They spilled fertilizer, split bags of mulch, broke the branches off shrubbery, and drove the lawn tractor over rakes.

Brianna was helpless, always standing around until someone told her something specific to do. When Lillian spoke sharply to her on her third day, she burst into tears and left.

The fourth (now third) new hand, Jeanie, a young single mother with creamy brown skin and hair in intricate cornrows, was the only one of any real use. She had a practical mind, an eye for detail, and some experience with gardening.

The second week, the cleaning crew arrived and made the big house shine from top to bottom with their usual dispatch. Gaela was so grateful she gave them a bonus. Then she hired a skeleton house staff with orders to be prepared for the descent of the owners any time.

The third week, Jake quit, having felt the sharp edge of Chuck's tongue one time too many, so Gaela hired two more to take his place, and actually got two reasonably handy ones. Ali and John didn't know much about gardening, but were quick to grasp instructions and equally quick to see where a helping hand was needed. Gaela teamed them with Chan and hoped something would rub off.

She could only get to her office and paperwork in the evenings. The budget looked pretty good this year, and she had every intention of sitting the Sullivans down, with Ted to give her moral support, and making them think seriously about better security. The house itself had security alarms, but couples regularly sneaked in to park by the lake, where cars were not allowed. One of them had made a fire on the rocky beach, and the greenhouse had been slightly damaged by vandalism on the night of April first. Gaela was definitely feeling less safe in her hideaway, and it wasn't all because of Caine, who still hung out a lot at Eden, had no visible means of support, and for all she knew, might be sleeping in the Secret Garden despite her stern warnings.

She saw him a couple of times, and spoke to him briefly once. He stopped by where she was planting pansies and started asking her questions, just like any visitor. Gaela was delighted to be able to converse with him on a subject in which she felt comfortable.

She decided it was way past her turn to startle him, so she said unexpectedly, "I'm not the only one who has my religion mixed up." The surprise on his face gave her great satisfaction.

"Oh?"

"Cain didn't get cast out of the garden. His parents did. He wasn't even born yet."

Caine's face darkened, and he stood. "Read a little further. Cain was cursed to wander the earth, and could never grow anything, ever again."

He strode away, and Gaela watched him helplessly, wishing she'd kept her mouth shut.

She still prayed for him daily. She didn't think it was her imagination that he seemed just a little less prickly and angry. At least, if she stayed off touchy subjects. Of course, who knew which subjects would prove to be touchy?

Once, late in the evening, Gaela thought she heard his music from her cottage. She went out on her little porch and listened. It seemed to be coming from the woods, some distance away. She had been right—he was staying here. Or was he camping perfectly innocently in the adjacent state forest? She twisted her head and tried to gauge the distance. Impossible, of course. Should she follow the sound and try to find him?

She couldn't do it.

Shivering a little in the chilly air, Gaela folded her arms and paced the three steps to the end of her little porch. She decided not report it, at least not for a while. He wasn't hurting anything, after all.

Then she wondered uneasily if she was betraying the trust of the Sullivans, who paid her to look after Eden. She paced the three steps back to the other end of the porch. Was her interest in this wayfarer interfering with her duty?

But what would she report, and to whom? "Hello, police? There could be a man staying here, or maybe not... where? Well, I don't know exactly, can you come and track him down? You can follow the sound of the recorder. Recorder. It's a medieval instrument..."

Ridiculous!

And she felt so strongly that he needed, somehow, to be here. For a while, only, she told herself, adding a new request to her prayers. "Don't let Caine hurt anything!" Oh, dear, was that even a right thing to pray?

She locked her door when she went in, as was now a habit, then continued to pace restlessly, worrying about the rest of the estate. When she finally went to bed, it was with the reminder to herself that nothing untoward had occurred yet, and Caine could have been staying here almost a month, already.

Or in the state forest. Or wherever.

Maybe she could just ask him. She fell asleep trying to figure out exactly the right, innocuous, non-accusing words.

Chapter Six

On a rainy, muddy April afternoon several days before they were expected, the Sullivans' huge recreational vehicle (more like a railroad passenger car, in Gaela's opinion) pulled into the drive honking its deafening horn. The few visitors who had braved the morning sprinkles had been chased away by the afternoon deluge, so Gaela had sent several workers home. She, Lillian, Chuck, Ted, and the best of the new gardeners, Jeanie, were the only ones there to go splashing out and greet the long-lost owners. The new house staff stayed inside, with instantly telephoned instructions from Gaela to "fix food. Fast!"

The door of the RV opened and a merry voice that might have been either male or female called, "Heavens, what a flood! Don't just stand there, come on in!" So they trouped up the steps and stood in each other's way, dripping on the luxurious wall-to-wall carpet, while hugs, introductions, and explanations were offered in a cacophony that made Gaela cringe.

Georgiana Sullivan, tall, square, and deep-voiced, dominated the conversation, if that's what it was. She enumerated in exhaustive detail all the reasons why they were early, turning her elegantly, if rather mannishly, coifed head and spearing each of her listeners with her eagle glance. Gaela grinned to herself at the stunned looks on the faces of those who had not yet met their elusive employer. Even Ted, who had met the Sullivans once last fall, looked a little glassy-eyed. Everyone's head, her own included, was bobbing attentively, like those toy dogs in the back windows of cars.

"Oh, how remiss of me!" boomed Mrs. Sullivan suddenly, turning to sweep an arm expansively toward a glamorous-looking person Gaela couldn't imagine ever getting wet or bedraggled. "Our niece, Ivy Sullivan! She has always wanted to visit Eden's Gate, haven't you, my dear?"

Gaela surreptitiously swiped at a rivulet of rain running down her neck from her streaming hair. Ivy looked like a super model, with smooth, blonde hair and eyes so green they certainly had help from colored contacts. She gave a small half-smile that made Gaela think of Mona Lisa. Who could understand the famous mystique of that stuck-up female? Glancing at Ted in hopes of sharing silent amusement, Gaela saw his eyes on Ivy's long legs and forgot the joke. Well. Good. That would take his attention off her. That was what she wanted, wasn't it?

At a nudge to her elbow and a quieter voice in her ear, Gaela turned. Sam Sullivan, short, round, and cheery, motioned to the driver's compartment of the big coach, and she smiled gratefully and joined him there. The two seats could be turned around to add to the amazingly roomy living room when the rig was parked and the tip-out was pulled out. Right now, they still faced forward in driving position, and made a welcome semi-refuge from the noise behind them.

"So, how's it going, my favorite garden elf?" asked Mr. S, as he liked to be called. Gaela privately believed he had illusions of wearing his initial on his chest. He'd need it, to deal with his larger-than-life spouse, with whom he seemed to get on famously.

"It's going well," Gaela told him, feeling insensibly warmed and comforted by his twinkling eyes and laugh wrinkles. "The weather warmed early this year, and there have been more visitors than usual. We've put in some new beds." She described some of their work in general terms, knowing he would have come home eager to share all kinds of new ideas he'd gleaned from their travels to famous gardens all over the country.

Mr. S had just begun to regale her with a description of a waterfall grotto he thought they might adapt at the spot where the biggest creek entered the lake when his wife interrupted them.

"There you are, Gaela! Now don't let Sam closet you away and bend your ear forever! Plenty of time for that! Dear girl, we've decided to stay home all the way to Memorial Day! Now what do you think of that?"

Gaela knew she didn't have to answer this with more than a smile. Truthfully, she greeted the news with mixed feelings. Mrs. Sullivan went on without pause to an invitation to everyone to note that the rain had slackened and they might all go up to the big house for tea. She fully expected the staff to be up to this challenge the instant she arrived on the scene, and thanks to Gaela's early warning system they were. At least, she hoped they were.

The bunch, who all seemed to be on the best of terms, splashed to the house, where the gardeners became suddenly aware of their muddy condition and huddled together near the door.

"Oh, come on in, come on!" called Mrs. Sullivan. "Floors can be cleaned!"

The staff looked at Gaela, and she grimaced and motioned to them to at least take their shoes off before venturing on to the cream carpeting of the dining room. Cream carpeting in a dining room! Sure, carpets could be cleaned. Mrs. Sullivan had never done so, however.

They spent an hour around the dining room table, stuffing themselves on a wide array of snacks that the staff had assembled in record time (Gaela would be lavish with praise when she got the chance) and listening to the travelers' tales and conflicting plans for their month at home.

"No, dear, it was in *February* that we saw Biltmore again! You remember, I wanted to see whether their bulbs came up before ours. They didn't, I might add. Gaela, they had the most darling gazebo! I think we should-"

"That wasn't Biltmore, George, that was that place in California. Dunwoodie, or something."

"No, I'm sure it was..." An arrested look came into Mrs. Sullivan's sharp eyes and she laid a strong hand on her even stronger chin. "You know, you're right, Sam. That was Dunsmuir. In the Bay Area, wasn't it? What a lovely place! Anyway, the gazebo was heavenly. I want one just like it on the lawn! We should be able to get it done next month, before Memorial Day, don't you think?"

"We don't need a gazebo, or at least not immediately. I want to copy the waterfall grotto we saw at that Japanese garden, and wouldn't it be great to have boat rides on the lake? A few boats wouldn't cost much." Catching Gaela's eye, Mr. S laughed and added gaily, "Oh, well, if our own people don't have time to row, we can hire some boatmen!"

Ted and Gaela shared a glance and shuddered in unison, trying not to laugh. The insurance alone would keep a sane person up at night.

On the way out the door, after they were finally released, Gaela gave Jeanie an encouraging smile. "Don't worry. They almost never last a whole month here. Anything they tell you to do, bring to me."

On the way back to her cottage that evening, Gaela wondered again what it was that kept the Sullivans on the road. She knew they loved to travel, but it was more than that. Lots of people loved to travel, even spending months on the road. But when they had a home like this, and one they obviously loved, why did they get so patently discontented whenever they stayed here any length of time? She had seen it happen every time. They'd both fling themselves into projects that were guaranteed to be mutually exclusive. This would lead to arguments, mostly good-natured ones, but gradually growing more acrimonious. Then she would start seeing one or the other of them alone in some corner of the gardens, sitting and gazing at nothing. If she were close enough, she would see an ineffable sorrow in their faces, unless they looked up and saw her. Then, at the flip of an invisible switch, the happy mask would light up, hiding everything but the eyes.

Soon after, they would be off again. She wondered what they were looking for, and if they would ever find it. Surely all the healing anyone could need was to be found right here in Eden.

At this point in her ruminations, Gaela reminded herself that she was different from the run of the human race, and that her life would be a burden if the Sullivans, much as she loved them, ever did decide to stay.

The next day Gaela put on a green waterproof poncho and went out in the rain to visit the Secret Garden, something she loved to do and didn't want anyone to know. They already thought she was nuts, the way she talked to the flowers.

She wasn't entirely surprised to see Caine there, but she didn't for one second admit to herself that she had half hoped he would be.

He grinned crookedly at her. "So, not only a dryad, you're also a naiad?"

"Something like that. What are you doing here on such a wet day?"

"Hoping to see you."

Gaela raised her eyebrows. "You expected to see me out in this?"

"You're here, aren't you?"

"Well, yes, but most people would have thought I wouldn't be. I mean wouldn't have thought I would be. You know, I spoke perfectly good English until you showed up!"

Caine laughed, a rusty but very creditable laugh. Gaela was transfixed by the change it wrought in his face, what she could see of it through the thicket of black hair.

Finally catching the sense of his words, she asked, "Why were you hoping to see me?"

"Because I like you."

"Well. That's . . . nice." She thought she might like him, too, sort of, almost. She was afraid to say so, though. He moved, and she saw a new restlessness in him, different from the restlessness that was always under his skin. A nervousness. It made her nervous, too. She hadn't been nervous in his presence for a while.

"Who's here?" he asked.

"What?"

"Who's at the big house? I saw the RV."

"Oh! That's the owners, the Sullivans."

He paced back and forth. "Do they come a lot?"

"A few times a year. They say they're here till Memorial Day this time, but I doubt it."

Caine looked at her curiously. "Why?"

"They never stay. They're always on the road."

He nodded. "Like me."

"Kind of, now that you mention it. Are you looking for something?"

He laughed shortly. "If so, I haven't found it. Are they?"

"I think so."

There was a minute of silence, then they both spoke at once.

"Of course, you know-"

"I think I-"

He laughed again. "You first."

"You know my theory. Everything worth looking for is right here."

His eyes lit on her, and that dangerous feeling she hadn't felt in a while was suddenly back. "Right here?"

"In the garden. In Eden." She spoke so quickly she stumbled over her words. "What were you going to say?"

"When?"

"A minute ago. You know, when we both—"

"Oh, yeah." He looked at her for a minute longer, then turned away jerkily. "I was saying, I think it's time for me to hit the road."

Gaela was shocked at her sense of disappointment. Given his ability to read her mind, she was terribly glad he was turned away from her at the moment. "Oh?" was all she could manage.

"Yeah. Still looking." Caine walked rapidly away from her, toward the gate. He stopped. It seemed one of them was always stopping at that gate to say some last word. For a minute, she thought he wouldn't say anything. Then, quickly, he muttered, "You could keep praying, if you want."

And he was gone.

Gaela sat in the silver rain for a while, watching the ripples intermesh with each other on the bird bath in the center of the little garden and listening to the raindrops' music. There was something wrong with the symphony today. She finally figured out it was missing the lead solo, and went home, disconsolate.

On the first sunny day, Ted and Gaela, each armed with clipboards and pencils, took two separate exhaustive tours of Eden's Gardens, one with Mr. S and one with Mrs. S. Afterwards, they sat at the workbench in the main workshop and compared notes, trying to determine if there was a way to reconcile the couple's opposing desires.

"There's always one major thing each one wants," said Gaela. "This time, Mr. S wants the grotto, and Mrs. S wants the gazebo. We should be able to do both those things, don't you think?"

"Before Memorial Day?"

"No, they don't really expect that. Both should be underway, that's all."

"Well, I could head up a crew to do the gazebo, if they want to hire extra help. The problem is whether it has to be identical to the one she supposedly saw at Biltmore."

Gaela laughed. "Not Biltmore. Dunwoodie."

Ted grinned. "Whatever. I'll get the details."

"Just the general idea. I'll pump her more to find out if it was round, square, or what. That sort of thing. I wonder if she brought back brochures. As for the grotto, it shouldn't be that hard. Mr. S is easier to get along with, for one thing. I think I understand those drawings he made. Chuck and I should be able to manage that, if we get someone to do the concrete 'stonework'."

It went without saying that the projects they'd had in hand before the Sullivans arrived were on indefinite hold. Gaela was only grateful that she worked for owners who let her have a free hand with gardening design and execution ninety percent of the time.

"I want you to go with me to talk to them about security," she told Ted, and his eyes lit up.

"You finally believe me?"

"The vandalism on April Fool night convinced me," she admitted.

"What about that guy you saw several weeks ago? He never showed up again?"

Gaela kept her eyes on her notes, shrugged as noncommittally as possible, and said truthfully, "He's gone."

Ted put his big hand over hers on the table. "I hope you've noticed how over-protective I *haven't* been lately."

She lifted her eyes to his and smiled with some difficulty. "I've noticed. And don't think I don't appreciate it."

"You matter to me, you know." His eyes were warm, hopeful.

"Ted—"

"I know, I know. You love me like a brother." He took his hand away and gathered his notes. "Story of my life."

Gaela watched him walk away and asked herself for the hundredth time why she couldn't fall for him. He was kind, gentle, good-looking, intelligent, *and* a gardener after her own heart! What more could she want?

They scheduled the security talk for the next day, before the Sullivans' zeal could begin to flag. When they went to the big house, Ivy met them at the door. Gaela realized she had forgotten Ivy. Would the presence of their niece affect the usual pattern of their stays? So far, she seemed to stay indoors. Probably a TV fan, Gaela thought disparagingly, watching Ted watch Ivy again. And if she didn't want Ted herself, why on earth did she care who he looked at?

When the Sullivans heard about the vandalism and the fire on the beach, and when Ted impressed on them their liabilities if anyone came in during off hours and then got hurt, they agreed to have a security company come and look things over. There would at least be a new, state-of-the-art system at the house and motion-sensing lights in secluded corners. The security company would also see about the possibility of wiring the four-foot wall that surrounded the entire fifty-seven acres so that a person who climbed it would set off an alarm, but a raccoon, for example, wouldn't.

It wouldn't affect anyone who simply hid out during the evening check, and stayed, thought Gaela. But then, there was no such thing as perfect security in this world. She wasn't sure there should be. The price of perfect safety would be too high. And wasn't *that* an interesting thought for someone who had spent her life hiding! It was her terrible need and fear that had made her pay attention and realize God was there.

The thought of terrible need and fear made her think of Caine. She had considered talking to Mr. S privately about him but it didn't matter anymore, now that he was gone. Gaela was secretly relieved. Confiding in people didn't exactly come easily to her.

At night, when she prayed for him, not to mention every time she went into the Secret Garden or anywhere near the rock at the lake's edge, Gaela could no longer pretend to herself that she didn't miss Caine. It wasn't that she actually missed *him*, she argued with herself. Just that she wondered how he was, wondered whether her prayers made any difference in his life. Not that it was any of her business. She would probably never see him again, anyway.

She did try hard to deny the sadness that thought caused.

For two weeks, the crew was caught up in building the grotto and the gazebo. Mr. and Mrs. Sullivan each hovered over the preferred pet project and harassed each other over the other, "unnecessary" project. Even Ivy began to languidly appear at both, mostly wherever Ted was working, Gaela noticed. Ted was supposed to be overseeing the gazebo, but managed to be at the grotto whenever possible, especially when Gaela was doing something he considered dangerous. She tried not get annoyed with him, because she could tell he was trying hard not to be annoying. It seemed as if every time she climbed a ladder or swung a pick he looked disapproving.

They were digging a temporary channel for the creek so that they could create an artificial drop where it usually entered the lake. This would be built up with concrete "rocks" that would echo and amplify the sound of the falling water. Gaela had already chosen ferns and water plants that would love the damp, enclosed space, and was becoming excited about the project. If they did it well, it would be a very inviting feature at Eden, especially on hot days. They could place a couple of benches at strategic spots and plant willows and maybe a river birch.

But it did require some swinging of picks. And pouring of concrete into the elaborate forms that would make it look, they all hoped, like real, natural boulders nature had put there.

Luckily, Ted happened to be on hand, looking disapproving, the day Gaela fell from the top of the forms.

Chapter Seven

Gaela perched at the top of the concrete forms, directing the mixer truck. She thought her footing was sturdy. She was taking particular trouble to be careful, since Ted was being such a mother hen. This was a big day. Besides the grotto work crew, all three Sullivans, as well as Ted, Randy, and even Lillian were there, not to mention a small crowd of visitors. When her footing suddenly shifted, Gaela's first instinct was to glance guiltily over her shoulder to make sure Ted didn't see her waver, but that small movement was her undoing. He was, in fact, looking directly at her, and his alarmed shout mingled with her involuntary yelp as she flailed her arms helplessly and fell straight backwards.

To Gaela's perception, the fall happened in slow motion. She sailed backward through the air, while several people yelled and slogged toward her, all moving slowly except Ted, who seemed to launch himself instantly from a dead stop to a wide receiver's thundering gallop. He fielded her as neatly as a football, but she got a clear look at his face, and that terror didn't belong in any ball game. Gaela felt a strange mix of guilt, relief, and longing, all washed away the next second by a sense of utter safety as he stood, panting, clutching her to his chest so that she could hardly breathe.

As a clamor of voices began, she put her arms around his neck and squeezed, fighting tears. Wide-eyed faces appeared in her field of vision over Ted's broad shoulder. For some reason Ivy's stood out, looking white and bereft.

Once everyone was certain she was in one piece, Ted was finally prevailed on to put her down, but he didn't let go of her until the pouring was complete. Exercising immense self-control, Gaela was sure, he didn't scold her.

Everyone trailed over to the gazebo next, where the framework was up and the roof was going on today. An even larger crowd watched this operation. Gaela divided her attention between watching Ted's muscles and watching Ivy watch Ted's muscles. Her insides felt as if they had fallen into the mixer truck.

She left, looking for something that needed planting or tending or something, and found Lillian at her elbow.

"That Ivy's a nice girl," said Lillian, à propos of nothing. "Just hurting right now."

Gaela looked at her in surprise. "Hurting? Ivy?"

Lillian nodded sagely. "I guess she has a past, or something. Most folks do, at that."

Hurting. Supermodel Ivy.

"Somebody's got to go to town for some stuff for the break room," said Lillian. "Don't you need a break?"

Gaela did, but it wasn't town she'd had in mind. Her cottage was calling her, with its silence and peace. "I'll go," she said.

She got the list and took one of the Eden's Gate trucks. She didn't own a car of her own--had no need for one.

While she was in town, she went to the music store and actually found a CD of something called a "Recorder Concerto." Then, discovering to her surprise that plastic recorders were only four dollars, she got one of those, too, and an instruction book.

By the time she got back to Eden, some sort of a delayed reaction was setting in, and all she wanted was to go home and play her CD. Ted took one look at her as she put away groceries in the break room refrigerator and unwittingly seconded her inner desires. "Go home," he said, not mincing matters.

"I will. Ted . . ."

His face contorted. "If I ever have to live through a minute like that again-"

She hugged him, and he held her convulsively. "I always said you were my hero, didn't I?"

Ted took her shoulders and held her away from him. "Go home," he repeated.

She went, thinking that it was past time she made up her mind once and for all about Ted Waite.

In her cottage, Gaela locked the door even though it was still light, put on the CD, and listened with open-mouthed astonishment to the music one of those little plastic things could make. Though, no doubt, this one was wood-- what was it? Fruitwood? Yes, "high-brow fruitwood." She could hear Caine's voice saying the words. Gaela turned up the volume on the CD player and went to fill her bathtub, an acquisition of her own which filled half her bathroom. She pushed the "repeat all" button and got in the tub with every intention of staying there until she became a prune.

Soaking in suds and hot water, she let her thoughts roam where they would, and a very strange mixture it was. Prayers, Ivy's lost white face, now why did it seem lost? Ted's strong arms, what *was* that feeling? Was it love? The beginning of love? Brotherly love? More prayers, Caine, (a brother who needed love, if ever a brother did), Mr. S and his grotto, the look in Mrs. S's eyes sometimes when she didn't know anyone was watching. That look reminded Gaela of something, she didn't know what. Recorder music, and Caine's hand holding it out to her. "I'll teach you, it's easy." A bum and a backpack and her first pink African Violet, whose descendants lived on her kitchen windowsill to this day, a kitchen knife in her hand and a scream of anguish—Gaela sat up with a jerk and a slosh of lukewarm water and realized she had fallen asleep in the tub. Good grief, next she would drown herself, and Ted really would never speak to her again.

She dried off and went to bed, to dream of Ted with ivy climbing up his legs and arms.

ॐ   ॐ   ॐ

Many miles away, under an overpass, Caine slept fitfully, dreaming of Eden, of paradise lost. "It's not my fault!" he screamed. He saw a face, a young face with wide blue eyes, but the eyes turned brown and stared accusingly at him. He raised his fist, and the face turned away in horror. Caine woke with a start, covered with sweat, thinking desperately, "I have to get back to her! I have to tell her it's not my fault!"

"What's not my fault?" He sat up, and consciousness slowly returned, scattering the last shreds of the dream.

"You can never go back to her, you idiot," he said aloud, savagely. It would have to suffice to remember her there in Eden, praying her innocent prayers.

The wind whispered around him just as it had in her garden.

I am here.

Caine turned over irritably. He must be falling asleep. Why couldn't he drop all the way into forgetful slumber? "You can't be here and there, too," he muttered foolishly.

God, if there was such a thing, could be everywhere. Oh, for pete's sake. Now he was hearing voices, and telling himself it was God. He really was ready for the loony bin!

He turned over again.

I am here.

Caine sat up. "You hanging out under overpasses, now, God?"

He could have sworn the breeze chuckled.

He gave up on sleep, shouldered his pack, and slid down the gravel slope to the road, looking both ways, trying to remember where he was. Looking up, he found the north star. Now he remembered — left was north. Chicago, or Cleveland, or New York City. Maybe even Canada. Freedom. Right was south, the way he had come, the way he would never go again. He turned left, and a gleam caught his eye. He looked down. At his feet, narrowly missing being squashed by his boot, was a dandelion, smiling bravely up at him as if it had no idea he could kill it with one stomp. Then he laughed. No, dandelions were tougher than they looked. The blossom might die, but the root, undaunted, would send up another. And another. And each would make a million seeds. On a whim, he bent and picked the flower, pale in the moonlight, and touched its fuzzy face. While he toyed with a useless and unloved weed, his feet turned south.

ରେ   ରେ   ରେ

May Day. Gaela's favorite day of the year. She and Jeanie and Lillian had spent the last week making May baskets to give to all the guests. Each tiny raffia basket held a paper cup of potting soil, with a johnny-jump-up or a violet or a buttercup, some small wildflower planted in it.

For the big house, they had made a much more elaborate planter. They set it by the front door early in the morning, rang the doorbell and ran, giggling like schoolgirls. From the shelter of a lilac in full bloom, Gaela craned her neck between Jeanie's and Lillian's shoulders to see who answered the door. It was Ivy, and her face lit like a candle when she saw the basket. She picked it up and looked around, trying to see who had left it, then called, "Thank you, whoever you are!" Still giggling, the three gave each other high fives.

Signs by the entrance told guests where to go to pick up their complimentary May baskets, and the staff took turns staying near the main workshop for most of the day, ready to hand out baskets and cheerful words. They also happily accepted compliments on the beauties of Eden, which, the guests avowed, grew lovelier by the year.

Early that evening, Gaela saw Mr. S sitting alone by the lake, gazing out over its ripples. Her heart sank.

Already? She went to him, and he looked up, happy mask firmly in place, and thanked her for the May basket. "Ivy and George love that stuff!" He always called his wife "George."

"Like you don't?" Gaela chided him, and was rewarded with a smile.

"I do, I'm just too manly to admit it. I used to go out with May baskets." His voice trailed off, and the happy mask slipped.

"With someone else?" Gaela ventured, and almost thought he would confide in her, for a second. Then he stood briskly. "Heavens, yes, with someone! A girl! You don't think I'd do such a thing by myself, do you?" He puffed out his chest and flexed his biceps, and she laughed obediently. To her surprise, he hugged her before he walked away. Then he turned back and said with determined cheer, "I'm going to admire my grotto. Care to accompany me?" He held out a courtly arm.

Gaela smiled back and took it. "Certainly, kind sir!" She dared to squeeze his arm just a little, hoping her wish to somehow comfort him would translate, even a little.

They walked up the lawn that swept from the lake toward the southwest side of the house. The sun had dropped behind the woods to the west, and long shadows stretched across the grass. Between those darker swaths, the lawn was blindingly green. They approached the octagonal gazebo, a lacy structure that looked as if it could have floated down from the clouds. It had been carefully centered between the two curving wings of rose garden that reached out from each end of the house.

"It's going to be so beautiful when it's painted all glossy white," Gaela said. "You were smart to put Ted in charge of the plantings. He has great ideas."

"He does, doesn't he? I told him I wanted it to be someplace brides would like. Pink, maybe. But he says yellow. He's going to plant climbing yellow ever-blooming roses on each upright, with that fluffy white stuff, what's that called again?"

"Baby's breath?"

"That's it. Funny names these flowers have. And lots of greenery. It'll be great."

"It will be breathtaking. And brides aren't the only people that will love it. I can't believe the grotto and the gazebo are both almost complete already!"

Mr. S grinned at her. "What with me and the missus arguing and holding things up?"

Gaela primmed her mouth and tried to look innocent. "I didn't say that. The weather has cooperated, and the crews have outdone themselves!"

"I don't suppose the competition between the two teams hurt any," Mr. S pointed out with a smirk.

"True."

"So, what do you say? Let's go to the grotto and see if we can't get in George's hair." He chuckled like a naughty child.

Gaela went along with him, laughing, but the grotto was deserted, to her secret relief.

This spot was the gazebo's opposite in every way, cool instead of warm, shady instead of sunny, tucked away instead of standing in the middle of everything.

"That concrete really does look like natural rocks," said Mr. S admiringly, willing to praise, since "George" wasn't here to harass.

"I know. It's amazing." Gaela watched the creek tumble over the lip they had made for it as if it had always done so, making a fine splash and seeming to enjoy itself immensely. Around the sides of the little enclosure, perhaps eight feet across, she had already placed some ferns and pieces of moss, which would soon spread and look as if they had been there since the Indians roamed these hills. Inside the edge of the grotto, the "stone" was shaped into a ledge for sitting on each side.

"Let's sit a few minutes," suggested Mr. S. "It's hot enough we won't mind the occasional splash, will we?"

Gaela sat with him, looking around contentedly, half dreaming, half planning. There was room for children to wade a bit. Benches would be placed under the birches that would soon be put in a little to the east, where the lake curved east and south giving a nice view of the grotto, out of reach of spray. She knew she would spend more time in this cool and quiet place than in the gazebo, charming though it was. She stayed a while when her boss excused himself and wandered away.

On the second day of May, it rained, but Gaela found Mrs. S in the Secret Garden, crying quietly. She teetered on the brink of offering solace, but what could she say? Mr. S had simply hidden his feelings when she showed up. Maybe they would prefer to be left alone with whatever grief they felt. Backing away, Gaela quieted her conscience by praying for peace for them both. Was that a cop-out?

Two days later, on one of the wooded paths, she saw someone she took at first to be Mrs. S again. The figure was wearing a large hat, and Mrs. S sometimes affected garden hats and flowing gowns when she was at Eden. Nobody had the heart to tell her these costumes only made her more overwhelming than ever. Then the figure moved, and Gaela saw that it was Ivy. Before her eyes, Ivy fell to the ground, apparently giving in to a storm of weeping.

So Lillian's radar had been on target. Gaela stood indecisively. Should she go and try to offer comfort? But they had hardly spoken to each other. Surely Ivy would only be embarrassed. Gaela certainly would.

While she dithered, Ted appeared. He went immediately to Ivy's side, and Gaela sighed with relief. If anyone knew how to deal with a weeping woman, it was Ted. Come to think of it, there might not be too many men you could say that of. Just another of his numberless talents. She watched Ted pick Ivy up and lead her to a bench. Ivy drooped against Ted's broad shoulder, and Gaela began to feel like a voyeur, so she went about her business.

That night, she added Ivy to her prayer list. "Oh, Mother/Father, what a lot of pain there is in the world! Can't you do something?"

Or was she supposed to be the one to do something?

Chapter Eight

With an eye to distracting herself and preventing pacing, Gaela put on her recorder CD. She wished she knew how Caine was doing. When the concerto ended, for the first time she found the nerve to do more than look at her own new plastic recorder. She tried a few notes. They sounded horrible! Nothing like the clear, sweet trills Caine had produced. Maybe this wasn't a "well-made" plastic recorder. Or maybe she just didn't have the touch. She persevered for a while, dutifully playing the notes on the first page of her book. She sounded like a kid playing with a whistle!

Putting both away, she wandered out into her garden, rather neglected of late. A little wandering and tending didn't bring her the peace and contentment it usually did, so she went back inside and read, and finally trailed discontentedly off to bed, to toss there for a while.

Gaela awoke late, and hurried to work. The next few days were sunny and busy. The head caretaker couldn't do anything without having visitors peering over her shoulders and asking questions.

"Whatcha doin'?"

"Feeding these little baby flowers so they can grow big and strong."

A delighted squeal. "*Feeding* them? What do flowers eat?"

Gaela grinned at the impish little boy, his hair springing in all directions and eyes sparking like live wires. "Well, this food is made out of animal manure, soaked in water to make what we call manure tea."

"*EEEEEEWWWWW!! YUCK!!* Mom, did you hear that? Those flowers eat—"

"Yes, dear!" said Mom hastily. "Now doesn't that make you feel better about having to eat vegetables?"

Gaela chuckled to herself as the boy ran off.

"Excuse me, miss, what variety of Lobelia is this?"

"Ma'am, why won't my Bradford pears blossom?"

"Are there public restrooms?"

She answered them all patiently, reminding herself that this was one of the things she *liked* about her job. Really. It had been very hard at first for a congenital introvert, but now she thought of it as passing the gardening torch on to others, whether to a new generation, or to older people who had never learned the joys of planting and tending.

But for some reason, she was jumpy lately, and feeling crowded. She had been thinking a lot about Ted, and had realized something important. She couldn't imagine Ted in her tiny house. Or any man. And she didn't want to. She loved her solitary life, in fact would have liked for it to be more solitary than it was. Days like this, she missed the old days, when it had been just herself and the occasional part-time worker, wandering around Eden's Gate and feeling as if she really had found lost paradise.

Gaela went to the back lot on the northwest corner of the property and planted the rows of multi-colored Indian corn, pumpkins, and gourds they would need for fall decorations. It felt good to be alone for a while.

Maybe she would never marry. That would be just fine with her. Which was good, since Ted and Ivy were spending more time together. She couldn't help wondering if her decision was being made for her.

On the twenty-first of May, just over one month since they'd arrived, the Sullivans packed up and left. The grotto was finished, though still looking a little raw. The gazebo was painted, but not planted yet. The Sullivans left a note thanking the staff for their hard work and adjuring them to keep it up — Eden's Gate depended on them all. There was a nice bonus for Gaela to divide up among the crew.

Gaela sighed, wishing she could have said good-bye. The Sullivans didn't usually leave this abruptly, but they did it often enough that she wasn't shocked, as the newer staff were.

Ted looked dazed. "Can we contact them? Did they leave a forwarding address, or anything?"

"They have a cell phone. Sometimes they even answer it. We can get them if we need to. And they can reach us, of course, any time." Feeling sorry for him, Gaela put her hand on his arm.

He looked at her as if he hadn't seen her for several days, and said, "Well, it doesn't matter. I was just surprised. Walk me to the gazebo?"

She smiled and went with him. This was probably a good time.

"Lookin' good, isn't it?"

"Beautiful," she agreed. "They trust you to do it right, that's why they can leave when it's not quite done."

He grinned down at her. "I may not know the Sullivans as well as you do, but I do get the general picture. I never expected them to stay this long. You don't have to reassure me, but it's nice of you. What are you doing tonight?"

She hesitated. She had so hoped he would fall for Ivy and forget all about her.

"Hot date, huh?" He was preparing himself for her usual refusal.

"Ted, you know I love you, right?"

"Uh-oh," said Ted.

"Oh, come on, it's not that bad." Gaela's heart was pounding, despite her determined cheer. She would so much rather just ignore things and hope they'd go away. But she was turning over a new leaf. She didn't want to sit on a bench when she was sixty and cry over lost choices or mistakes. Not that she had any idea what the Sullivans cried over. *Come on, Gaela, you're putting it off.*

"Like a brother, right?" Ted's voice was also heavy with determined cheer.

"Ted, I know that's usually a put-off, but really, I do love you like a brother. Isn't that a good thing? You certainly take care of me in a way none of my brothers ever did!"

"Sure, that's a good thing. Why do I have the feeling this is a dear John sort of moment? Look, if this has anything to do with Ivy, she's going through a hard time right now, that's all."

"This has nothing to do with Ivy. I'm just finally sure of my own heart, and I apologize for taking so long about it. Although I tried hard not to raise false hopes."

"No, chief, you never did. Don't worry. It's all my own false hopes." He sighed.

"I admit," said Gaela, "I had rather hoped that Ivy might . . ." He didn't answer. "None of my business, though. Listen, we've both got work to do." She turned away, but he grabbed her and hugged her right off her feet. She hugged him back, feeling both their hearts pounding. Then he set her carefully down.

"Sorry. Couldn't resist."

"That's okay."

She left him by the gazebo, and went looking for something in need of tending.

It was a disorienting sort of day. They were all trying to remember what projects they had been planning and working on before hurricane Sullivan descended on them. Visitors had to ask questions twice, and Randy mowed the lawn again that he had just mowed three days ago.

Gaela went in the house and dismissed the staff, thanking them heartily for their service and assuring them they would be called again the next time the Sullivans came. She gave all the perishable food to a local food pantry, checked the fifteen rooms, and set the new security system. She still had to read the manual each time, not having done this many times yet. Ted had had to be content in the end with this, the new lights, and an alarm on the gate. He wasn't happy, but it was more than they'd had before.

Gaela went to the office and thought about hiring more summer help. It was about that time. Memorial Day and the end of school were looming nearer. She placed an ad and went outside to make a circuit of the garden and decide what needed doing next.

She was standing right next to Ted, talking about the east rose garden, when she saw a dark, bearded man and couldn't choke back a gasp.

"What? Chief?" Ted looked from her face to the man, who was walking quickly away, and grabbed her arm. "Is that him? It is, isn't it?" Ted let go of her and headed in the man's direction.

"No! Ted!" She grabbed him and held on, not impeding his progress in the slightest. "Ted, will you listen? It's not him! I mean, it is, but-"

Ted stopped so abruptly that Gaela's death grip on him was the only thing that kept her from falling. "What do you mean, it is, but it isn't?" he asked in an ominous tone. Gaela gulped and wished she were a better liar. Drat Caine! If only she'd been better prepared, she wouldn't have blurted out a truth she'd rather Ted never knew.

"He--we became friends. Not friends, exactly, but—I was only ever scared the first day I saw him."

"And just how many days have you seen him?" growled Ted.

Suddenly Gaela squared up to him, hands on hips. "What business is it of yours? I only told you about him because I believed he was a threat to me. When I learned differently, I was embarrassed I ever told you anything. Believe me, Ted, I appreciate your protectiveness. It saved my life on at least one occasion, and I don't forget it. But this time, I am not in danger. Okay?"

Ted regarded her darkly. "I thought you said he was long gone."

"He was. I guess he's back. Leave him alone. Eden's a public garden, remember?"

"Your mantra. Which I notice you only invoke when this guy is around. Fine. I'll mind my own business. Just know that if he threatens you in any way, he's dead meat. You may not love me, but I still love you!"

With that parting shot, Ted stormed away, leaving Gaela with her mouth hanging open. Now she'd hurt him worse than before. She rubbed her hand over her face. Life was just not fair.

Looking around, Gaela realized she and Ted had been under observation practically the whole time. Cheeks flaming, she faced the knot of visitors, who began to guiltily sidle away. "Show's over," she said with a bright smile. "Next performance in an hour!" This got her a polite chuckle, and with that, she made her getaway.

Her feet took her directly to the Secret Garden. The gate was open, and Caine was there before her, but apparently wasn't expecting her. She caught him in an attitude so much like that of the Sullivans that she finally realized what Mrs. S's eyes had reminded her of. Caine's eyes! They both looked as if they'd lost something they would give anything to regain. Caine looked up when he heard her steps, and she caught her breath.

For an instant, she thought it wasn't Caine at all. His beard had been neatly trimmed, and his black hair, trimmed, parted, and combed, lay on his shoulders in glossy curls. He stood, looking at her almost shyly, and she took in his new jeans and green cotton shirt. Even his boots were new. Gaela's eyes found their way back to his face, lingering on the strong lines of his cheekbones and jaw. His eyes, which had always made her insides quake, looked even bigger, softer, and more defined by lashes she only wish she had. Gaela couldn't find her voice. Caine was shockingly handsome!

"Hey," he said finally. His soft voice made her shiver.

"Hey, yourself. My goodness! Is that you?"

"It's me. Scary, isn't it?"

Scary wasn't the word that sprang to mind. *Please, God, let me not be blushing! My face feels hot.* With great willpower, she didn't press her hands to her face. Instead, she took her usual seat in the swing and asked as casually as possible, "So, how have you been keeping?"

"Okay. You?" He seated himself on the log, which she hadn't hauled away for that very reason.

"Fine." This was scintillating. "The owners stayed long enough to turn the place upside down and add some new features, and then left. You'll have to see their contributions."

"Do they just let you do what you like around here?"

"Pretty much, yeah. Within a budget, of course."

"Cool. It's like your own place, without having to make the money."

"True. But then, as I understand it, they didn't have to make the money, either. They inherited it. Something to do with coal, I think. Or oil."

He nodded. "Both, probably. And more."

"Probably."

Conversation languished.

"Hey, you know, I found a "Recorder Concerto."

Those dark eyes were definitely more dangerous than ever now that they weren't surrounded by underbrush. "Did you? Giuseppe Somartini?"

"Something like that, I think." She couldn't find the nerve to tell him she'd bought her own recorder. Anyway, he'd renew his offer to teach her, and she didn't want him to hear the squeaks she made. "Well, believe it or not, I am supposed to be working. The Sullivans are lenient, but they do expect me to do something for my paycheck." She stood, and he did, too. She went to the gate then turned back with a grin. Her turn. "I never thought I'd say this, but I'm glad you're back."

Caine smiled, but didn't reply. She couldn't decide if he was glad, too, or not.

She went back to her checking, but although she carried a clipboard around the garden, she didn't make many notes on it. She couldn't get over how incredibly gorgeous Caine was, underneath all that disguise. Nobody would take him for a bum now, although she had no reason to suppose he was any less homeless than he had been when she met him. Come to think of it, she had never known whether he was homeless or not. Standing still, gazing blindly into the topiary garden, Gaela decided that since Caine seemed to want to be friends, sort of, and since she had gone out on a limb and informed Ted they were friends, it was time they knew some small things about each other. Normal things. Small talk things. Nothing nosy.

"Where do you live?" she imagined herself asking him. No. *"Where are you from?"* That was better. *"What do you do?"* He at least knew both those things about her. *"Where did you learn to play like that?"* There. That was a nice, safe question. People liked to talk about their hobbies. She certainly couldn't ask what she really wanted to know. *"Have you found peace yet?" "Have you learned to pray?" "What is it you're looking for?"*

"Where's the bathroom?"

"What?" Gaela turned with a start. A woman with three children, one of whom was jiggling urgently, regarded her strangely. "I asked twice. Where's the bathroom? Can't you see it's an emergency?"

"Oh, I'm so sorry! Just thinking! You have to go back up through that trellis, toward the house, and out to the parking lot. They're behind the tall, narrow trees." Eyeing the jiggling boy, she whispered sympathetically, "Don't tell, but if you're really desperate, there's a nice, fat elephant right over there." She pointed to the biggest example of topiary at Eden, and the boy disappeared behind it like magic while Gaela and his mother shared a laugh and his sisters chorused, "Gross!"

☙ ☙ ☙

Caine stayed so long in the Secret Garden he had to hide when the big guy made his security rounds. It was ridiculously easy. He waited for dark and slid quietly through the woods until he was within sight of her house. Somartini's Recorder Concerto was playing, and he smiled, pretending she had done it deliberately, to give him a welcome. He never should have come back. Why had he?

He crawled in under an evergreen with low-hanging branches, where he had left his pack earlier. Scrunching around until he was relatively comfortable, his head on the pack, he settled himself for sleep.

As he drifted off with the whispering of the wind in his ears, he wondered if she was praying for him.

Chapter Nine

By Memorial Day, Eden had a full staff of sixteen, with hour-long morning staff meetings during which Gaela checked up on progress, fielded questions and suggestions, and handed out the assignments she'd made up the night before. She didn't get to do as much gardening as she liked, this time of year. If she turned some of the bossing over to Ted, maybe she could remedy that a little.

Three of the new people were great at handling the public, so that became their primary responsibility. As soon as they were trained, they could take over most garden tours, the ones for tourists who just wanted to see everything in the most efficient way before they got back on their air-conditioned buses. She herself would continue to lead the much more inspiring educational tours for serious gardeners.

For the rest of the summer Randy and two high school kids would do practically nothing but mow and trim. Gary and John could now take care of specific gardening tasks if they were laid out for them in list form. But they were getting pretty fed up with babysitting Chan, as they put it.

One day Lillian peremptorily ordered Chan to help her in the greenhouse. That evening, Lillian came to Gaela. "Well, you'll never believe it, but our man Chan is a dab hand at gardening under glass."

Gaela raised startled brows. "A dab hand? I would have said ham hands!"

Lillian clucked admonishingly. "It's a matter of giving people chances, and a little education, until you see what they like and are good at. For your information, those ham hands are downright expert at bonsai, no matter how tiny."

"You're kidding!"

"Not a bit. And you'd better believe I kept an eagle eye on him at first, too."

"Well, great!" said Gaela. "You have no idea what a relief that is to me. I didn't want to fire him. John told me he supports his mother."

"Well, if he keeps on this way, you'll have to give him a raise."

Gaela took a minute that week to go and watch Chan. She couldn't help grinning to see his sleek black head and Lillian's salt and pepper one bent together earnestly over something small and green on a work table. With a satisfied nod, the "chief" left them to it.

Chuck, as always, worked alone, dividing his time between the topiary garden and the lake. He was attempting a family of topiary swans walking in a row, though they presently looked like nothing more than an oddly shaped and oddly spaced hedge. When he wasn't clipping exotic shrubbery or training ivy to huge metal frameworks, he was stalking along the lakeside growling at anybody who had the temerity to wade, or to feed junk food to the geese and the Mallard ducks who were now nesting.

For the summer, there was one stretch of pebbly beach, marked off with buoy ropes, where wading was allowed. Guarding this stretch was the job of choice for the younger workers, so Gaela measured out turns scrupulously, adding extra lifeguard duty as a reward for excellent work on some other assigned task, such as the infinitely less popular litter patrol. Each year she thought she was getting a better handle on this boss stuff.

She and Ted seemed to exist in an awkward truce. She was sorry for it, and delighted the day she brought in the mail and it included a thick envelope for him, addressed in an elegant, loopy hand. Even without peeking shamelessly at the return address, Gaela would have known it was from Ivy Sullivan. She put it in his cubbyhole on the wall, hoping it would cheer him up.

Caine was still around, but she didn't get to talk to him much except in the evenings. During the days he sometimes showed up while she was gardening, asking questions like any visitor, and twice he joined a tour she was leading.

She still felt an electric shock every time she saw him. He seemed like an entirely different man than before. It was so embarrassing. Outward appearance had never mattered much to her. *Great, Clancy!* she berated herself, *Now? At this late date, you're going to turn into some schoolgirl swooning over a "hunk?"* Or so her younger assistants elegantly described him. She heard their giggles on more occasions than she liked.

"There's that hunk again! Man, I wish he'd just *look* once at me!"

Worse yet, "Oooh, that guy is *so* hot!"

And worst of all, "Ms. Clancy, I think he likes you! He looks at you all the time!"

To which she had replied with a distinct snap, "Who likes me? That's ridiculous! Did you finish watering the new beds around the gazebo?"

Her most devout and fervent hope was that their sharp eyes would never see her looking back, or notice the flush that she unmistakably felt every time he came within fifty yards of her. Luckily, she tanned brown enough to be able to *hope* no telltale red was visible.

Gaela had discovered during the first week Caine was back that he was usually to be found in the Secret Garden in the evenings, so she carefully limited her own evening visits there to no more than twice a week. This was not so easy, and not just because she missed the garden, either.

Her first attempts at small talk had not been wildly successful.

"Where are you from?"

"Around. You?"

"Upstate New York."

A light of interest in his unfathomable eyes. "Really? I've been through there a few times. I kind of like those snowy winters, myself."

And the next thing she knew, he had her talking about the little snow house she'd made in a corner of the back yard when she was nine and there was two feet of snow.

"Where did you learn to play the recorder so beautifully?"

"I taught myself, actually. Are you sure you don't want me to teach you? Come on, give it just one try."

And Gaela the private, the tell-nobody-any-secrets-they-might-use-against-you was actually tricked into revealing that she now possessed her own recorder, and coerced into letting him give her just one lesson. Her squeaks became notes, and she began to believe she had met her master in more ways than one.

However, there was still one way in which she was his master. He didn't know the first thing about growing things. One day when she was planting apple-scented geraniums and he was asking questions, she said, "Here, give me a hand."

"Me?" He looked as startled and nervous as if she'd handed him a newborn baby instead of a plant.

"Sure. I've already dug the hole. Spread the roots like this, so they can grow freely." While she talked, Gaela carefully restricted herself to sneaking sideways glances. But she didn't miss the softening of his face as his hands carefully spread the roots the way she did and pressed the moist dirt around the stems.

There were children watching, and they immediately set up a chorus.

"Can we help?"

"Me, too?"

"Yes, you can help. *You* can dig a hole, just like this, and *you* can put in the next plant, and *you* can water the ones we've already planted. Careful, don't drown them."

Gaela and Caine each gained several lively satellites, and she also didn't miss his gentle way with children. The bed eventually got planted, not too crookedly.

When the children's parents dragged them away after Gaela assured them everything was done and thanked them for their help, she turned to Caine and looked at him appraisingly. "Why was I ever afraid of you?"

He smiled a little grimly. "Don't let your guard down, Pixie."

Gaela was momentarily distracted. "That's the second time you've called me that."

"It's because you're so little and brown. The first time I saw you, with your brown hair and brown hands and brown coverall, I thought you were a pixie like my nanny used to talk about."

A clue! She was careful not to let her face show a single glimmer of her interest, but she would definitely figure out a way to follow up on this. A memory snagged her, and she exclaimed, "So that's why you said that about my brown eyes, the day you held my ladder. You said you were glad they were brown."

"I remember."

"I thought you were nuts!"

"I am, and don't you forget it."

"There, now, you see? That's what I mean. Why do you persist in trying to make yourself out to be some kind of bogeyman? You're just trying to scare me."

"Gaela, if you knew the truth about me, you'd run screaming."

"Well, I keep trying to learn about you. You won't even answer a simple question, like where are you from?"

"Why do you want to know?"

"Because I'm starting to think we're friends, at least a little. Friends tell each other things."

They had been walking toward the sheds, and Caine stopped and faced her. "Why do you want to be my friend?"

"Because—" she hesitated. Why did she? Would he get upset if she told the truth? "Because I think you need one."

"Ah." He walked on. "I'm a project."

"No!" Gaela trotted to catch up. "What's wrong with needing a friend? Anyway, that's not the only reason."

"Well, why, then?"

Now she was in for it. "Because I like you."

"You like me? You don't even know me!"

Full circle. And Ted was approaching with a wheelbarrow and the grim look he reserved for Caine. "I want to know you," she said doggedly. "But of course, I can't force any confidences, and I would be the last person to want to. I value my privacy myself. If you'll excuse me. Hey, Ted, wait a second." And she trotted over to Ted, leaving Caine frowning after her. Let him frown. Why *did* she like him, anyway? "Ted, one whole circuit of sprinklers down on the lawn has quit. We'll have to check the water main and the breakers."

Caine wasn't in the Secret Garden that evening when Gaela went, hoping to mend fences. She didn't see him again for two days, which was just as well, since there were four weddings in those two days, besides three busloads of tourists to see the famous Eden's Gate. They still couldn't get the sprinklers going, and two gardeners quit, having found lifeguard jobs where they could stay on a real beach and watch real bikinis.

Then Ivy showed up unexpectedly, throwing Gaela into a tizzy until Ivy reassured her.
"Don't hire anybody, and don't worry about me. I only need one room, and I can take care of myself. There should be plenty of food in there for a couple of days, and if there isn't,

I'll get some. Just refresh me on that new security system, will you?"

Gaela showed her how to get into the house and left her there. It would be interesting to see if Ted's face would lighten up any.

The next time she heard recorder music on the rock by the lake, she climbed up and confronted Caine. "Where are you staying?"

He lifted an eyebrow. "Hello to you, too! Did you miss me?"

"Don't put me off. Where are you staying?"

"I've taken a room in town, if it's any of your business."

"Good."

"Why?"

"Because I suspect you have stayed here at Eden in the past, and I can't let you do that anymore. Do you have enough money for food?"

Caine laughed. "What is this, feed the hungry month?"

"Will you for once answer a direct question?"

"Sure, honey, I have plenty of money. I robbed a bank."

Gaela ground her teeth at him. "I am *trying* to offer you a job!"

For once Caine's face showed pure astonishment. "What?"

"A job. You know, where you show up every single day and do as you're told. Surely you've had at least one in your life?"

"You're asking me to work for you?" He couldn't seem to believe it. She wasn't sure she did, either.

"On a probationary basis. Two of my workers quit, and you show promise as a gardener. Or at least you can fetch and carry and help with heavy work if you don't want to garden."

He just looked at her for a minute, and she decided this spur-of-the-moment impulse had been about as dumb as most impulses were. Then he said slowly, "Actually, I'd love to garden, if you're serious."

"Great. It's just minimum wage, you know."

"Fine."

"Good. Can you start tomorrow at eight?"

"I'll be there. Why are you doing this?"

She figured it wouldn't be a good idea to say any of the things crowding to the front of her mind. *I think you could use a job. I think you could use some self-confidence. I think you need time in a garden. I want you where I can keep my eye on you.* So she told him the other truth. "I'm desperate!"

He grinned and she left him, hurrying back to the big house where she was meeting her next gardeners' tour.

ଔ ଔ ଔ

Well, now he'd done it. Caine sat on the rock until his seat went numb, trying to make himself just go away and never come back. But he'd given her his word. And she'd said she was desperate. He was beginning to see the scope of the work to be done on this place, and it was no sinecure. She needed him.

Nonsense and poppycock! She needed any warm body with a strong back, preferably one that wouldn't quit after two weeks. The problem was, she was beginning to like him, or so she insisted. He had always liked her. And if she knew the truth--if she knew the things he'd done--if she had so much as a hint as to why he was drawn back to this place, or what he had done the last time he was here!

Why couldn't he just leave? And no nonsense about voices in the wind, either. If there was a voice here, it was probably an evil voice--the same dark, desperate one that had chased him for years. The one that saw to it he kept right on making the same destructive choices, no matter how many resolutions he made. The one that would make sure this time it was himself he destroyed.

Caine scrubbed at his face with the heels of his hands. It hadn't felt like an evil voice. Not this time. And there was something about being here. The gate of Eden. He thought of the sign in town. "Beauty for the eyes and peace for the soul." Wasn't it starting to be true, just a little? Wasn't he different? He felt different. Or was it only because he was around his pixie? Was it a spell she put on him? When he was alone, it wasn't peace he felt. All the old torment and hatred threatened to overwhelm him again.

Not always.

Caine turned his head, seeking the source of the sound, if sound it was. Not always what?

A picture filled his mind. It was a clear memory of just a little while ago, before Gaela came and made him an offer he couldn't refuse. He'd been sitting here, on this rock, playing an old Gaelic lullaby that the thought of her name had brought to mind. And he had, yes, he had been at peace.

He shouldn't stay. But he couldn't seem to go. And if there was any chance at all--if even a little of what she insisted was true, and there was any healing to be had here . . . could he afford to pass it up?

When Caine finally stood, he was so stiff he had to do some serious stretching before he could even attempt to climb down from the rock.

Chapter Ten

The first job Gaela gave Caine the next morning was to help unload a truckload of cedar mulch, potting soil, rock phosphate, and sundry other fifty-pound bags. Ted moved two bags for every bag Caine moved, giving both men reason to glare at each other. When Gaela passed Caine on her way to the workshop, he bent over and pretended to hobble like an old man, and she grinned unsympathetically.

"Gardening's hard work," she said cheerfully.

"That's not what she always tells us," Lillian contradicted, happening to be within hearing. " 'In a garden,'" she quoted, and six voices joined her for the rest, " 'all work is pleasure!'"

Caine rolled his eyes, and Gaela laughed and said, "I never said it wasn't hard work, however. Tote that barge, lift that bale!" She grabbed a fifty-pound bag herself, and Caine watched disgustedly as she toted it competently to the stack they were making under the overhang of a shed roof.

"That thing is bigger than you are!" he growled. "Go plant something!"

"She's the chief, and perfectly capable. Don't baby her!" growled Ted, the perennial mother hen, and then Gaela really did laugh.

Ivy came around the corner of the shed smiling expectantly and asking, "What's the joke?"

"Oh, nothing." Gaela wiped her eyes. "These galoots think I should go paint my nails or something and leave them to be the big, strong men." Then she eyed Ivy, wondering if she'd put her foot in it.

Ivy eyed her right back. "Why shouldn't women be strong? I wish I were as strong as you are."

"Nothing to it," Gaela assured her. "Exercise and a little belief in yourself." She continued to eye the tall, slim beauty speculatively. Did she dare? Why not? "Are you busy today?"

Ivy looked positively eager. "Not a bit! Do you need help?"

"Tote that barge, lift that bale!" put in Caine, passing with another bag on his shoulder.

"No, no, we wouldn't want to make you guys look bad or anything," said Gaela sweetly. "Can you take sun, Ivy?"

"As long as I have my hat."

"Are you up to helping me spread some of this stuff?"

Ted stopped by them with his hands on his hips. "Ivy isn't one of us peons. You don't have to put everyone you see to work."

"Nonsense, she's volunteering. And you can stop any time you want to," she told Ivy.

Ivy lifted her delicate chin at Ted. "I'll let you know if I start wilting."

Ted shook his head and went back to the truck. His back said eloquently that if they were going to gang up on him, he was washing his hands of them both.

"Good choice," said Caine in a confiding tone, but Ted ignored him.

So Gaela found Ivy some gloves and they loaded up a golf cart and headed out to work side by side, shoveling cedar bark under shrubbery and around summer plantings.

Gaela decided to practice her small talk skills on Ivy. Maybe she would be an easier subject than Caine was. "So. . . what do you do when you're not shoveling mulch?"

Ivy grimaced. "Not much, at the moment." She grunted as she tried to dig the tip of her shovel into the pile of shredded bark in the back of the golf cart.

"You don't have a job, or go to school, or something?"

"I did school. Boy, did I do school. Phillips Exeter. Vassar. All the best for Mother's little darling." Ivy's blond hair swung past her face as she deposited her shovelful under a yew shrub and worked to spread it evenly.

Gaela was considering going back to being a recluse who only spoke when necessary. "So, um. . . do you have a degree, then?"

Ivy laughed. "I have a Master's degree in how to be a beautiful, useless ornament to society." She straightened and shoved her hair out of her face, leaving a streak of dirt across her carefully made-up cheek. Gaela straightened, too, and saw tears in the green eyes.

Why had she ever tried to open up? She was no good at it.

"To tell you the truth," Ivy blurted, "my life is pretty much a shambles right now. My mother thinks she can control every second of everything. I mean, she always has, but for some reason I hate it more and more lately. Then, this spring, my fiancé left me at the altar."

"How awful!" was all Gaela could manage.

"I mean, literally, at the altar, in the $15,000 dress, with the 2,000 guests looking on, the whole comedy routine!" Ivy waved her gloved hands and almost lost the forgotten shovel.

"You're kidding!"

"Believe me, it was too horrible to make up."

"What a jerk!"

Ivy's face twisted and Gaela winced. *Tactful, Clancy!*

"I guess he was, but I thought he loved me." One of the tears escaped, making a muddy track through the dirt on Ivy's cheek.

"I'm so sorry."

"I guess nobody's ever loved me. Nobody except my dad. Maybe nobody ever will love me like my dad."

"It's good that you have him," Gaela ventured.

"He died eight years ago." Ivy delivered this in a dead, hopeless sort of voice, turning back to continue mulching.

Gaela spent a few seconds privately vowing a return to hermit-hood. She loaded her shovel and worked in silence beside Ivy, wondering if there were people who would actually know what to say when a relative stranger opened her heart and dumped its contents all over the garden with the compost.

"Mom hardly waited until he was buried before she moved us back east so I could go to the Right Schools."

Gaela seized on the least hazardous detail of the conversation. "Back east? Where did you live before?"

"California. I was born here in Ohio, but we moved out there when I was still practically a baby. Dad loved it. I want to go back there someday. Although I am glad I've gotten to know Uncle Sam and Aunt George. They're wonderful."

"Well, that's good." At least she had somebody to turn to.

"We've hardly ever had any contact until now." Ivy stopped and leaned thoughtfully on her shovel. "I always thought there was some. . . something. . . between my dad and Uncle Sam."

"Oh, really?" Gaela knelt to push mulch under spreading branches.

But there didn't seem to be any more confidences, thank goodness.

A while later, as Ivy matched her shovel for shovel, Gaela asked, "Why did you say you wished you were as strong as I am? You look like a pretty good mulch-slinger to me!"

Ivy mopped her face and sighed. "I'll be a basket case tomorrow. I'm not exactly used to this kind of work. I guess I've just been shoveling my anger, you know? They say it's really therapeutic. I didn't know how right they were."

"Do you feel better?" asked Gaela.

"I do. I really do." Ivy stretched her back, lifted her face to the sun, and smiled.

"Good. I'm glad."

As Ivy left, Gaela called after her, "If you ever need a job, let me know!"

Ivy grinned over her shoulder. She still looked like a supermodel, even all sweaty and with dirt on her face. "Bet I could get Aunt George and Uncle Sam to pay me more for it!"

Gaela laughed. "Don't you dare steal my job. You'd regret it, you know."

"Don't worry! It'd kill me!"

Ted showed up from somewhere, and Gaela watched Ivy make what appeared to be an embarrassed swipe at her dirty cheek. Ted just laughed at her, reaching out to touch the streak and turning to walk her back to the big house. As they went, Gaela could hear Ivy joking about her hard-working morning with more animation than she had yet seen in that young woman.

"Nicely done," said a voice behind her. She turned and saw Caine. "Another project well underway," he added, and walked away.

Gaela made a face at his back. Showed how much he knew. All she had been trying to do was learn to be a little more open. Reach out a little. Not dig around in the guts of people's private lives.

That night in the Secret Garden, after a particularly successful recorder lesson, she actually played Mary Had a Little Lamb. Caine seemed as delighted with her as she was with herself. He put his recorder to his lips, and Gaela looked away suddenly and put her hand to her stomach. She wished his beautiful mouth were still hidden by whiskers. Ridiculous, the affect it had on her!

"Play it again!"

"What?"

"The song, silly! Play it again!"

So she started, and he began to play a harmony. But the feeling that he was depending on her to have the right notes and timing unnerved her. Before she even got to the second "little lamb," Gaela dropped out and put her face in her hands.

"No, don't quit," said Caine, "Come on—again. You can do it. Don't worry about mistakes. I'll cover for you. And don't be afraid to lose the beat. I'll play with you, no matter how slow or fast you go."

So she tried again, doing her best to ignore him and play as if she were alone in the garden. This time she came to the end flushed with delight. Or possibly with breathlessness.

"Excellent!" declared Caine.

"Again!" begged Gaela. "I want to listen to us this time."

They did it three more times, and by the time they were through, they were playing a real duet, together. Gaela was amazed at how marvelous the feeling was. "You make me sound good!" she exclaimed.

"You sound good all by yourself," Caine told her.

She put down her recorder and looked him in the eyes. "You're such a good teacher. Patient, positive, never scolding. So why do you put down other things I do?"

"What do you mean?"

"Ivy wanted to work with me today, and I let her. You made it sound like some kind of goody-goody thing. You call yourself a 'project' and try to make me feel guilty for liking you or caring what happens to you."

He wasn't looking at her anymore. "I'm sorry. You're right, I do that, don't I? I don't know why, but I'll try to quit."

He had never answered any of her "small talk" questions. She wondered what he'd do with one of the real ones. Greatly daring, she asked quietly, "What are you afraid of?"

He was silent so long she was sure he wasn't going to answer. She hadn't really expected him to, so she was surprised when he said, "I'm afraid you'll like me too much."

"How much is too much?"

"More than I deserve."

"How much do you deserve?"

Caine stood suddenly. "Look, you worked me to death today. I'm tired. I'm going back to my palatial dwelling now."

With his hand on the gate, he paused, but didn't look back. "Keep up the good work," he said, and was gone. Gaela sat alone in the dark garden for a while. What good work? The recorder? The friendliness to Ivy? To him? Nagging him to answer questions he had no intention of answering?

Keep praying.

Gaela had no trouble recognizing the voice on the wind.

"I will," she promised.

Chapter Eleven

It was strange, seeing Caine all day every day and not having to feel secretive about it. He soon fit into the routine of Eden as if he'd always been there. She even knew his last name now. Caine Hunter. It was an odd name, but she'd heard worse. She'd changed her own, come to that.

Rather to her surprise, he got on well with the other staff, and soon even Ted seemed to stop disapproving of his presence. This could have been partly because Ivy stayed longer than she had originally planned, and helped with the work fairly regularly. Ted's face, as Gaela had hoped, began to lighten.

One sunny afternoon, Gaela and Ted saw a crowd around the gazebo and went to investigate. They found Caine sitting cross-legged on the top step, playing Irish dance melodies on a tiny recorder no more than ten inches long. It had a high, light voice like a bluebird, and not a person in the audience wasn't smiling and tapping a foot.

Ted looked at Gaela. "I can see why you like him. He's quite a mystery."

She watched his face for any hint of mockery in this statement, but didn't see any. "He sure is. I think he's been through terrible trouble of some kind. I know you thought I was crazy, hiring somebody without a single reference. But I keep hoping the garden will help him."

"Might be the garden," said Ted agreeably. Gaela gave him another suspicious glance, but he was watching Caine and tapping his foot.

From then on, Caine's impromptu mini concerts were a regular feature, or rather, an irregular feature — wherever and whenever the mood took him.

The long June days began to grow hot. Everyone who hadn't yet gone to shorts did so, except for Chuck, who never did. Caine put his hair in a ponytail, and the greenhouse became a shadecloth-covered screenhouse. Gaela watched the skies. July and August were always dry, so they hoped for a few rains in June. Not that they didn't always have water. The garden systems were set up to pump water from the lake to the plantings, and they had all sprinklers running again. Still, she preferred as much natural watering from the sky as possible.

The shady pergola, a long, arched tunnel covered with wisteria and lined with benches was usually well-populated. The grotto was now a favorite spot, too. And the lake was always a good place to spend a hot afternoon. Chuck stepped up his vigilance, if such a thing was possible. Someone had to walk the trails through the woods daily and pick up litter. Somehow people seemed to think if you couldn't see them drop it, it wasn't litter.

There were eight weddings at the new gazebo during that favorite of all bridal months. The climbing roses were a little spindly yet, but no one seemed to care. Gaela thought it would be stunning in a couple of years. If she ever got married, maybe she'd do it there, herself. But *not* while Eden was open to the public! Some people seemed to enjoy having a crowd of strangers gather—and one always did. Not she, thank you.

One day, after no fewer than three weddings, two at the gazebo and one in the topiary garden, with the happy couple dressed as zookeepers and exchanging vows under the upraised trunk of the elephant, Caine asked her, "Do you ever go to church?"

Startled, Gaela looked at him. "Every day, God and me and the flowers. But, honestly? Not with other people as often as I should."

"Why not?"

"This is one of those questions you wouldn't answer if I asked," she pointed out. "In fact, you'd probably get all huffy on me."

"You're welcome to do the same."

Perversely, she didn't. Instead, she thought about why she didn't go to church very often. It was something she felt guilty about, as a matter of fact. There were plenty of excuses, the most popular being that she was too busy, especially in the summer.

"I don't like crowds," she said. "My spiritual life seems like a private thing to me."

"Of course it is," Caine agreed readily. "I thought church was supposed to be where people went to have a chance to share a different kind of spiritual life—a group life."

Gaela gave him a curious look. "Why on earth are you bringing this up? I thought you didn't even believe in God."

"Of course I believe in God. I think what you should do is have Sunday morning services at the gazebo."

She could only stare at him. Was this Caine, the frightening, dark, moody stranger of a couple of months ago? Or had a body-snatching taken place while she wasn't looking?

He reddened and moved uncomfortably. "Nothing major. A couple songs. A poem, or something. You know. There wouldn't be that big a crowd, not that many come on Sunday mornings, anyway."

"I think it's a great idea! But who would do it?"

"I thought maybe Lillian."

"Lillian?" she exclaimed.

But Lillian proved to be delighted with the idea. "And Caine can play his little flute."

"Oh, no," said Caine, backing away and looking panicked. "Not me!"

"It was your idea. You know better than to suggest an idea you don't want to help implement," said Lillian firmly, and dragged him away to make plans.

Gaela was intrigued with this new side of Caine, not to mention Lillian. How much did she really know about the people she worked beside all year?

She and Ivy were on their way to deadhead roses when they came across a heated discussion in progress between Caine and Lillian, with Ted as an interested contributor.

"I do not sing!" Caine was declaring emphatically. "And certainly not in public!"

"I'm not talking about a solo or anything," Lillian scolded. "We just need someone to lead a few well-known songs, and keep us on key. I know you can do that. You are a musician, aren't you?"

"I'll help," Ted offered. "I can stay on key."

"Good, then you do it!" growled Caine, looking like a man ready to run, in Gaela's experienced view. She stepped forward, hoping to head off a crisis, though not sure what to say. *She* certainly wasn't about to sing in public!

"I can sing," said Ivy.

There was sudden silence as the group turned to stare at her.

"What? Don't you know it's an absolute must for aspiring ornaments to society to be able to sing?" Ivy demanded, raising her perfect brows and using her most snotty uptown voice.

"Well, then, there you go!" exclaimed Lillian in relief. "You're off the hook, Caine!"

"I never was on the hook," Caine informed her, still looking a little dark in the face.

"Oh, lighten up, Hunter. You can be the orchestra," said Ted.

For a second, Gaela held her breath, but Caine apparently decided to take this in good part. She made good her own escape before she could be roped into performing some terrifying deed of public churchliness.

As her contribution to the enterprise, Gaela had leaflets printed up and distributed in town, advising the public that next Sunday at eleven a. m. there would be a short devotional service at the gazebo. "Come to church in the Garden of Eden!" she put across the top in large letters, rather pleased with this gambit.

Apparently others were enchanted with the idea, too. There were over thirty people around the gazebo by ten forty-five the following Sunday, at least three times the number they would usually expect in the gardens on a Sunday morning. To Gaela's amazement, Ivy and Ted led a round of singing with two perfectly wonderful voices. Ivy, in particular, simply sparkled with charisma, drawing the people not only to join in, but to sing out in lively four part harmony. The planned three songs grew to six, with two old favorites called out from the cheerful crowd. Caine accompanied all six with increasingly complicated syncopation.

Then Lillian gave a ten-minute talk on finding God in the "Garden of Eden" that grew at the center of one's own life, and Caine played a lovely, plaintive piece that could have been a prayer itself. Lillian apparently thought so, too, because she closed the service with a few moments of silence and a simple, "Thank you, Mighty Lord. Amen."

All day the service stayed in Gaela's mind. It seemed to make the air of the garden a little sweeter. Caine was absolutely right--group spirituality had a whole different feel from personal spirituality. Both were important. She knew that. She had been neglecting the public side of her spiritual growth because it was not an area of comfort for her. Trust Caine to unerringly ferret out her areas of discomfort. Then again, it had been neatly turned on him, hadn't it? How had Lillian bullied him into participating in something so uncharacteristic? For that matter, how did

Gaela know what was or wasn't characteristic for Caine? Hadn't he known all six songs by heart?

Her mind turned over other questions like a garden fork turning up fresh soil. Who knew Ted and Ivy could sing like that? What was the piece Caine had played? Where had Lillian learned to speak, and why had Caine known it when Gaela didn't? Why had the whole thing been Caine's idea? Back to that. What did she really know about Caine? Until he filled out his employment papers (scantily, it must be said) she wasn't even sure if Caine was his first or last name.

And where was he today? She hadn't seen him since the little church service.

Sometime later, she finally asked Ted, who said, "He asked for the rest of the day off. I tried to call you," his eyes went to her belt, which was bare of its holster, let alone a phone, "but I figured he'd earned it, and you wouldn't mind."

"No, that's fine." She looked at her belt. "I guess I forgot. Sorry. I'll go get it right now."

She went through the woods to her cottage, worrying all the way. Had he quit? He'd left before, with less notice.

The rest of the day blurred. Her peace, enriched by the morning service, was gone.

In the evening after everyone had left, she went to the Secret Garden. He wasn't there, of course. Having accidentally revealed an almost personal side of himself, he would probably exit, stage left and she'd never see him again.

She was sitting on his log with her arms around her knees, trying to decide if she was making him into a "project," when she heard his step. It was almost dark, and she could only see a shadowy form when she looked up.

"Do the flowers talk to you?" he asked.

Gaela laughed a little damply and hoped he couldn't tell she'd been crying. "You always start conversations with these sudden leaps," she said. "Usually strange ones. What do you mean, do the flowers talk to me?"

"Just what I said. I hear you talk to them all the time, and sometimes it seems as if they answer. So I thought I'd like to know." He dropped cross-legged in front of her. They were sitting much closer than they ever had before. Gaela was glad she couldn't see his eyes. She didn't think she could bear them at this distance.

As always, she had to think before she answered him. Did the flowers talk to her? "Not exactly," she said finally. "I mean, I don't think plants are really conscious or sentient, as some people believe. But I do think there's something—a sort of communion—I don't know the right word, if there is one. I learned gardening from the plants themselves. Not because they said, 'I'm thirsty,' but because they wilt when they're thirsty. I always say anyone can learn to garden if they just learn to listen."

"I know, I heard you say that on a gardeners' tour. That's another reason I asked if they talk to you."

"If you mean in real words, though, I'd say it's more like they put me in touch with the One who made them, who can really talk to me. The flowers taught me there is a Creator."

"You mean you weren't raised believing that?"

"Well, yes, I was, but it wasn't really a personal thing. We went to church faithfully. Now that I think about it, maybe that's one reason I have a jaundiced view of church. I didn't learn about God in a church. I learned about him in a hospital."

She stopped, and there was a silence. It was a comfortable silence, but a listening one, and she realized she could probably tell him her story. But she wasn't about to open up quite that much, not to someone who remained so closed himself.

"And I got to know him in this garden," she said. "This morning, when Lillian spoke of finding God in the

Garden of Eden in your heart, I thought of this place, the Secret Garden. I often think Eden—this estate, I mean—Is like our hearts. There are lots of different kinds of places—public places, sunny places, shady places, wilderness areas. There's always plenty of work to do, and some of it is work that others can share. Then there's a secret place in the middle, a walled garden where no one else can go. It's there you really build your friendship with God—with the Great Gardener. It's there you plant good things, and weed out bad ones, and there you go to cry when you need to, or hole up and let yourself be nursed, or forgiven, or whatever. Anyway, that's what I think."

Feeling awkward, she shut up.

"Does *he* speak to you?"

"Who, God?"

"Yeah."

"Well, I think so. Sometimes."

"How?"

Gaela gave a little laugh. "I have no idea. Not out loud, not to me, anyway. Sometimes I think I hear him when I read the Bible or other spiritual books, or through my own thoughts. I just sort of... get an idea, and I think it's from him, so I ask him, and after a while I'm pretty sure, so then I act on it and watch to see if, you know, if the results bring peace and love, or whatever. Not that *that's* always easy to tell!" She shook her head. Brother, this was personal enough! And why was Caine still asking the questions, and she obediently answering? A little disjointedly, she concluded, "To me, of course, he talks through the flowers, and just, I don't know... a whisper on the wind."

Caine seemed to stiffen. "A whisper on the wind?"

"Sometimes, why?"

"Nothing. It's just—nothing. I've got to go. You should go to bed, it's been a long day." He rose abruptly.

"Caine?"

He kept going, so she went after him. "Caine!"

He stopped with his hand on the gate.
"Have you heard him?"
No answer.
"Have you heard his voice on the wind, Caine?"
Caine left without speaking.

Chapter Twelve

During the next few weeks, Caine seemed rather distant. He refused to have any further part in the Sunday services which grew in popularity weekly, although once Ivy left, Ted had to lead the singing by himself. Caine was usually nearby, appearing to listen almost against his will, but he always disappeared before anyone could demand any music from him. Gaela sent him to the fall garden, where the corn always needed hoeing. Maybe solitude would be good for him. It always was for her.

They never met in the Secret Garden anymore. That would teach her to preach! Gaela tried only once to practice her music `alone at her cottage. Then she hid the recorder in a drawer. Maybe out of sight would eventually be out of mind.

In July the heat grew oppressive, and not only plants showed the strain. Gardeners were forever hauling hoses to beds that weren't on the irrigation system, which most weren't, and tempers were threadbare. Another worker quit. Ted calmed two family fights and tossed out some belligerent teenagers. Three times, the emergency squad had to be called because someone fainted.

One was an actual heart attack, and Caine covered himself in glory by keeping up a calm, steady CPR until the squad got there. Then he disappeared, threatening never to come back if he so much as heard a whisper of any press or media whatsoever.

"I still think that guy's got something to hide," Ted told Gaela.

"Don't we all?" she responded, drawing a strange look from him.

One night, sick of tossing in bed, she put on a short, white cotton shift and went out to walk by the lake. It was midnight, but the moon was full, and bright enough to cast a shadow. She went through the woods on the familiar path to the big rock, and from there began to walk east along the side of the lake. As she passed the wading beach at the foot of the lawn, she heard music over the swish of the water. She stopped and listened. Sure enough, he was here, somewhere up ahead. Gaela tightened her lips in irritation. Hadn't she told him he couldn't stay here anymore?

She quickened her steps and soon realized he was in the grotto, playing over the sound of the little waterfall. It sounded lovely, and some of her irritation faded. Still, she had to make it clear to him that during off hours, he was not allowed to be here, at least not without permission.

She came around the corner of the grotto and saw him. He sat with his back to her on the smooth floor of the cave-like enclosure, just at the edge of the water. He was playing something complicated and haunting, and she realized again how really skilled he was. This time, the recorder was longer, with a deeper, richer voice. It sounded like something the lake would play if it could, as if Caine had given the water a voice. Was this the kind of music that had given rise to the legend of Pan?

Gaela wasn't sure how to let him know she was there without startling him, but when he finished the piece, he turned as if he'd been aware of her all along.

"That was breathtaking," she told him, "especially with the water playing accompaniment."

"Breathtaking is a good word for it," he agreed, pantomiming being out of breath. Turning off compliments, as usual.

"I do have to ask, though-"

"I know, what am I doing here at this hour?"

"Well?"

"I'm not camping out here, if that's what you're worried about. I left once, actually, but I couldn't sleep, so I came back. How about yourself?"

"Same problem, I have to admit. It's the weather. If we don't have a storm soon, we'll all explode." She ought to turn away and look at the lake or something. If she'd ever thought him gorgeous, (and she'd never got over thinking so) moonlight made him absolutely . . . absolutely! There was no word. Dreamy was way too corny. His hair was down, but his shirt was open for coolness, and she was getting hotter by the second. He looked like Pan himself, with his dark curls and beard, and skin polished to marble by the moon. She wondered if he'd have goat feet if she looked, then broke the spell with a giggle.

"Something funny?"

Oh, don't look at me! Gaela managed to wrench her eyes away. "Nothing. Sorry." She took a deep breath and held it, hoping to keep further giggles at bay.

"Go away."

That shook the giggles out. She turned back. "What?"

"Go away right now." He was looking at his clenched hands and sounding a little strangled.

She'd strangle him. "You're the one who's not supposed to be here."

"Okay, you're right, and I'm going. But you go away right this minute, I'm warning you." And he looked up.

He shouldn't have done that.

She could no more move than she could fly to the moon. And by the look of him, he was just as unable to be still. A current she could almost hear crackling held their eyes locked on each other. She watched him carefully put his recorder down and stand. He was coming toward her. *Run,* she begged her feet. *Run!*

Her feet obediently began to move, but in slow motion. They stepped forward until they met his boots, and stopped. His strong musician's hands came to her face, and hers found their way to his chest.

"I don't think-" she managed to whisper.

"Me neither," he said. "I'll think later."

He bent a little at the knees, and she stood on tiptoes. His lips were on hers, his mustache tickling her nose, his long hair brushing her cheeks. He was right--she could think later. Breathe later, too.

His arms locked around her and her feet left the ground. She pulled her arms out from between them and wrapped them fiercely around his neck. The storm that hadn't come was all in this kiss, thunder and lightning, music and waterfalls, tears and loss and paradise passionately sought. Caine pulled back first, and she laid her head on his shoulder and tried to remember how to breathe.

"I told you to go," he said hoarsely after a while.

"I tried," she answered weakly.

"Not very hard."

"No."

He put her down resolutely, and she tried not to cling. "I quit," he said.

"What?"

"I quit. I'll be gone tomorrow. You can find someone else to mulch your beds." He had swung away to pick up his recorder.

She stood stock still in shock. "You've got to be kidding me."

Caine turned on her, and she saw the frightening dark stranger was back. She flinched before the fury in his eyes. "Gaela, you have no idea what a truly terrible idea this is! It's not your fault, it's entirely mine. I should never have come here, and I knew it, and once I had left I should never have come back, and I knew that, too." He turned away, then said over his shoulder, "But I want you to know, that kiss was worth it all. I'll never forget you, my Pixie."

"You're a coward," she said coldly.

His back stiffened, and he stopped. "What did you say?"

"I said you're a coward, Caine Hunter, if that's really your name. You run away every time there's a hint of trouble or difficulty." He had turned back and was glaring at her in a way that would once have had her trembling from head to foot, but she was in a fine rage and had no intention of stopping now. "Don't you think I know what it feels like to be afraid? Don't you think I know how it feels to want more than anything to just escape? I tried suicide!"

Caine's mouth opened, and all her rage deserted her. Well, that was a graceful way to bring the subject up.

"You tried to kill yourself?"

"Twice. Want to see my scars?" She held up her wrists and he came and took them, not looking, but feeling the scars with tender fingers.

"I've seen them before. I wondered."

She leaned against him, suddenly exhausted. "Remember when I told you I learned about God in a hospital?"

"I remember." He picked her up and carried her inside the grotto to one of the cool stone benches, where he sat down with her.

She told him about her stay in the hospital, about the pills and group therapy and about her plant. "I wanted it to live, so it wanted me to live. It was a long time later that I learned it was an African Violet. It still lives on my kitchen windowsill, along with its grandchildren. I'll show you someday."

"But what made you want to—" He hesitated.

"To die? You can say it. It's really hard to explain. I'm not sure I understand it." She paused to gather her thoughts, trying not to be too distracted by the fact that Caine was stroking her scars with a feather touch, as if to make them disappear.

"I was born smack in the middle of a nine-kid family, and not a single one of them understood me. Nor I them. My poor parents must have thought I was a changeling. My brothers and sisters were after fun and adventure, and all I wanted was to play all by myself somewhere. They played pranks, and I cried. They fought out their differences, and I pretended I never had any. Whatever anybody wanted, whatever happened, that was fine with me. Of course, it wasn't, really, but I didn't want to yell to make myself heard, and I didn't know how to get anyone to listen. After a while, I started to be invisible. Then—" Gaela's voice stopped dead in her throat. Suddenly becoming aware of her bare legs below the edge of her shift, lying across his lap, she stood abruptly. She couldn't go on.

"Gaela?"

She turned her back to him and looked out at the lake. He was standing, coming up behind her, and she wanted to run. "Look at the moonlight," she said foolishly. "It makes a path on the water. A person should be able to climb that, don't you think? All the way to somewhere that's always safe."

His hands closed over her shoulders and she felt her heart speed up. "You're safe here, Gaela."

Oh God, oh God!

"Did someone hurt you?" She felt his fingers tighten, then loosen, and knew that he was deliberately controlling himself, deliberately trying not to frighten her. The knowledge somehow shut off her panic as if with a switch.

"There was a guy. He followed me." She gave a mirthless laugh. "Black hair and beard, by the way." Caine's fingers tightened again, but this time she didn't mind. "I was fourteen. He never did anything. Just watched me. Followed me."

"What did your parents do?"

"I didn't tell them." She thought the fingers might shake her, but they stilled again. Would she have bruises tomorrow? "What was to tell? He didn't do anything. But one night, I was coming home from a late study session at the library, and he chased me." Was this her voice, cold, emotionless? "I tried to tell my mother then, but she said it was my imagination. Or—" Gaela choked and almost couldn't continue again. A breath. Another. "Or maybe my skirt was too short."

She heard a curse behind her, and kept her eyes on the moonlight path. "I stayed up all night that night and let down the hems of every dress and skirt I owned. But he still followed me, and finally he caught me. I kicked and struggled... I hardly remember. I don't think I even screamed. It was like a nightmare, like it wasn't real. I knew it was finally true—I was invisible."

She would have bruises. Caine seemed to have completely forgotten his hands, clenched on her shoulders. She was glad of them. They kept her clamped to reality.

"I got away."

"Thank God!" A warm breeze fanned her cheek, and she realized he'd been holding his breath. "So then did your family listen?"

"I didn't say anything."

"*What?*" Caine turned her around to face him. Her shoulders tingled now that the pressure was gone. The hard fingers were around her arms now, and she thought he really would shake her. "You didn't say anything?"

Gaela felt the first tears. "I wanted them to notice by themselves."

"Notice—?"

"I had a black eye and a cut lip, and bruises on my arms." Gaela leaned forward until her face met Caine's chest. "I just wanted them to see me!" she wept.

His arms were strong enough that she could just let go. She didn't have to be strong, or silent, she didn't even have to hold herself up on her own feet anymore. After a few minutes, her sobs stilled. She could hear Caine's heartbeat under her ear.

"Did they notice when you tried to commit suicide?" he asked grimly.

She laughed a little against his shoulder. "That's what the psychiatrist said. At least I got attention." She lifted her head and looked up at him, wiping at her cheeks with the backs of her hands, feeling like a baby. "You have to understand. They loved me."

He snorted.

"They did, really. They were terribly upset."

"I hope so! But did they change?"

"Did they ever! Now I couldn't blow my nose without someone noticing. I hated it. It wasn't until a long time later, when I came here, that I felt like I was starting to be myself, or even figure out who myself really was. I even changed my name."

"You did?"

"After a fashion. My parents named me Gale, spelled like a strong wind. Now I ask you, does that fit me? I had found an interest in Celtic things, and changed it to Gaela, spelled like that ancient and mysterious language I want to learn someday."

She yawned suddenly, and stepped back a pace. "Heavens, what time is it? I can't believe I'm telling you all this dreary stuff. I've never told anyone else. I mean, except for paid shrinks. I just wanted you to know that I know what I'm talking about when I say God can heal and forgive. He can make you a whole new person. He can make you visible. And I don't care what you've done."

She yawned again. "Oh, my. Sorry. Wearying business, this baring of souls, isn't it?" Her voice became a squeal—"*What* are you doing?"

He had scooped her up like a two-year-old. "Taking you home."

"That's silly. I can walk." He ignored her, so she pretended she wasn't embarrassed and put her head back down on his shoulder. It was kind of nice being in his arms. She felt--what was that word the counselors had always used? Cathartic, that was it. "I've been catharticized," she said, and giggled.

Caine chuckled softly. "I'm glad to hear it." He walked along the beach and up the lawn to the house, past the west rose garden, then ducked through the pines behind the work sheds.

"Aren't I getting heavy?" Gaela mumbled sleepily.

"All those fifty pound bags you make me tote," he explained. "Now last month, it would have been another matter." He pretended to stagger and she giggled again. "What do you weigh, eighty-five pounds?"

"Think I'm going to answer a loaded question like that? You can go right on thinking eighty-five."

"Here we are." He stood on her porch, seeming reluctant to put her down. "Sleep late, okay?"

"I never sleep late."

"So try something new for a change."

Finally he kissed her forehead and put her down, tousling her hair as if she were a ten-year-old. "Good-night, Pixie."

He was gone almost immediately. How did he do that?

"Good-night," she whispered.

She went right to bed, but not to sleep. She kept reliving that kiss. What had she done?

ଔ   ଔ   ଔ

What had he done?

Caine found the wall by long experience and swung over it with ease, heading for town and his drab room. But when he got there, he didn't stop. He walked on by and kept walking.

This is how it starts. Now she's shared her heart, and she thinks you've shared yours. She thinks she's safe with you.

I've never told anyone else.

Confound her clever little soul, anyway! She was trying to own him with lines like that.

But he knew better.

I don't care what you've done.

The faces that were never far from his mind rose up before his eyes in the darkness. No! This is different! This is nothing like the other times! That kiss alone . . . !

He tramped another mile just thinking about the kiss. No other kiss in his experience had borne any resemblance at all to that kiss. What was the difference?

It didn't matter! He had to get out of here. Never mind that she would call him a coward. Better that than the things she might call him. He had to leave. It was unforgivable that he'd hung around this long, making her trust him, learning to love her.

Oh, God! Love her? When and how had that happened? It couldn't continue. He had to find the way to cut it off now, before it was too late.

I don't care what you've done.

If only she knew.

Caine walked the rest of the night.

But at eight o'clock the next morning, damning himself for his weakness, he showed up for work at Eden.

Chapter Thirteen

The long-awaited storm broke that morning. The staff dashed around bringing in what could be brought in, tying down what could be tied down, and generally trying to see that Eden would weather the blow as well as possible. They blew into the workshop just ahead of the hail, and stood for a minute by the windows gazing awestruck at nature's fury. White balls bounced across the lawn, clanged on the dumpsters behind the shed, and battered the roses they could see in the west rose garden.

"Whew!" breathed Gaela. "Some of you might as well go home. It will storm most of the morning, and the main work this afternoon will be cleanup. A couple can stay and help Lillian in the greenhouse once the hail stops, and I can use one in the office. Ted, what do you have on?"

"Tractor work in the maintenance building. I can use a hand."

They sorted out who was staying and who was going, while Gaela and Caine assiduously avoided each other's eyes. It turned out that more went home in the afternoon, since the heaviest of the storm had abated, but the rain showed no signs of stopping.

Late in the afternoon, Gaela found herself alone in the shop with Caine, and was overcome with shyness. This was stupid! She had to figure out something to talk about. Something besides deep, inner secrets. Something normal, and nonchalant.

"I've been wanting to ask you something."

"Oh? I mean—yes? What is it?" He was more tongue-tied than she was, which made her laugh inwardly and loosen up. Who would ever have thought she'd meet a man who was even more afraid of intimacy than herself?

"About those recorders." Never mind the fact that she had put hers away and tried to forget it existed. It was a neutral subject. "Why are they different sizes, and how many do you have, anyway?"

"The smallest one is called a sopranino. It's the highest, and is in the key of F. The regular sized one that people are familiar with, the one you're learning on, is a soprano, and is in the key of C." She nodded, remembering that with all finger holes closed, her recorder played middle C. "The next larger one, the one I had—last night—uh—" He cleared his throat, and Gaela couldn't help grinning.

"Yes?" she said sweetly. "Last night?"

Caine laughed, too, and his eyes suddenly regained their dangerous glint. "The one I played in the grotto last night," he enunciated with great aplomb, "is an alto, in F. I have an even larger one, a tenor, which is in C, and they have basses in F and contrabasses in C, which are huge and cost a fortune, even in plastic. Don't misunderstand what it means to be in a certain key, though. Recorders are capable of sharps and flats, so you can play music in any key, so long as it's within the range of the recorder you're playing."

"I never knew they were so versatile."

They were still talking music when Lillian joined them.

"I've had the most fabulous idea, just right for a rainy day! Let's plan a miniature garden! We can have bonsai, and plants that naturally have miniature growth habits. Reindeer moss, for instance, could be bracken and ferns. Regular mosses can be grass and baby's tears can be ivy, and there could be tiny little pools, maybe even a fountain. The kids would love it!"

"Everybody would love it, probably to death! Where would we put it, and how could we protect it? Do you think of it as an inside garden, in the greenhouse? Or portable, even?"

Their three heads were bent over a map of Eden and a piece of graph paper when Ted and Randy came gasping in the door, rain pouring from their ponchos. Ted dried himself off and came to look at their plans, but Randy said he might leave early.

"You're just not interested in anything that can't be mowed with a riding mower," Lillian accused.

Randy laughed. "Should I be?" He pulled his hood closer around his face and plunged into the downpour.

The next day they went out to assess the damage. Gaela's fears were realized. She had suspected the worst just from what she could see on the path to her cottage the evening before. Fallen branches lay everywhere, flowers drooped to the ground, Ted's roses on the gazebo were nearly stripped. Four panes had broken in the greenhouse, but they knew that already. Parts of beds had washed out, and mulch was heaped on the lawn. The creek was running so hard through the grotto that some of the ferns had actually been washed out into the lake. One of the new trees leaned precariously, its soil having been washed out from beneath it. Half the parking lot was under water.

Gaela looked around miserably. "Well, let's get to it," she said. "And try to stay off the lawn where you can. It'll turn into a sea of mud."

All hands went to work. A few visitors showed up, but left before long.

The second day, the water was lower in the creek and off the parking lot. More visitors came, and two of Gaela's staff spent all their time keeping people out of damaged areas. Gaela and Ted finally chased everybody away and closed an hour early.

Gaela found Caine down by the lake throwing rocks into the muddy water. Hands in her pockets, she joined him. "Depressing, isn't it?"

"I have to quit." He threw another rock with great concentration.

"Oh, come on, it's not that depressing."

"This is no laughing matter."

"I'm not laughing."

Caine put his hands in his pockets and stood facing her. She wondered if they both thought if they kept their hands in their pockets they would be safe.

"You were wrong," he said. "It matters what you've done."

"I never said it didn't matter what you'd done."

" 'I don't care what you've done.' That's what you said."

"I said there is forgiveness and healing, no matter what you've done. It certainly *matters* what you've done, both to yourself and to other people."

"For murder?"

He said it so baldly that for a second she didn't get it. Then a chill started in her belly and spread. "Yes."

He gave a scornful laugh and turned away to pick up another stone. "You little saints. That's what you're taught to say. Everybody's all forgiven, and everything's all daisies, *no matter what.* It's hogwash." He threw a stone so hard she thought he was trying to hit the other side of the lake. *Oh, God, what do I say now?*

Nothing came to her, so she said nothing.

"Would God have forgiven Hitler?" he demanded.

"Yes."

"You've got to be kidding me."

"If Hitler had wanted forgiveness, he could have found it. You know, forgiveness doesn't say it's okay."

"What's that supposed to mean?"

"Everybody thinks forgiveness is the same as excusing. It's not. If there's an excuse, if you step on my toe, or something, you say, 'oh, excuse me!' and I say, 'that's okay.' No forgiveness needed. It's only if there *is no excuse* that you need forgiveness. Forgiveness is for sin. Forgiveness is for when something is so wrong, it's unfixable. Usually, we wait till things reach that state, too, more's the pity. We finally get desperate enough to cry out to God. And he answers."

"I killed my sister," Caine said conversationally.

The chill had reached her limbs, and Gaela hugged herself.

"It was right out there." He pointed. "In the middle of a lake, just like this one."

He threw another stone, and grunted with the effort. "I didn't mean to. I never mean to."

She waited. She couldn't feel her stomach.

Caine threw three more stones, wrenching his whole body in a half-circle. Then he said, "We were just horsing around. I was rocking the boat to make her scream. Then I pushed her in. She screamed even louder then, but I laughed." His face twisted. "Then I tried to pull her back in, but she tried to pull me overboard, and I jerked away. I didn't know--" He choked and his voice hardened again. "I killed her. My own sister. I even left her there. Tell me there's forgiveness for that." And Caine turned and walked away.

Did he really think she'd let him just leave? She'd run after him. Just as soon as her feet would move.

"Yes," she said, but it came out in a whisper. *Oh, God, help!* "Yes!" Gaela screamed, and her feet were unlocked. She ran and grabbed him, dragging him to a stop. "How old were you?" Now why had she asked that?

"Old enough to know better. Are you imagining a nine-year-old?" His eyes, his dear, dangerous, black eyes were dead.

She shook him angrily. "How old?"

"Sixteen."

"What didn't you know?"

"What?"

"You said — a minute ago. You jerked away from her. You didn't know — what?"

"It doesn't matter." He tried to walk away again, and when she couldn't pull him to a stop she hit him until he stopped and looked at her. Then she grabbed fistfuls of his shirtfront. Muscles from every heavy bag she'd ever toted came to her assistance, and she manhandled him back against the outside of the grotto. "You listen to me, Caine Hunter," she growled into his face, not caring that it was a foot above her. "I am not going to let you run away this time. Do you hear?" He didn't seem to, so she shook him again. Tears were blinding her. "*Do you hear?* You are going to stand right here like a man and tell me the whole thing."

Gaela couldn't believe she was doing any of this. She seemed to be taken over by some unstoppable force of love and fear.

"That's not my name," he said.

"I don't care!" she shouted at him. Then she lowered her voice. "Now, let's try this again. You're sixteen, your sister is . . .?"

"Fourteen," he supplied dully.

"You're in the boat, and you're horsing around. She falls in — "

"I pushed her."

"Fine! You pushed her! Then you tried to pull her back in, and she tried to pull you in the lake. Tell me, was she trying to kill you?"

"Of course not!" It was the first life she'd seen in him for several minutes, and she exulted in it.

"Of course not. Okay, so you pulled away from her, and you didn't know — *what?*"

"She hit her head. When I pulled away, she hit her head on the boat. I swear I didn't know it." There was definitely life coming back into his eyes. Gaela sympathized. She remembered how horrible it was when you started to feel again.

"Then what did you do?"
"I left her."
"Why?"
"I went to get help. It was stupid. I panicked. Of course she would die before I could get back. But I couldn't see her, and I panicked. My mother never yelled at me like that in my whole life, and she was a yeller." His voice was cracking. "I already knew I killed her. Mom didn't have to tell me."

"Oh, my dear."

"Dad didn't say much of anything. He never did when she yelled. Later, she said she was sorry. She said she didn't mean it. But it was true, whether she meant it or not."

"Did you forgive her?"

"My mother? She didn't forgive me."

Gaela smiled a little. "Well, actually, that's two separate questions. But, are you sure?"

"Sure of what?"

"Are you sure your mother didn't forgive you?"

"I don't know. I guess so. She said she did. I left home the minute I graduated."

"You've *never* seen your mother since you were — what? Eighteen years old?"

"Seventeen. I've seen her. But she never knew it. She's dead now."

"So she lost both children."

He looked at her for the first time. "Yeah. So you see, I have a lot to be forgiven for."

"And something to forgive. Have you really forgiven your mother for lashing out at you?"

"How can I forgive her now? She's dead!"

"Forgiveness starts with the forgiver, and even if it can't be complete the way it should be, you still need to forgive. Have you?"

He thought about it. "I guess so, yeah. It was understandable."

She shook him. "No, that's excusing. That's the other thing. There are reasons, extenuating circumstances, but there's no *excuse* for a mother to lash out like that at her child. She did it because she was a faulty human being—a sinner. She needed forgiveness. And you can only get it from God. We can hope she let *him* forgive her. *You* still need to. And your dad, too, for letting you down. But you have to accept forgiveness from God yourself before you can give it." She still had hold of his shirt, and she pulled at it until he looked at her again. "Now you listen to me, and listen closely. Even if you had murdered your sister deliberately, with malice aforethought, in cold blood, even if your parents never did forgave you, *God could still forgive you.* God is the Father and Mother of all fathers and mothers, the only One who can love and forgive perfectly. Do you hear me? He can forgive, because he's the one we've really sinned against. He wants to forgive us so much that he deliberately gave the life of his own *Son* so that he could say, 'Caine, my child, the penalty's already paid! I took your rap. I forgive you!'" She shook him again. "Are you listening to me?

"God forgave David, in the Old Testament, didn't he? *He* killed a whole bunch of people, deliberately! If God could forgive him, he can forgive you. Of course it matters what you did, and why you did it, if only because different people need different treatment. God dealt with David his way. He deals with you your way. In your case, it was an accident, Caine. An *accident.*"

She was not getting through. *Oh, God, help!* An idea came to her. She leaned into his chest, clutching his shirt with white knuckles, and stared into his eyes as if she could transfer directly into his heart the truth she was desperately trying to share.

"Would you forgive me?"

Chapter Fourteen

"What?" Confusion warred with the deadness in Caine's dark eyes.

"If I had done it. Let's say it was your sister, and I was in the boat with her, and the exact same scenario happened. I'm sixteen, I push her, I don't know she's hurt, I panic and go for help, and she dies. Would you forgive me?"

His troubled gaze slid away from her face, toward the lake. She could see the wheels turning slowly in his mind and almost watch the scene unfold behind his eyes. "I'm really, really sorry," she told him, and tears stung her eyelids as if the story were true. "It's devastated my life, and I'd give my own soul to go back and make it not happen. Could you forgive me?"

Slowly, his eyes came from the lake to her face. The spark was back, though a little drowned. "Yes. I could forgive you. But I don't know if I can forgive myself."

"You don't have to. God will. When I tried to kill myself, it was very deliberate, all planned out. It's a miracle I didn't succeed. It's a much worse sin than yours, on the face of it. But he forgave me, and not only that, he healed me and gave me a whole new life. I promise you, he'll do the same for you."

Under her hands she felt a long sigh raise his chest and then release it. "But that's not the worst." She just waited, so he went on. "When I left home, I became a horrible person."

"You became the person you believed yourself to be."

Caine smiled sadly, and raised a hand to touch her cheek. "My little pixie, always looking for good. Sometimes there's none to be found. I won't bore you with all the gory details. Let's just say I made a lot of stupid choices. Among other things, I started seducing and discarding women. Oh, I never meant any harm. That became my stock in trade. I'd always be convinced I loved this one, and I'd convince her she loved me, too. But it never lasted. I'd move on. I don't know what I was looking for."

Gaela knew what he was looking for, but she didn't say anything.

"I got one pregnant." He laughed scornfully. "One that I know of, that is. I made her get an abortion. My own kid." His voice broke, and he tore away from her suddenly. "I never even knew if it was a boy or a girl."

Gaela saw the anguish on his face before he ran. He ran and ran, and not all her calling could bring him back.

She went to the Secret Garden and waited there a long time, praying harder than she'd ever prayed, but he never came. Finally, totally drained, she went home and to bed. Lying there, weeping into her pillow, Gaela made herself a promise. She would call her folks tomorrow.

☙   ☙   ☙

Caine crashed through the woods, teeth clenched so hard he thought they'd crack, trying desperately to gulp down a lump the size of all the anguish he'd carried all these years. He was not about to bawl like a baby. What in blazes was wrong with that woman, anyway? How dare she pull out all his guts for the world to see? Women always did that, dragging out your inmost secrets in the name of a "closer relationship." Who needed it?

He stumbled over a root and fell gasping to the ground. He thought he might throw up. How *dare* she make him relive that hell all over again?

But it had been his own idea. He had brilliantly thought if he spilled a carefully selected part of the truth, it would disenchant Gaela and she would let him go. She was what kept him here--nothing else. Her spells, her toils, her nets for his unwary feet. He couldn't go until she let him go, and he had to get out of here. Sooner or later, the rest of the truth would be revealed. A breeze ruffled his hair. Caine grabbed the ground with both hands and struggled to control his harsh breathing. He would not cry!

I am here.

"No!"

Yes.

Gaela's little hands in his shirt, holding him in place like iron. He tried to laugh, and the first sobs came out instead. He bawled like a baby, shuddering and heaving and wetting the leaves under his face. After a long time, he rolled over and dug in his pockets for a handkerchief. "Why do you want me? You have everything."

I don't have you.

He gave a gulping laugh. Well, that was unanswerable.

He blew his nose and crawled shakily to his feet. A grown man, weeping all over the place and talking to himself.

The breeze cooled his hot cheeks and dried the last of his tears. "Okay, here's the deal. If it's you, and this is real, I'll give you a try. But if I don't see some kind of great, magical difference, I'll know it's my own imagination. Take it or leave it."

There was silence.

"Yeah, I thought so." Caine walked wearily home, fell into his lumpy bed, and slept ten hours.

ೞ ೮ ೞ

Gaela was worried when Caine didn't show up for work. Surely, after all that, he hadn't run? She was nervous all morning, snapping at her helpers and then apologizing abjectly, until Ted dragged her aside and demanded, "What gives, chief?"

"What do you mean?"

"I mean, you're moping around here like you lost your best friend. I notice Hunter didn't show. Should I find him and take his head off for him, or what?"

Gaela couldn't help laughing. "Ted, you're a dear, but you don't know what you're talking about. If he's left, you couldn't find him, anyway."

"So, it is about him."

"Yeah, I admit it, it's about him. I found out some of what's eating him. You could pray, if you care to. Believe me, he can use all the prayers he can get. And speaking of prayers, how's Ivy?"

"Doing well, actually. She might be coming again in September."

"That's nice. I like her."

Ted put his arm around her shoulders and gave her a gentle squeeze. Gaela had mixed feelings. Did it mean he was getting over her and this was a brotherly hug, or did it mean he still wished? She only let it last for a minute before saying, "Well, we'd better get back to work."

The morning wore on, getting hotter and hotter.

Gaela and several others were in the work shed when Caine flew in at ten-thirty. A rush of relief made her feel weak in the knees.

"I slept so late! I never slept so late in my life! I'm sorry!" He was looking at Gaela, and she knew he wasn't apologizing so much for being late, as for making her think he'd run again.

She sank onto a stool at the work table.

"Are you all right?" asked Jeanie.

"Fine! It's the heat." Gaela fanned her face in what she hoped was a convincing manner. This man was growing entirely too necessary to her. He had finally shared a part of his heart, but she still didn't even know his name, for heaven's sake! She put on an unconcerned face. "No problem, Caine, we've got it covered. I think all the storm damage is pretty well under control. The part we can fix, anyway. The rest is up to the garden. I think maybe Ted could use a hand in the shop."

He went obediently, but gave her another apologetic look over his shoulder. Gaela lowered her eyes. If only he weren't so dratted good-looking! She determined to avoid his company today.

So, of course, she found herself seeking out sights of him whenever she could. What had happened after he left her? Had he made any attempt to find forgiveness? She wished their conversation--or confrontation, or whatever--hadn't ended so abruptly.

At lunch, for the first time ever, Caine joined the others as they draped themselves over benches and grass in a little private spot between the sheds and the woods that they had claimed as their lunch area. Gaela often went to her cottage, but made an effort to eat at least a couple times a week with the staff. She was trying to watch her tendency to solitude. A good leader mingled. She was lying on her back trying to interest herself in the contents of her paper bag when Caine appeared, upside down over her head.

"So, I see I've found the cafeteria."

"Cafeteria slash sauna," drawled Lillian from the depths of a folding lounge chair. "I thought that storm was supposed to cool things off."

"It did," said Ted, "but we were so busy running around picking up after it that we were too hot to notice."

"Are there people out there?" asked Gaela.

"Slightly wilted, but still recognizable as people," said Caine, sitting down in an unoccupied spot on the grass and digging into a sack from a fast food chain.

"Rats. I suppose that means some of us should take over for those who are doing the sunshine patrol and let them come and eat. You look awfully fresh," she added, pulling herself up on her elbows to regard him with suspicion.

"Heat never bothers me," Caine said apologetically.

Gaela dropped back. "Good. Then you go relieve the others. You can have all shifts from now on."

"Hear, hear!" said Lillian.

"Way to go, chief!" That was Ted.

Weak applause sounded from the others.

"Sure. Do I get a lunch break?" Caine asked with his mouth full.

"Oh, I guess," sighed Gaela, dragging herself to her feet. He hadn't had any more sleep than she had--why did he look so cheerful? She started to leave, then stopped suddenly and looked back. Caine was sharing the contents of his bag with Chan and two of the younger guys. He *was* cheerful, wasn't he? Something had happened. An open door, at least. Gaela forgot the heat and lifted her face into the sunshine for a grateful second. Then she went back to work with a spring in her step.

Caine's playing became a regular and favorite feature of the Sunday morning services at Eden.

As August rolled around, he began sharing bits about himself. Just tidbits, enough to keep her wondering, but it was a start.

"I'm from Ohio, originally," he said one day, à propos of nothing.

"You are? Around here?"

"Pretty nearby." He was laconic, and she decided not to push it.

"Were you rich?" She was thinking of that "nanny" remark. And they'd had a boat, maybe.

"Why do you ask that?"

"Well, whatever. Were you poor? Middle-class?"

"Rich, I guess. Silver spoon and all that."

"Was that fun?"

"Sometimes."

Another day, he told her he'd played in the orchestra in high school.

"Now, that's no surprise. What instrument? Not recorder, I assume?"

"Clarinet."

"Oh, I like clarinet."

"I know. Debussy." He grinned at her, and she grinned back, remembering her terror when he'd invaded her hideaway.

"Want to see my house?" she asked.

"Sure."

So she invited him in, and he wandered around exclaiming over her needlework pillows, admiring her fireplace, and looking out the bay window. He looked at the picture of her family she had on a table, and asked what it was like to live in a crowd.

Gaela rolled her eyes. "Like living in a crowd. I love them, but I'm glad I don't live too near them."

"Do you get along with them better, these days?"

"Better. I called them recently. I'm going to try to stay in touch more than I have. I wouldn't want to have to say, someday, that I hadn't seen -" She stopped suddenly, realizing where this was taking her.

He gave a half laugh. "Learning a lesson from me? Good old Caine, an example held up to youth." He put the picture down and strolled into the kitchen. "I might try to contact my dad one of these days," he said casually. She didn't have a chance to reply, even if she could have thought of something to say. Caine had begun a ceremonious speech to the violet on the windowsill, thanking it for saving her life.

That night, reliving his visit, she realized he fit nicely into her little house.

When she asked his real name, though, he wouldn't answer. A dark look could still come into his eyes sometimes.

Gaela discovered she was glad to think Caine was not his real name. She never had liked it. She looked up the story of Cain in her Bible. "Your brother's blood cries out to me from the ground. . . . Cursed is the ground because of you . . .when you cultivate the ground it will no longer yield its strength to you; you will be a wanderer and a vagrant on the earth."

"Oh, my dear," she sighed, alone in her living room. "God never meant you to take this story to heart. The circumstances are entirely different." She remembered that he had said he'd been cast out of paradise and could never grow anything again, and knew instinctively that when he'd left home, he'd taken this name. Cain, the outcast, and Hunter, the seeker. He'd been seeking for a long time. She hoped he was beginning to find.

Gaela found an opportunity to stand looking worriedly at a patch of ground when Caine would catch her at it. He came over and asked what was the matter, exactly as she'd planned. She hoped it was okay to manipulate just a little, for a good cause.

"There should be something here, don't you think?"

"Sure, why not?"

"But I don't know what. Do you have any ideas?"

"Well, it should be something bright, because of those dark evergreens there."

"True. And something easy, because we don't have a lot of time for another bed."

"What about those geraniums you showed me?"

She allowed her brow to clear a little. "The cranebill geraniums? That would be nice. What else?"

Caine looked up at the sun. "Do you think this spot is well-drained enough for geraniums and also well-watered enough for hosta? I've never seen those two together, and I've always thought they'd look nice."

Gaela looked at him in unfeigned surprise. "That's a great idea! It ought to work, if you mulch the hostas. And use Royal Standard. They have white blooms. The lavendar ones of most hostas would clash with the geraniums. The problem is, I'm so busy. Do you think you could take charge of it? It'll take a lot of looking after. This is a bad time of year to start stuff. But it's just a small spot."

She hoped there was no suspicion in the glance he cast her. "Sure. Can I tell Lillian you said I could have what I want out of the greenhouse?"

"Go for it. Thanks! I'll come and see how it turns out as soon as I can." And she made her escape before he could figure out she'd given him his own garden.

Gaela saw him there several times, hovering over his plants, which did look very nice together. She could swear she saw him talking to them at least once. She hoped they were talking back.

Chapter Fifteen

On August 10 Gaela entered the workshop in the morning to a chorus of "Surprise!" She jumped and covered her face. Oh, no. Laughter and cheers surrounded her, and she peeked through her fingers and saw a crowd of people, a pile of brightly wrapped packages, and a sheet cake covered with frosting flowers and the words "Happy Birthday, Chief!"

Ted pulled her hands away from her face, and she frowned at him. "This has to be your doing. How did you discover my birthday?"

"I have my ways," said Ted with a sinister leer.

Gaela hated surprise birthday parties. If there was one thing she dreaded more than another, it was being the center of attention, fussed over and expected to show eager joy about presents you had to open in front of everybody. It wasn't that she didn't appreciate them, but she felt silly.

Well, nothing to do but fake it as kindly as possible. She smiled brightly around the room and gushed, "You *shouldn't* have!" and everyone laughed. Caine's smile seemed almost sympathetic, but that had to be her imagination. He couldn't know. Nobody else in the world disliked birthday parties!

Gaela avoided his eyes and went to inspect the cake, which was made in the form of a garden, with beds of multi-colored frosting flowers, paths made of licorice jelly beans, a pond of blue frosting with two oversized plastic ducks on it, and a little plastic trellis in one corner. "This is really great! Who's idea was it, as if I didn't know, Lillian?"

Lillian grinned smugly and thumbed over her shoulder to Chan, looming behind her like a linebacker.

"Chan? Really?" Gaela stared up at the embarrassed young man. The interesting shade of fuschia blooming on his face seemed to indicate that he had, indeed, been the perpetrator of the cake. "Wow, Chan! I'm so impressed! Did you make it, too?"

"Oh, no!" Chan declined hurriedly, to the laughter of the others. "I just sort of made a, you know, like a sketch, and took it to the bakery."

"Well, it's beautiful," Gaela declared, touched.

"Come on!" Jeanie pulled her to the table. "Open your presents!"

Gaela picked up a large blue package, prepared to ooh and ah to the best of her ability. "To the chief, from John and Gary." She ripped at the paper and discovered a set of hand garden tools. "Hey, great, just what I need!"

Gary and John shuffled their feet, and it occurred to her that some of the crew might be as uncomfortable as she was. How well did they really know each other, after all? Had Lillian and Ted roped people into this?

"We tried to get really tough ones," Gary told her.

"Almost as tough as you are," Ted put in, and everyone laughed again.

Gaela stuck out her tongue at him and picked up a gift that was so tall it was leaning against the table, its long, wooden handle visible, its triangular business end wrapped in striped paper. " 'Happy Birthday from Jeanie.' Hmmm, I wonder what this could be?" She was getting into the spirit of this celebration. Tearing the paper, she gasped theatrically. "A hoe! I *never* would have guessed!" Her tone changed as she got a good look at the too. "Hey, wait—this is that super-duper, guaranteed forever Dutch one I saw in that catalog, isn't it?"

Jeanie nodded, and Gaela could almost have hugged her. "Thank you! I really wanted one. This is great!"

A tiny package beautifully wrapped in silver paper turned out to be a spectacular cloisonné pin in the shape of an orchid. "Oh, Lillian! Oh, my goodness, look at this! Put it on me!" Lillian did, and then hugged Gaela. "Thank you," gulped Gaela, hoping she wouldn't disgrace herself.

Randy had bought her a toy lawnmower, "so you could have one of your very own," he explained, over more laughter.

"How did you know I was jealous of you?" Gaela demanded. "I thought I kept it pretty well hidden."

She opened several more garden tools, a packet of seeds of a rare flower she had never seen, and an Audubon field guide from Chuck, wrapped in Christmas paper with red poinsettias all over it.

Almost over, and it hadn't been so bad. Of course, she hadn't expected anything from Caine.

She regarded the last gift, a large, oddly shaped item wrapped in colored Sunday funny papers.

"Well, open it!" said several voices eagerly.

"I'm afraid to!"

"Come on!"

Gaela picked up the package gingerly and turned it over. It was from Ted, and she gave him a sidelong glance, but he was concentrating on looking cherubically innocent. She pulled the paper aside—not very difficult, as it appeared to have been taped together by a four-year-old—and revealed a large megaphone. Everyone looked as bewildered as she did until he explained helpfully, "It's for when you forget your phone." By now everything and anything made the whole crew dissolve in laughter.

Gaela waited until they wound down, put the megaphone to her lips, pointed it at Ted, and bellowed, "Ted Waite, report for duty! Tote that barge, lift that bale!"

He winced and ducked away from the blast, and she said with satisfaction, "Yes, that works nicely! Thank you so much, Ted!"

Then twenty-seven candles had to be lit and blown out with great ceremony. Gaela couldn't quite forbear a glance at Caine when she was loudly enjoined to make a wish. When she blew them all out with one breath, Ted remarked, "Great lung power, for such a little thing. I've always said so."

Lillian cut the cake and produced ice cream. The "chief" tried to hold something resembling a staff meeting while they ate, as it was past time they were out on the grounds. She thanked them all again for the party before dismissing them to their various tasks.

Sighing with relief as they trooped out the door, she turned and found Caine waiting behind. "I have a present for you, too, but I thought I'd wait till later. I didn't think you'd like this hoopla all that much."

So he had guessed.

"You were very right. Six years, I've managed to avoid even letting them know when my birthday was. I wonder how Ted found out? So, now that you know the deep dark secret, when's yours?"

"My what?"

"Come on, fair's fair. I promise not to do to you as has been done to me. Unless of course you had a hand in it?" She gave him a threatening glare.

"Not me, chief, ma'am, on my honor! March thirteen."

"Aha. And how old will you be?"

"I will be thirty-three, oh nosy one."

"And—" did she dare? — "will you still be here?"

He held the door and they walked out. "Oh, who knows?" he said breezily. "I never plan anything that far ahead."

And he pulled one of his disappearing acts.

That night in the Secret Garden, he silently handed her a rectangular package. Opening it, Gaela found a book of simple recorder melodies and duets.

"Oh, Caine, this is great! Thank you!" She leafed through it eagerly.

"Since you didn't give me a present this year—" Gaela looked up with an outraged expression—"you can give me the pleasure of playing some of these with me."

She dropped pretense and beamed at him. "I'd love to!" Surely, if he gave her duets, he planned to be around at least for a while.

Then he pulled out another, smaller package. "That was the useful present. This is the frivolous one."

"Two presents? Oh, Caine!"

She slipped off the paper, and saw a hardbound, illustrated copy of Robert Louis Stevenson's *A Child's Garden of Verses*. She hoped her face expressed her joy, because she couldn't find any words. Her throat threatened to close up on her if she spoke.

She looked up, and found him standing way too close. He leaned forward and planted a kiss on her lips, than backed off hurriedly and said, "Well, happy birthday, Pixie. I have to get out of here." And he escaped.

She stood looking after him, thinking if either of them was magical, he was the one. He seemed able to transport himself instantly out of danger. And how was it that he always knew exactly what she would like?

How could he seem to know her so well, when she didn't know him at all? She rethought that. She did feel she knew him, sort of. Recognized him, or something. Well, that was a silly thought. Straight out of a B movie. *"Two souls, destined to meet,"* she mocked herself in a whisper. When she added up what she actually knew *about* him, it tallied up to pitifully little.

One day a week or so later, pruning roses, she thought she heard Somartini's Recorder Concerto. She lifted her head and listened. Yes, it was the theme, anyway. Coming from . . . the gazebo? She walked closer, and saw a much larger crowd than usual. Caine was perched on the railing this time, running through those incredibly difficult, incredibly fast trills without apparent effort. Gaela just stood and stared. This man was a *master* musician! Unaccountably, it made her angry. She stomped back to the roses.

She was sitting in the swing in the Secret Garden with her arms folded when he came to see her that evening. This time she was the one who jumped into a conversation without preamble. "What do you want to know about me?"

"I beg your pardon?"

"What do you want to know? You have my birthdate, my hometown, would you like the names of my brothers and sisters? My parents? My dad is a building contractor, and my mother is a housewife *par excellence*. My brothers and sisters are, let me see -" She began counting on her fingers. "A plumber, a teacher—"

"What is this all about?"

"I'll tell you where I went to high school, and what I thought I wanted to be when I grew up, and all my deepest secrets—*oh yeah!* I already told you those, didn't I?"

"Gaela-"

"Come to think of it, you told me yours, too. Some of them, anyway. It's just the really *private* things you can't bring yourself to share. Your name. Your family. What you do. The fact that you could play with the New York Philharmonic. Or, for all I know, have done so!" She was yelling now, dismayed to discover tears on her cheeks.

Caine came and knelt before her, unfolding her resisting arms, taking her hands in his.

"You know Samartini's theme *by heart*?"

"I'm sorry."

"You'd better be sorry. I'm falling—" Gaela clamped her mouth shut so fast she bit her tongue. The words she had almost said shouted in her head. *I'm falling in love with you, you idiot!* If he could read her mind as well as usual, she hoped he picked up those last two words loud and clear. How could she possibly fall in love with a man whose name she didn't even know?

Caine put his forehead against their joined hands. "I know. I know. I'm sorry. You have no idea. I want to tell you everything, but I just can't bring myself to. I know it's stupid. I've already told the worst. It's not that I don't want to tell you. It's that there's something I've got to do. And until I can bring myself to do it, I can't come to you. I just can't." He let go of her and rose to his feet in a swift movement. "You'd be better off without me. I always said so."

He moved toward the gate, and she hissed furiously after him, "If you run away this time, Caine Hunter, I'll never speak to you again."

He laughed softly. "It's your spells that keep me here, Pixie, and your spells that always bring me back. I've tried to get free from you. I really have. But I don't seem to be able to, so unless I get a lot stronger, I don't think you have to worry. Though you should worry more if I stay. I never stay anywhere long, you know." Hand on the gate, he looked back. "I stayed in Cleveland three whole years once. I played clarinet in the symphony there." And he was gone.

That was three times in one day! Gaela was so mad she cried, now that there was no one there to see her.

For two weeks they existed in a holding pattern. Caine and Gaela interacted more as employee and boss than as friends, let alone anything more. Several staff left as college classes began, and Gaela felt even more amazed than other years that the summer was drawing to a close already.

August 24 dawned like any other day. The skies were blue, the air had not yet begun to chill for fall, and the leaves were still green. Mums were in full bloom in the borders, and birds were busy in the ornamental cherries. The staff meeting went without incident, and the workers scattered over Eden's Gate, intent on their tasks. Gaela and Jeanie were moving hoses from one bed to another when they heard the first screams.

Chapter Sixteen

Gaela jerked upright and almost fell over. She had never heard such anguished shrieks. They seemed to be coming from the general direction of the big house. She started to run, trying to tell if the screams were words. One word, repeated over and over. She saw Ted racing up from the lake and realized that was the word. "*Ted! Ted! TED!*" As she skidded through the pergola and rounded the wall of the Secret Garden she was shocked to see Ivy flying across from the parking lot, her feet hardly touching the ground. She collided with Ted and seemed to try to climb up him, sobbing wildly.

Guests were gathering. Breathlessly, Gaela moved to disperse them. "All right, folks, let's move on. Everything is okay. We have it under control." At least she hoped Ted did. "Take her to the house!" she called to him. He had managed to pick Ivy up despite her desperate clinging and was moving away with her. She could hear his murmuring underneath her sobs and gasps. More staff had arrived by now, and Gaela left them to deal with the curious crowd and followed Ted, trying to decipher what Ivy was wailing. She thought she heard the words, "They're dead!"

Caine passed her, his face white, and she heard him telling the visitors that he would be playing in the gazebo in five minutes. Bless Caine!

Ted was fumbling with the security lock on the big house door, and Gaela passed him and opened it, her own fingers trembling. Lillian showed up with a glass of water.

Ted tried to put Ivy on a couch, but she wouldn't let go of him, so he sat down with her in his arms. "Cry, then," he said tenderly. "Go ahead and cry. We'll wait until you can talk."

Gaela looked around and found a box of tissues. It looked as if Ivy would need the whole thing. Lillian sat down by Ted and started rubbing Ivy's back in slow circles. Gaela stood helplessly, feeling cold. Who was dead? A vague, wordless prayer began to run through her consciousness.

After a few minutes, Ivy's sobs became hiccups and then broken sighs. She sat up on Ted's lap and blew her nose, drank some of the water, and tried a grateful smile, which quivered out of shape. "I'm sorry. I'm ashamed of myself."

"Nonsense!" said Lillian. "Whatever for?"

Ivy made a half-hearted attempt to get off Ted, but he held her in place. "What's going on, Ivy?"

"Aunt George and Uncle Sam-" Ivy's face broke down again.

"Oh, dear Lord," whispered Lillian, and Gaela hugged herself. Her heart thumped heavily.

"They had an—accident in the RV," Ivy managed.

Gaela backed up to a chair and dropped into it. "They're . . . dead?" Her voice sounded strange.

Ivy nodded and started to cry again. Ted pulled her head down on his shoulder.

After a long moment in which nothing was heard but Ivy's weeping, Gaela pulled herself to her feet. "You stay with her, Ted. I guess I'll . . ." She looked helplessly at Lillian.

Lillian stood too. "I'll come with you to tell the others. I wonder if we should close the place?"

It seemed like an impossible task to find everyone and put them out, but Gaela shuddered at the thought of trying to go on with the whole day, which had just begun, acting as if nothing had happened. She wanted Caine.

"You go west, I'll go east," she said to Lillian. "Try to find everyone. Call an emergency staff meeting as soon as everybody can get to the workshop. Visitors will just have to fend for themselves for a little bit."

Her first stop was the gazebo, where the crowd listening to Caine were still eyeing the big house curiously and whispering. Gaela realized practically every guest in the garden was probably here, and took opportunity by the horns. "Ladies and gentlemen," she said, when Caine paused for breath. "There has been an emergency, and I'm afraid Eden's Gate will have to be closed for the day." A murmur of disappointment spread through the crowd, and someone called out, "What happened?"

"I'm sorry, sir, I'm not at liberty to say," Gaela told him. "If you will all—"

"Did I hear that woman say somebody died?" called someone else.

"Yes." She kept her words vague. "There was a death in the family. Now, if you will all please go to your cars, we will be taking a look around the gardens to let everyone else know they need to leave now. We're very sorry for the inconvenience, and hope you will come back to Eden another day."

"Will you be open tomorrow?"

Gaela hesitated. "Actually, I am not sure. You'd better call ahead. Thank you for coming." Together, she and Caine herded them away, and they began straggling reluctantly toward the parking lot. Other staff members had been hovering nearby, and came forward for instructions. "Go find everyone and get all guests out of the garden and close the gate. Then tell all workers to come to the workshop as soon as they can get there."

She grabbed Caine's hand as he started away, and he turned to her with a strangely closed look on his face. "Caine-" she hesitated. She had been hoping for comfort. "The Sullivans. Ivy says—" she couldn't say the words, but he nodded once.

"I know. I heard her. They're both dead?"

"Yes. I don't know any details yet."

He turned away again, and she let his hand go. "I'll check out the woods trails," he said, and left at a trot.

Gaela watched him go. She should have known. He always closed up when trouble threatened. She headed for the grotto and the topiary garden, which were deserted, and stuck her head in the Secret Garden, where a young couple with a baby were startled to be informed that Eden's Gate was closing early due to an unforeseen incident. They obediently gathered up their paraphernalia and departed.

Gaela was one of the last to arrive at the workshop. "Is everyone gone?"

"Yes, we think so. There weren't many here yet. We turned away two cars at the gate," Randy told her. "We need to put some kind of sign up. People will be upset."

"We could call an announcement to the local radio station," suggested Jeanie.

"And say what? We don't know anything."

"We don't need to say much. Just what we told people already. There's been a death in the family, and the garden will be closed until further notice."

"What did happen, anyway?"

Gaela took a deep breath. "According to Ivy Sullivan, the owners, Sam and Georgiana Sullivan, were in an accident in their RV and are dead."

There was a low whistle of dismay.

"What will happen to Eden?" asked Randy, and Gaela looked at him startled. She hadn't even thought that far.

"I . . . I don't know. I guess we will have to close until we find out, at least. Jeanie, will you call that in to the radio station? Gary and John, will you find something to make a big sign with? Um, the rest of you, well, I guess if you're in the middle of an important job, finish it, and then you can choose whether to hang around here and wait for news, or go home. I'll let you know as soon as I know more."

The door opened and Ted entered.

"The Sullivans are dead, and Ivy thinks there may be trouble with the will. The place may have to be shut down indefinitely." He spoke gruffly, as if trying to control his own emotion.

Gaela felt the earth move under her, opening a chasm into which she just might disappear. "Well, then," she heard herself say in a more or less normal voice. "There you have it. Finish up anything you left hanging and go home, and I'll let you all know as soon as I learn anything definite."

The staff filed out with anxious murmurs and glances at each other.

Gaela watched Caine go with them, and turned to Ted. "How's Ivy?"

"She's lying down resting. She didn't want me to leave, so I'll be going back up there."

"Does she have anyone at all?"

He shook his head. "Her mother. She expects her to descend on us like a bat out of you know where. Gaela, how are you doing?" He put a hand on her shoulder, and she covered it gratefully with hers.

"Okay, I guess. I think I'm in shock. I can't quite take it in yet. Ted . . . do we have jobs?"

"I don't know, chief. Ivy knows the name of the lawyers, and we're going to call them when she's feeling a little more up to it. Come on up to the house when you can."

"Okay."

She stayed in the workshop for a while when he'd left. Questions that hadn't occurred to her at first were coming thick and fast now. Did she have a job? Did she have a home? Did she have a life left? If she had to leave here, where in the world would she go? Who would love and care for Eden? And where, oh, *where* was Caine when she needed him?

She did a run-through of the garden, telling herself she was checking to see if all visitors were out, checking to see if the garden needed anything right away, checking to see how much help she could get by with if the garden were closed down. She knew she was really looking for Caine, and failing that, looking for comfort from her gardens themselves. The same vague, wordless prayer had been running in the background of her mind since she'd first heard the announcement. She sat down on Caine's log in the Secret Garden and began to pray aloud. "Oh, God, help! Help Ivy, help us, help everyone connected with this." She tried to breathe calmly. "Show me what to do next, and help me live a moment at a time and not panic. Give peace to the staff, and help us find other jobs, if that becomes necessary. And what about Caine, God? What about—" but she had run out of words.

In a while, she got up and went to the big house. Chuck and Randy stood awkwardly in the tiled hall.

"Lillian and Ted are upstairs with Ivy," Randy told her.

Ted came down the stairs. "Lillian's with her. They'll come down in a little while. What needs doing outside?"

"Nothing," Gaela told him. "Everybody's gone but us, I think. I did a walk-through, and everything looks okay. I—" she looked around the little group and swallowed. "I don't know what to do."

"None of us does," Ted pointed out. "It's not exactly a normal situation. Why don't we get some drinks or something, and sit down?"

They sat, silent and uncomfortable, around the big table in the kitchen, holding glasses of water or juice or soft drinks. Nobody was very thirsty. The clock on the wall ticked solemnly. Gaela stifled a nervous laugh.

Finally they heard footsteps and Lillian and Ivy entered the room. Ivy looked composed, though pale. Ted stood and went to her, and she leaned on him for a moment. "Let's all sit down," she said, shaking her head at Ted's offer of a drink.

"I was at home when I got the call," she began. "I was supposed to be with them."

This called for a moment of horrified silence as she hung on to her composure.

"I wanted to come here again, so I had gone home to pack some things. Mother will be in a fury at me when she arrives, probably today or tomorrow. All I could think was to get in my car and drive like a maniac to get here."

Gaela shuddered at the thought of Ivy making a long drive in the condition she'd been in when she arrived. But she understood perfectly Ivy's instinct to get to Ted any way she could. She'd give anything to be able to run to Caine like that, and she wasn't even the one who was bereaved. She saw Ivy's sidelong glance at Ted and easily interpreted it to mean she knew she'd have a scolding coming as soon as Ted thought she was up to it. Gaela knew it would be a half-hearted one. Ted was glad Ivy had run to him.

Ivy had figured out her next sentence. She seemed to be stringing them together one or two at a time, with effort. "I'm sure you're all wondering about your future. I happen to know something about the will. My aunt and uncle talked to me about it on our last trip together."

Again a stop and a struggle. Ivy cleared her throat determinedly. "They wanted this place to go to me, if it couldn't go to their son."

There was a stir in the room. "Their son!" exclaimed Lillian. "I never knew they had a son!"

"Most people don't. I've never met him, myself. There was some kind of a huge fight years ago, and they've been estranged ever since. They don't even know if he's alive or dead, and they never talked about him. I guess there's some kind of a provision in the will for a search for him, but I don't expect he'll turn up. They never found him in all these years."

"People turn up when there's money in it," Chuck pointed out drily.

"That's true." Ivy appeared to consider this for a minute. "Anyway, if they find him in a certain amount of time, or something like that, he gets it all."

"No matter what kind of person he is?" objected Ted.

"Well, I'm not sure. Maybe there are other provisions. Anyway, if he doesn't turn up, they wanted me to have it. But I'm not sure I want the responsibility, at least not yet, and I told them Mother wouldn't be fit to live with if she didn't get it."

"What claim does she have?" asked Randy.

"She doesn't, not really. My dad was Uncle Sam's brother, and she always lamented that the brothers should have had half share in the place when Grandmother died. Never mind that Dad didn't want it. I have always suspected he moved us to California when I was a baby partly to get away from here, or from his brother, or something. I don't really know, but there was something. . . something they never would talk about." She paused, then added with a twist of lips, "I think Mother actually hoped something like this would happen, with them traveling all the time. Then she could trail around playing lady of the manor. Oh, I guess that's pretty harsh. I shouldn't—" Ivy sighed, and Ted's hand moved comfortingly on her shoulder.

"Anyway, Uncle Sam and Aunt George said no, Dad was perfectly happy with his cash inheritance, and the estate was to go to Sam's son. But I was second in line. They said they'd have the executor continue to watch over things for me until I'm thirty, so that Mom couldn't make things too miserable for me." Her face crumpled again. "But she *can*! She can make me wish I *could* turn it over to her! I don't want it without Uncle Sam and Aunt George, and now I'm stuck with it!" She turned her face into Ted's shoulder and sobbed quietly.

"If the son doesn't show," said Randy thoughtfully.

A bizarre thought crossed Gaela's mind. Caine –? No, impossible! Her heart sped up anyway. What if he was? He'd said his mother was dead, though. He'd lied before, but he wouldn't lie about a thing like that!

The conversation swirled around her, unheard. Suddenly she remembered his sister. If she'd never known they had a son....

She opened her mouth and the question came out. "Did the Sullivans ever have a daughter?"

Ivy sat up and sniffed, reaching for a tissue. "A daughter? No, why?"

Gaela felt her heart settle to a more normal rhythm. The others were looking at her curiously, so she tried to be nonchalant. "Oh, I just wondered. A son appears in the picture, why not a daughter?" She couldn't decide if she was relieved or disappointed that Caine couldn't be the long-lost heir.

"Honey, we need to know what our next step should be. If you give me the lawyers' number, I'll call them for you, if you want me to," offered Ted.

"The number should be in the index on the desk in the library," Ivy said. The two went to retrieve it. The others waited in the kitchen with the ticking clock until they came back, Ted holding Ivy's hand.

"One of the lawyers, a woman named Elizabeth Crandall, says she's been named executrix of the estate. She'll come and meet with us tomorrow. She asked if we could get by with the winter staff if the place stays closed, and I said we could." Ted looked at Gaela, and she nodded. "The jobs of the rest of the staff are in limbo at the moment, because everything depends on what the heir wants to do, and it could be up to a year before that is settled with certainty. So that's how it stands tonight."

They all sighed and stood up. Ivy begged Ted and Lillian to spend the night in the house with her, and Randy and Chuck went home.

Gaela wandered for a while and waited in the Secret Garden. Caine was nowhere to be found. Naturally. She finally went home. The peace and security she usually found there was missing. Would this be her home when the dust settled?

She lay in bed unable to sleep for the pictures dancing in her head. Mr. S's rosy face, Mrs. S's bossiness, their melancholy, now partly explained, Caine's long fingers on his recorders, on her hands, on her face. She finally cried, and once she started she couldn't stop. She hadn't even got to say good-bye to them this time.

And where was Caine?

Chapter Seventeen

Gaela didn't sleep well. She was in the Secret Garden at dawn, trying to pray, trying to believe the best of Caine, trying to accept the fact that it didn't make any difference what she thought of him, he would do what he was going to do.

She called all the staff and asked them to be at the house at eleven, so they could learn first-hand what the executrix had to say about their jobs. She supposed it wasn't that much of a disaster for some. Most of them were only working for the summer, anyway. Students had left already; the rest would have stayed on through October. There were only five who worked here for a living.

And only one whose whole life was here, more closely bound up with Eden's Gate than even the Sullivans' lives had been.

Elizabeth Crandall was scheduled to arrive at ten-thirty, but Gaela saw a car pull in the drive an hour before that. It was white, as long as the pergola, and flashed with chrome. This would be Ivy's mother. Gaela decided to hang out in the gardens until she was called. She had heard more than enough about Ivy's mother to make her thoroughly terrified of her.

No one called her, so she cleaned up at ten-fifteen and watched for another car. When it arrived, she went to the back door of the big house and knocked. It seemed strange, knocking, which she never did even when the Sullivans were home. Nobody answered anyway, so she went in and followed the sound of a strident voice to the library, where Ted, Ivy, Lillian, a strange, stuttering man, and a no-nonsense-looking woman in a navy suit confronted a tall female that had to be Ivy's mother. Gaela figured out immediately why model-beautiful Ivy was so shy.

She had clearly inherited her looks from her mother, but this woman wore beauty like a weapon. She appeared to have sharpened it over the years. Her nose was sharp, her chin was sharp, her clothes and her high-heeled shoes and her glance were sharp. Her tongue was certainly sharp, and she was wielding it with furious energy on the suited, gray-haired woman. The strange man kept echoing the last two words of everything she said. Who could he be? Ivy hadn't said anything about a second husband.

Ivy herself was shrinking into Ted, who had a protective arm around her and was visibly controlling his urge to forcibly shut her mother up.

The suited woman, who had to be the executrix, was stolidly ignoring the flow of words, opening her briefcase on the neat desk in the library.

Lillian was standing back and observing, appearing to find the whole tirade amusing. Gaela sidled in next to her.

She shouldn't have moved.

"-- anything so ridiculous in my life! Aha! And there you are, miss! Aren't you the head gardener, or caretaker, or whatever you call yourself? Speak up!"

"Speak up!" barked the strange man.

Flanked by Lillian and Ted, Gaela could smile coolly. "I call myself Gaela Clancy. And you are?"

The woman looked shocked. "I am Vivian Sullivan, and I would like to know what you think you are doing allowing your hired help to consort with my daughter, luring her away from her home and practically shacking up with her? I never did understand what my brother-in-law saw in you, and I assure you, your employment here is terminated immediately, as is that of all your *helpers*!" She clearly meant cohorts in sin. Gaela almost giggled.

"All your helpers!" said the man, nodding officiously.

The executrix cleared her throat. Ignoring her, Vivian Sullivan drew another breath, and Ms. Crandall gained the admiration of everyone else in the room by saying calmly, "If you'll all have a seat—Mrs. Sullivan, I believe I have the floor! Have a seat please." After a shocked second, Vivian Sullivan sat. Gaela felt like applauding.

The rest hustled to seats as Ms. Crandall's gimlet eye found them. She cleared her throat again, and opened a file folder. Vivian opened her mouth, encountered the gimlet eye, and shut it.

"Now, then, I am Elizabeth Crandall, the appointed executrix and trustee of the estate of the late Samuel and Georgiana Sullivan. May I say how sorry I am to hear of their untimely demise. I did not believe I would be called upon to perform this duty so soon." Ms. Crandall's eyes softened noticeably when they rested on Ivy. "I have here a copy of the will, which you, Miss Sullivan, should have received by now."

It was Mrs. Sullivan who answered. "I certainly have! I brought it with me, and I assure you, my lawyers will be looking into it. I have never heard of anything so foolish, so irresponsible—"

"Irresponsible—"

"No doubt that is why your brother-in-law and his wife found it necessary to appoint me," said Ms. Crandall with finality, and Vivian gasped and shut up again. "In order to effectively understand my duty, I would like to be introduced to those present," said Ms. Crandall.

Gaela spoke up. "I am Gaela Clancy, the head caretaker, and these are Ted Waite and Lillian Gifford, my assistants. Naturally we understand that this business concerns the family, and not us. We are only here to learn, well, frankly, whether we still have jobs. I have asked the rest of the staff to assemble to learn what you have to say, as well."

"Then I shall speak to you first, Ms. Clancy. I appreciate your concern, and only wish I had something more definite to tell you. I believe I spoke to Mr. Waite yesterday?" Ted nodded. "Yes. I have checked into the matter, and I have the authority to tell you that the winter staff, I believe you said five, may stay until they hear otherwise." Ivy's mother stirred, and the executor speared her with a look. "The rest of the staff, I am afraid, are dismissed; however there may be some remuneration if they have difficulty in finding new jobs on such short notice. You will, of course, give such references as you deem necessary. The estate will remain closed to the public, so your duties will merely be to keep the grounds in good condition pending the final decision as to the disposition of the inheritance. I shall wish to speak with you later regarding financial details, the budget under which you have been operating, what care is given to the house, and so on. If you will be so good as to leave me your number."

Gaela gave it to her, and asked nervously, "There is one more thing, Ms. Crandall. Perhaps you are aware that I live in a small cottage on the estate?"

"Ah, yes, I had forgotten. Thank you for reminding me. I believe it will be a good idea for you to stay. We will discuss details of that later, as well."

"Thank you. I think that answers our questions as well as they can be answered at the moment." Gaela and Lillian stood to leave, but Ivy hung on to Ted.

"Ms. Crandall, Mr. Waite and I are . . . have a friendly relationship. He is here at my request. Lillian stayed at the house with us last night. I want Ted to stay in here with me."

"Very well."

Gaela and Lillian shared a glance outside the door. "Whew! What a battle-axe!"

"Good thing," averred Lillian. "Wonder where the Sullivans found her? She's exactly what's needed to deal with that Vivian woman."

"And give courage to Ivy. I liked her, I must say. Who on earth was the Greek chorus?"

"Oh, didn't you know? That's right, Ivy told me when we were upstairs. She was too distraught to remember to mention it when we were all together in the kitchen, poor little thing. That's her ma's new boyfriend. I guess he's a real estate developer, and Ivy's scared he has his eye on this place."

"Oh, no! He couldn't cut it up! They wouldn't!"

"Who knows what they'd do if they got their grubby little paws on it? Yep, you can thank the good Lord Sam Sullivan had the sense to hire that Crandall woman to watch over Ivy's interests. She's only twenty-one, did you know that? What a life she must lead with that harpy of a mother! At least now she'll be out from under her talons!"

Outside, they found the rest of the crew waiting. Gaela's eyes swept the group for Caine's face, and didn't find it. She told them the bad news. They took it calmly, going to gather their things from the workshop. Lillian went to share some words with her faithful helper, Chan. A few stayed to talk to Gaela about references or severance pay. Jeanie gave her a speaking look and a hug. "I'll see to it you get some funds to tide you over for a couple of weeks, at least," Gaela promised, thinking of the three little mouths Jeanie was responsible for.

An hour later, Gaela found herself alone in the summer for the first time in several years. Randy was off mowing a distant meadow that was mowed twice a year, Chuck was out on the lake in a skiff, battling duck weed, Lillian was in her greenhouse, and of course Ted was still inside with Ivy.

Caine had never shown up.

Gaela puttered around finding things to tend, and thinking about the Sullivans. They had never spent much time here since they'd hired her, although she gathered this had been their full-time home before that. They'd told her from the beginning that they wanted a caretaker so they could come and go as they pleased. The first year, while old Mrs. Sullivan still lived, they had been home perhaps half the time. Gaela and old Mrs. Sullivan had become quite good friends, though certainly not close enough to mention personal things like family battles. After her death, Mr. and Mrs. S were gone more and more until they only came home a couple of times a year. It was still hard to believe that all that time they'd been mourning a lost son. Gaela realized now how little she had really known her employers. Yet nearly every rock and plant had some memory connected to them.

Here was the tree on which Mr. S had taught her to prune. There was Mrs. S's "favorite rose," which only bloomed once in June, and for whose blooms she had never been home except one time. Yet she insisted it was her all-time favorite. The grotto and gazebo, of course, would always recall them, and so would the topiary garden and the pergola, two other projects over which they had squabbled. One of the benches by the lake was the place Gaela had most often found Mr. S when he went into his melancholies. Longing, no doubt, for the prodigal son. Did Caine's father sit and pine for his lost son?

A hopeful idea occurred to her. Maybe this fiasco had driven home to Caine the fragility of human life, and he had gone to see his dad. Dared she hope? Couldn't that have been what he meant when he said he had something he had to do before he could come to her? This thought lifted Gaela partly out of the despondency in which she was sinking. She decided she'd try to believe it until she knew otherwise.

She was sitting in the Secret Garden when she heard the gate creak and turned toward it with a leaping heart.

Elizabeth Crandall walked in. "Mr. Waite told me I would probably find you here."

"Oh, I'm sorry." Gaela rose from the swing so hurriedly that it hit her in the back of the legs. "You shouldn't have come all the way out here. You could have called—I have my phone."

"Don't worry about it. I have long desired a chance to see Eden's Gate. I have known the Sullivans for years, and never managed to make it out here. This is what they called the Secret Garden, isn't it?"

"Yes, it was built almost seventy years ago by Sam Sullivan's mother, Eden Sullivan, the one the gardens are named after."

Ms. Crandall gave her a strange look, but Gaela thought she'd imagined it when the other woman turned in a circle, breathing in the smells of leaf mold and budding mums and damp greenery, the late summer ambiance of the little walled garden. "Nice place. I can understand," she said inscrutably. "So you've taken care of the grounds for how long?"

"Six years."

"They're beautiful. You must enjoy your work very much."

"I do, ma'am. I don't think I'd ever want to do anything else."

Ms. Crandall sat on a bench near the swing. " Please—sit, be comfortable." She waited while Gaela sat, then added, "You must be very anxious."

"Rather. I think I could handle whatever I had to, if only I knew one way or the other."

"Yes, that is the difficult part. No doubt you know there is a codecil concerning the lost son."

"A codecil?"

"A recent addition to the will. They specified that a year and a certain sum of money be spent on a diligent search for him. In the meantime, there is a trust fund to cover care for the home and gardens. That is what you and I need to discuss. There is nothing I can promise you now except that you have a home and a job for that year, or until he is found, whichever comes first. Frankly, I do not believe in the last-minute, miraculous discovery of long-lost sons." Ms. Crandall nodded her neat, gray head decisively. "Between you, me, and the bedstead, one might say, Miss Clancy."

Gaela choked a little, startled by the eruption of slightly erratic colloquialism into Ms. Crandall's flowing utterances. She turned to watch a busy chipmunk for a moment, as the executrix continued.

"I believe, though as I have said I cannot actually promise, that your livelihood will be safe. Miss Sullivan has already stated to me that her wish, in the event, is that you remain and that the garden be reopened to the public. In that case I would still be trustee, watching over Miss Sullivan's interests until she is thirty, and I will do my best to see to it that neither of you need deal with Mrs. Vivian Sullivan any oftener than necessary. Otherwise, you may not enjoy the job as much as you have in the past." Ms. Crandall looked around appreciatively again and added scrupulously, "Let me add that, should it become necessary, I do not believe you would have any difficulty finding work once it became known that you had the care of this place."

"Thank you." Gaela took comfort not only in Ms. Crandall's assurances, but in the kindness that prompted them. One fact snagged in her mind. "You said they specified a year. I've been wondering—if they wanted to find him so much, why didn't they search while they were alive?"

"Ah, a good point. I believe that the Sullivans have been searching, in their way, for many years. Everywhere they went, they were, perhaps unconsciously, looking for their boy. However, they always believed he would finally come home of his own accord. Recently, they have been made aware of their own mortality, and have been less certain of that fact. They decided to search in a more thorough and official manner. Leaving no stone unsifted, one might say." Again the woman nodded decisively, and again Gaela found it necessary to turn her head to watch the flight of a cardinal. "In actual fact, the search had begun before their death, and the year will be completed next June. At that point, you, I, and Miss Sullivan will decide what is to be done."

Gaela took a deep breath and released it slowly. It really wasn't so bad. Ivy would certainly let her stay. And it would be nice to work together with her on the future planning of this garden. But she couldn't quite dispel her anxiety. What if the heir *was* found? What if he was awful? After all, what kind of person would feud for decades with nice people like the Sullivans? And what about Ivy's mother? "Can Ivy's mother make real trouble?"

Ms. Crandall, that bastion of respectability, snorted. "Mrs. Vivian Sullivan is quite capable of making a great deal of sound and fury. She has no power whatever, but she is certainly able to make her daughter unhappy. Perhaps you and I, Miss Clancy, will be able to protect Miss Sullivan somewhat."

Gaela found herself instinctively squaring her shoulders for battle and almost grinned again at the mental image of herself and Ms. Crandall, in full armor, standing nobly between Ivy and her mother.

"Mrs. Sullivan does not, I regret to say, clearly understand a trust, either. I believe she has some idea, first of wresting this lovely home from her daughter, then of selling it to developers."

"But she can't do that, can she?"

"Certainly not." Ms. Crandall rose. "Now, then, Ms. Clancy, if you will join me in the room I am apprised is your office, let us talk turkey!"

Gaela gulped back a giggle and led the executrix to her little office, where they "talked turkey" to such purpose that she felt quite relieved by the time they were through. The budget had been overhauled to account for the change in status to a private garden with a five-person staff. Her small expenses at the cottage and her stipend had been declared reasonable and would continue. Severance pay for certain of the staff had been settled upon. She wouldn't feel really safe until June had passed, but for a while, Eden was still hers.

Only it was more like the original, in that now it contained a resident serpent.

Vivian Sullivan ran her to ground in the topiary garden. "Of all the horrible ideas in gardening, I do believe chopping up helpless trees and shrubs to look like cartoon animals is the most repulsive!" She glared around at Chuck's masterpieces with a shudder.

Gaela was glad Chuck was still out on the lake.

"I believe in the *natural* school of gardening," Vivian informed her. "I think Mother Nature should be allowed to have her own way. Think of the habitats you've destroyed by all your invasive maneuvers! Archie, my intended, did you meet Archie? No? Well, he is Archibald Williamson, of Williamson, Incorporated!"

Gaela had never heard of either, but tried to look politely impressed.

"Archie thinks this whole area could be made into the most lovely, natural garden estates. One to five acres each, you know. The ones on the waterfront would cost more. There would be winding paved roads, so scenic and pastoral. Of course, *this* would all come out. Though perhaps part of it could be a park, where the little children could play and the senior citizens could walk of an evening. Perhaps, Miss Conley, you could still have a job here! There would be a great deal of mowing and such to do."

Her manner changed abruptly as she turned her dagger nose on Gaela. "However, I did not come to talk to you about that. I have come to make it clear, once and for all, that your hired help must leave my daughter alone, or there will be no employment for any of you. He, certainly, must go at once. I could sue, you know. Harassment, or alienating of affections."

Gaela had never been so glad in her life to see Ted rounding the corner of the hedge, looking fierce. As he strode to a point where his broad shoulders blocked her view of Mrs. Sullivan's sharp, angry face, she gave in to the grin. Ted *and* Ms. Crandall, both in full armor! Poor Vivian didn't stand a chance.

"Let me make a few things clear to you, Mrs. Sullivan!" growled Ted. "First, you have absolutely no rights here. Eden's Gate will be either the son's, or Ivy's. Never yours. In the meantime, it is under the care of Miss Clancy, who is perfectly capable of caring for it as she has always done, and who *will not* be subjected to your juvenile displays."

Sputtering with fury, Mrs. Sullivan tried unsuccessfully to talk over him, and then to walk around him. Ted thrust out a muscular arm between her and Gaela, who was listening appreciatively from behind his wide back. "Second, Ivy is of age, and can choose her own friends. If I had any doubts about my desire to rescue her from an empty and unhappy life, you have removed them."

Gaela gasped at this frontal attack. Mrs. Sullivan began to shriek like a factory whistle, and Ted stoked the fires further by laughing at her. Gaela made her escape, leaving them to it.

That night, standing by her bay window, Gaela murmured, "Well, God bless the prodigal son, wherever he might be, and whatever he might need. If he's still alive." She tried to pretend, even to herself, that her heart wasn't adding, *"Please don't let him be found unless he's nice!"*

Chapter Eighteen

So Gaela's days took on a new pattern. She got up leisurely, ate her breakfast outside in her little sunny garden unless it was raining, and went to have her devotions in the Secret Garden. Then she met with the other four, and often Ivy, at the workshop, and they divided up the day's tasks. Lillian kept everyone abreast of what was in the tabloids concerning the present nine days' wonder, The Mystery of Eden's Lost Son. Sometimes she brought in ridiculous headlines and they laughed together over them.

They would work in the quiet gardens, warning each other if Vivian Sullivan or Archie Williamson hove into view. Gaela had assumed that the house would be closed, awaiting its rightful owner, whomever that turned out to be. But apparently Ms. Crandall had decided that, while they could not actually live at Eden, Vivian and Ivy and Archie could stay for a while, as it was a family vacation home, of sorts. There must be no damage and no drain on the estate's resources. Vivian had brought in her own cook, and apparently believed Gaela and her staff would clean up after them when they'd left, since it would clearly be a drain on the estate's resources to hire a housekeeper.

The staff conspired to help Ivy avoid her mother, sneaking her into and out of various areas. The text function on Gaela's phone had never received such dedicated use. She was never without it, fully charged and turned on.

She had taken to inviting everyone back to her cottage for lunch. Vivian hadn't yet figured out where it was. They ate on her miniature patio or inside, spread all over the main living area. She found she liked having friends in her home. It was a new experience for her. Then they went back to their gardening. They also conspired to give Ted lots of time for walking with Ivy, or even taking her out on the lake occasionally.

In the evenings, Ivy went dutifully to the big house and dressed for dinner, the others went home, and Gaela had her evening quiet time in the Secret Garden. Sometimes she sat there long after the light had gone.

Tactfully, no one mentioned Caine to her. The tacit understanding was that he had been temporary help like the others, and his term of employment was over. Since the garden was no longer public, the staff took weekends off. Gaela went to the gazebo on Sunday mornings, wishing she could hear Caine play just once more. She couldn't bring herself to go to the small church she'd attended sometimes in the slow winters, knowing the congregation would have read about her in the papers.

September slid by, still warm, still green. No one actually made the squatters in the big house leave, so they didn't. These quiet days were much like the early days Gaela remembered, before Eden went public, and she would have enjoyed them very much if there had not been such a boulder of uncertainty hanging over her head. Some days, she missed the visitors, especially the children with their eager questions, and the serious gardeners, with whom she traded arcane tips and secrets. But her first love was always solitude, and she liked having the garden to herself while it was still warm and sunny, instead of having to wait for the cold months for some privacy.

If only.

If only Vivian Sullivan and her slimy cohort weren't there to spoil everything.

If only she knew to whom the estate — and her life — were going to belong.

If only Mr. and Mrs. S hadn't died in the first place! Of course, then she wouldn't have this privacy, these quiet days, or these if onlys.

If only Caine were here.

☙   ☙   ☙

Several states away, Caine sat in darkness among the trash on a curb and rubbed his grimy hands over his face. It hadn't taken long for him to revert to form. He was as shaggy and disgusting as he had been the day he showed up at Eden's Gate. What a horrible joke that had turned out to be! He had really believed for a while that he had found some peace there. He should have known better. Peace was not for the likes of him. No peace for the wicked. That was in the Bible somewhere.

Poor little Pixie. She really believed all that stuff about forgiveness and redemption. For people like her, it might be true. But when you were cast out of the garden, there was no going back. He ought to know that. "You will be a wanderer and a vagabond forever."

His punishment for trying to get out of his punishment was the cruelest of all. He'd been given a glimpse of real paradise. Her face was with him always.

I am with you always.

Caine lurched to his feet. "Go away!" he shouted. "I tried!"

A lone passerby, out late, gave him a furtive, nervous glance and hurried on.

The breeze tickled his ear, and he staggered away, swiping at it. It followed him everywhere he went. "Why won't you just leave me alone?" he almost wept.

A hand on his arm steadied him. "Who won't leave you alone?" asked a deep voice.

Caine tried to focus bleary eyes on a black man with a network of lines around his eyes. "God," he said. "God won't leave me alone."

The man smiled, and Caine realized the eyes were bottomless wells of kindness. "Oh, no, he never will," he said. "Lucky for us. Are you hungry?"

Hungry? Caine wasn't sure if he was hungry. "Do you know God?" he asked. He felt drunk, but he was pretty sure he hadn't been drinking.

"Yes." The man led him into an all-night diner and ordered him food. Caine looked at it, and decided he was hungry after all. The man seemed to like watching him eat.

Caine's head was a little clearer afterwards. He was embarrassed. What had he said to this man? He would thank him for the food and leave as gracefully as possible. He looked into the kind eyes and opened his mouth to thank him. "Do you think God can forgive anything?" he asked.

"Yes." The dark eyes saw him — really saw him, and didn't turn away. Why?

"Anything at all?"

The lines deepened as the man smiled and held out his hand. "My name is David," he said, as Caine automatically shook his hand. "I used to be a psychiatrist. I wanted to be able to control my life, and of course I couldn't, so instead I tried tell other people how to control theirs." David shook his head and grinned sadly. "Completely inimical to the whole idea of therapy, by the way." The smile faded. "I controlled my wife and daughter right out of my life. Then I seduced a patient. Oh, I never meant to. But I did." Caine's eyes widened, and he listened intently. David's bass voice rolled over him, cocooned him, like molasses. "I did that twice. Then I got caught. I lost my license and spent five years in prison. While I was there, I met the Eternal. And I learned he can and does forgive the most appalling things. I could tell you stories that would make your hair curl right up like mine."

Caine felt numb. "What do you do now?"

"I sweep walks. Pick up litter. Wash dishes when I get the opportunity. The truth is, I just got out. I'm not quite sure what to do next. Some one of these days, God's going to show me the job he has in mind for me. Right now, I guess you could say I'm a minister. Not in any formal way. I just look for people like you that I can share with. There's a lot of hopelessness in these streets. Most of these people, all they really need is someplace to go where they can get some peace. I can't give them that, but I can give them a hand, and an ear, maybe a meal. I can tell them their Creator won't give up on them, and that he can forgive them and give them peace right where they are. They look at me, and they can see I'm telling them the truth."

Caine thought about that. If this man knew so much, maybe he knew the answer to a question that had been keeping Caine awake at night. "Don't you have to go and find people and tell them you're sorry, too?"

"If you can, and if it wouldn't hurt them, that's a good thing to do. Lots of times you can't." David's eyes looked past Caine at something sad. "You wish you could, though, and that's a fact." He looked at Caine and Caine knew he understood, understood as Gaela never would. Thank God for that, he thought. He preferred her innocent.

"Can you hear God?"

David laughed, and the sound washed over Caine like a healing medicine. "One way and another, he makes himself heard. Tonight, for instance. He told me to go to you."

Caine stared at him. "He did? How?"

"I don't know that I could explain it. I just saw you there, and I knew I had to go to you." David's dark eyes softened. "Like a whisper on the wind," he murmured.

Caine put his fist to his mouth. On the ground in the woods, maybe, but please, God, not in front of another man! "I've got to go," he said in a strangled voice, stumbling out of the booth. I've got to--thank you--you don't know--thank you!" He gripped David's hand, and fled.

He walked as fast as he could until the urge to cry was gone. Then he kept walking. Maybe. Was it possible? No. It was too late now. Too late.

The wind was still with him.

☞ ☜ ☞

Gaela was in the grotto one evening, watching the sun set over the lake and reliving the one and only kiss it seemed likely she would ever have from Caine, when she heard a soft footstep. Her heart quickened foolishly, as it always did. It seemed to still believe he would be back. A man's form came around the side of the grotto, between her and the sun, and she held her breath until he spoke.

"Well, well, if it isn't the cute little gardener!" Gaela hadn't liked the two words "cute" and "little" used together in her presence since the age of six. She didn't even smile politely.

"Is there anything I can do for you, Mr. Williamson?"

"Why, no, sweetheart, your work is done for the day, isn't it? I just thought I'd come down and watch the sunset, and here I found myself a better view than I expected!" He leered, while Gaela watched in stupefaction. She hadn't known real men, outside of a movie screen, made faces like that. "I'll just leave you to watch the sunset in private, then," she said, and stood up.

He reached out and tried to take her arm. "Don't be in such a hurry. I don't mean you any harm. Can't a man have some company while he admires the lake?"

Gaela shook him off and tried to sidestep him, but he was quicker than she expected, and trapped her against the wall of the grotto. *Oh, God!* His voice changed as his hands bit into her arms. "Now, if you're going to be like that, then maybe you need a lesson in manners."

For just an instant, Gaela panicked, longing for Ted or Caine, or any of the men. Then, as Archie's face homed in on hers, she remembered all her own muscles, and how to use them. She smiled so he'd relax his hold, and then bit, hit, and kicked at the same time. Archie stumbled back with a howl of rage and pain. Gaela darted past him and scrambled up the hill beside the grotto. When she was well out of his reach, she shouted, "Touch me again, and I'll sue you to the moon and back!"

"It'll be your word against mine!" he yelled back.

Gaela looked down at him from above the grotto. "Oh, I think everybody will pretty much be on my side," she promised, and ran for home.

Behind her locked door, she started to shake. She ran a bath and soaked in it for a long time. Then she went to bed and cried. It was the first time since Caine left that she hadn't gone to the Secret Garden. "God is with me. I will be all right," she repeated to herself through her tears.

The next morning, she had bruises on her arms. She thought about covering them up, and decided not to. In the workshop, Ted took one look, grabbed her, and demanded, "What's this?"

"Oh, I'm going to tell you all about it, believe me, and I want every staff member to hear it," said Gaela. When all had arrived, including Ivy, she told her story. "I thought about calling Ms. Crandall, but it was a minor incident, actually, and I hate to get into any legalities. I just want you, Lillian and Ivy, to watch out for this creep. Naturally, if there's a second incident, we'll blow the whistle. Everybody keep your phone on."

Ted glowered at her. "We do already. If this had happened during the daytime, I assume you would have used yours. How are these safeguards going to help you once we've all gone home?"

It was a good question, one she'd hoped he wouldn't raise. "I won't go out of my house once you've all left. You can even walk me home. Vivian and Archie won't be here much longer, I hope."

"Actually . . ." It was Ivy's quiet voice, and they didn't hear her at first. "Actually," she repeated more clearly, and they looked at her. "This is the second incident."

"*What?*" roared Ted, and Ivy cringed.

"Settle down, Buck Rogers!" ordered Lillian tartly. "That's probably why she didn't tell you in the first place."

Ted took Ivy's face in his hands and turned it up to his. "So help me, God, if you're afraid to tell me things just because I get loud—"

"I'm not afraid of you," Ivy assured him. "It's Mother! We have a hard enough time. Can you just imagine?"

Quiet settled in the little room while they all imagined.

"That's it, then," said Gaela briskly. "I'll be the whistle-blower myself. I've even got bruises to show. We'll get him out of here, don't you worry, Ivy."

Ted demanded in a carefully quiet voice, "Did he hurt you, Ivy?"

"No, I promise he didn't. He just tried to grope me in the upstairs hall. I got away."

Gaela found the business card Ms. Crandall had left her and dialed the number on it.

It could have all been settled with a minimum of fuss and bother, if Vivian and Archie would only have agreed to go quietly. Instead, Archie bellowed slander and libel, and Vivian, for once, echoed him, screeching that she had always said Gaela and her crew had loose morals. Which was true, she had always said that.

Ms. Crandall pointed out they were only in the house on sufferance, and threatened to get the sheriff to evict them if necessary.

They called the sheriff themselves, and accused Gaela of a variety of crimes, from alienating the affections of a loving mother's only daughter, to blackening an honest man's good name, to embezzling estate funds. Gaela showed the officer her bruises. Archie showed them some of his.

The nine days was long over for the Eden's Prodigal story, but this was juicier than ever. The local press had a field day.

Then a tabloid with no movie stars to annoy picked it up.

ଔ ଔ ଔ

On a grimy city street, walking and walking, trying to find the courage to go back, Caine almost tripped over a torn newspaper the wind blew against his feet. He looked down, stepped on the paper, and walked on. Then he stopped and turned around. The paper was blowing up against the side of a building. Caine made a dash for it and looked again at the picture.

It showed Gaela, holding up her arms against the flash of the camera, Ted's arm around her shoulder. The headline proclaimed, CARETAKER BEATEN IN PARADISE! A slightly smaller subtitle read, STILL NO SIGN OF LOST PRODIGAL. There were helpful circles drawn around the bruises on Gaela's arms.

Caine dropped the paper and ran all the way to the bus station.

ଔ ଔ ଔ

The sheriff took everyone in for questioning, gave it as his disgusted opinion that Archie's was a "case for the circular file," and did his best to get Gaela to press charges. Even Archie's own pet lawyer told him he had no case, and would be laughed out of court if he tried to make one. Ms. Crandall obtained a restraining order and explained apologetically to Ivy that she was going to have to say no one could live at the big house until the investigation, which had so far turned up nothing at all, was complete.

"That's all right," said Ivy. "I'm getting an apartment here in town. Gaela says she'll recommend me for a job at the local landscaping company that helps her out a couple times a year. I might take some evening classes."

She and Ted exchanged glowing looks, and everyone present understood she might have other future plans, too.

Vivian and Archie threw fits and tantrums, but they left. Vivian gave Gaela to understand that her days were numbered. "Everyone knows there's no son!" she hissed. "I promise you it won't be long until I have the say around this place that I should have had from the beginning. Then we'll see what we will see."

"Then we'll see!" snarled Archie, casting Gaela a malevolent glance.

Gaela laughed.

It was pouring rain the day they left. Randy and Chuck had gone home early, so Ted, Ivy, Lillian, and Gaela ran through the downpour to the workshop to celebrate. They cheered and laughed and toasted each other with paper cups of tomato juice someone had left in the refrigerator. Ted turned on the old radio that never got good reception in the rain, and fiddled with the knobs until he found a scratchy university station. Through the static, Gaela could make out the strains of Debussy.

She turned away so the others couldn't see her face, wondering if the day would ever come when the agony of loss would lessen. The door opened behind her, letting in rain and wind, and her foolish heart tripped, as always. *If only.* The chatter ceased, and she turned to see why.

Standing in the open door, soaking wet, his hair dripping into his eyes, his chest heaving as if he'd been running, was Caine.

Chapter Nineteen

For a long moment, nobody moved or spoke. Then Caine strode to Gaela's side and took her arm in his wet hands, pushing her sleeve up. "Let me see," he rasped. His mouth twisted at the sight of her fading bruises.

Gaela laughed shakily. "You should see the other guy." Her attempt at lightening the atmosphere failed.

"Oh, I intend to," said Caine grimly.

Gaela wished he would put his arms around her. "How did you find out?"

A parade of conflicting emotions crossed Caine's face. "God told me," he said.

Gaela stared at him. Ted motioned to the others, and they faded away into the rainy evening.

Caine looked at her hungrily, almost the way he had looked at her the first day he came to the garden. Questions crowded her lips. *Why did you go? Why did you come back? Who are you?* She stopped waiting for him to put his arms around her, and walked into them. They closed around her, and a huge sigh escaped. She felt as if she'd been holding her breath for a month.

Home! All the fears and uncertainties of recent weeks faded into the background. She closed her eyes and pressed closer, soaking up his warmth and strength and dampness, smelling rain and city streets and wet wool and Caine. Water ran from his beard down the side of her neck, but she didn't care.

"I'm sorry," he whispered into her hair. "I'm so sorry. Will you forgive me?"

"Yes."

Another big sigh shook her, but she thought it was his this time.

"I have so much to tell you. I'm still all messed up, you know."

She pulled back far enough to laugh up into his face. "Are you? Well, you've come to the right place, because I am all together, neat, complete, and perfect. I'll fix you right up."

He tried to grin down at her, but she could see the old torment was back in his eyes. "I know."

She rolled her eyes. "Idiot."

He bent at the knees, and she stood on tiptoes. She could feel his arms tremble, and she thought his kiss would burn her up in its agony and longing.

When she could speak, she said, "Caine. My dear hunter, for heaven's sake, will you please tell me your name? I cannot keep calling you Caine when you are *not* an outcast."

"You'll never believe me."

"I'll believe you if you swear to tell the truth."

"It's Adam."

"You're kidding."

"No, my father named me Adam."

"Adam." She tried it out. "Well, I like it a lot better than Caine, believe me."

"He was still cast out of paradise."

"He'll be reunited. He was promised a deliverer." She was still standing in his arms, and she backed reluctantly out of them. His hands clung, then slowly let her go. "We have to talk."

He dug his hands into his pockets and turned away, giving her a panicky feeling. "No. Yes. I know. Not here."

Gaela wanted to ask why, but only said, "Where?"

"The gazebo. It has a roof, and we won't melt getting there. I'm soaked already. So are you, now." He looked somber.

"Oh, Caine — Adam. Adam! How weird. That'll take some getting used to. So, *Adam*, Is that why I had to practically force you to hug me? Because you were afraid to get me wet?"

"No, that's not why."

Nothing she said could get a smile out of him. He held his coat around her and they ran through the deluge to the gazebo.

"Now, talk."

"You first. I saw a gossip sheet that said you were beaten. Followed by some stupid thing about a prodigal?" Outside in the dark, his face looked grimmer than ever.

"You know better to believe anything you read in one of those. Though if that's what it took to bring you home, I'm glad. I wasn't beaten. And I was serious when I said you should have seen the other guy." She grinned. "He picked the wrong pixie."

His grim look remained, so she told him the whole story, exaggerating the funny episodes and downplaying her momentary fear. Caine—Adam—did smile a little when she told him that what outraged her most of all was that it had happened at their grotto. "And right when I was reliving the other heated experience I had there!"

"I still don't understand what all of this has to do with a lost prodigal."

"Oh, that. That's a curious one. It seems that all these years the Sullivans have been searching for their long-lost son. Ms. Crandall says she thinks that's what they were looking for when they kept traveling all the time."

Adam got up restlessly and walked to the other side of the gazebo to stand staring out at the rain. It was probably hard for him, all this talk about a prodigal son. She hoped one of the things he had to tell her was that he had made contact with his family, but if so, it must not have come out very well. He had been much more at home in his skin when he left than he was now. His voice was so quiet she almost missed it over the hiss and patter of the rain on the roof. "Why was he long-lost?"

"Well, that we don't know. That is, I suppose Ms. Crandall may know, but the rest of us don't, not even Ivy. She says there was some big fight years ago and they've been estranged ever since. She never even met him. Nobody knows if he's dead or alive, but the will specifies a year-long all-out search to be made for him, because they want the estate to go to him." She tried another small laugh. "Leaving no stone unsifted, Ms. Crandall says." No reaction. She sighed. "If they can't find him in a year, then Ivy gets it, but Ms. Crandall is to continue as her trustee and advisor until she's thirty. That's because her mother is making such a stink. I guess they knew she would. Seems she thinks she ought to get it all."

Adam turned. "Her mother and this creep who molested you and her own daughter?"

"Yeah, they want to 'develop' it. Can you imagine? I can't decide if I hope they find the son or not. I'm afraid he'll turn out to be a creep, too. But on the other hand, I've developed a soft spot for prodigal sons." His only reaction to this was to snort scornfully and turn away again, so Gaela continued, "Besides, I wish I could tell him personally that I know for a fact his parents forgave him for whatever it was he did. That every time they came here, they would sit alone and gaze sadly at nothing, or cry, until they couldn't stand it anymore, and they'd go traveling again. I saw them miserably missing their son. Maybe he'd like to know that. Maybe he needs to know it."

He didn't say anything, and Gaela realized in dismay that she was twisting the knife point in his own wounds, especially if he had tried to contact his dad and not been welcomed. Oh, why did she have to sermonize lately? It was not at all her style. "In the meantime, while the search goes on, all the staff have been let go except the winter skeleton staff, and the garden has been closed for the duration." Still no reaction. "I guess that means the bad news is, you no longer have a job, but the good news is, I have more time and we can talk and get to know each other better." More silence.

Gaela sighed. "That is, assuming you have come to your senses and are willing to let a person peek over those brick walls of yours."

A strange choked sound made her get up and go investigate. He wasn't talking because he was shuddering all over with suppressed sobs. She reached for him, stammering both his names, but he backed away from her. "I've read the story," he ground out in a voice that sounded like he'd been swallowing broken glass. " 'Then the prodigal son came to his senses, and he said, I will arise and go to my father.'" Adam took in a great, shuddering breath. "Only I can't. I can't! I was going to." His voice rose higher and higher. "I wanted to. I was given another chance. Now it's too late!" Gaela grabbed him just before he fell. They landed on their knees on the wet floor, and she held his head against her chest while he sobbed raggedly, gasping, "Dad! Dad! I'm sorry!" He clung to her like a drowning man, and she knew she would have more bruises tomorrow.

She rocked him and cried with him and murmured nonsense, while the rain fell around them and her legs went numb under her. Finally he loosed his hold on her and dug for a handkerchief, muttering thickly, "That's the third damn time, and it better be the last."

Gaela moved stiffly, trying to coax enough blood back into her legs to enable her to stand up. "The third time for what?" Her own voice was a little hoarse, too.

"Bawling like an infant, that's what." Heaving sighs still interrupted his sentences.

"I'm glad to hear it," said Gaela, pulling herself up on her knees by the railing.

"You would say that, you female, you. Did I break anything?" He managed to stand and to pick her up as well.

She giggled damply. "Crushed me to a pulp, you male, you."

They sat close together on the bench that ran around the inside of the gazebo. Adam's right arm was around her, and his left hand held both of hers to his chest. The rain could reach them, but they were both so wet it had become a moot point.

"Your turn," said Gaela firmly. "What gives, Adam?"

So he told her about the wind, and David, and the newspaper. "All of a sudden, it dawned on me that all this time, I've been thinking solely of my own needs. *I* couldn't come back. *I* was a lousy, mixed-up so-and-so. *I* was cast out of Eden. I even tried to convince myself my cowardice was better for you because *I* was such a loser. It was like a blinding light when I realized *you needed me*, and I hadn't been here. If I'd been here, none of it would have happened."

"How do you figure that?"

Adam laughed softly, sadly. "You still don't get it, do you? I'm Adam Sullivan. I am the long-lost prodigal son, the heir to all we survey."

Gaela heard the words, but they didn't make sense. "What do you mean?"

"Shocking, isn't it? A fine case of ironic fate."

"But — you can't be!"

"Why can't I be?"

"They didn't have a daughter! And you said your mother was dead!"

"My mother is dead. Georgiana is his second wife. Didn't that ever come up? No, I can see by your shocked face that it didn't. I am rather moved, in fact, by the complete way in which she seems to have taken on my father, lock, stock, warts, prodigal son, and all. I was never *their* son, as they appear to have claimed me to be. My parents' marriage broke up just before I left, although it was never very healthy. As for my sister, my mother made a shrine to her memory that made all who came near it feel ill. It was a travesty of the honest grief my father felt. Not to mention the unbearable grief and guilt that I carried every day."

Adam shifted. "But let us not go there, or I shall be blubbering gustily again. Anyway, my mother accused my father of not caring, one time too many, and he kicked her out. She took all her shrine materials with her. There was nothing left here to remind anyone my sister had ever lived. Except the name. I actually thought the lack of constant reminders might make me feel better, but it didn't. It may even have been a factor in my leaving home."

The earth was tilting under Gaela. She had to hold tightly to Adam just to keep her balance. She was glad she was sitting down. "What name?"

"Eden. The estate's named after her. Didn't you know? No, of course you didn't. My little sister was named Eden. Don't you think that's cute? Adam and Eden. We didn't. We had to band together at school to keep the bullies off our backs. But at least she had the excuse of being named after Grandmother. Naming the place Eden's Gate was one of Mom's ideas of memorializing her death. Dad let that stand, when she left."

Now that Adam had finally started talking, it was as if a dam had broken, and it was all pouring out at once. Gaela's head was spinning.

"I came back here on my birthday this year. I saw the sign in town and it promised peace. I was ready to try for some. Then I saw you, my garden pixie." Adam was quiet for a minute. "You know, I've given that a lot of thought. Why was I so obsessively attracted to you? I mean, aside from the undeniable fact that you are obsessively desirable." Gaela smiled obligingly. She didn't know if he could see her in the dim light of the security lights over at the house. But she could tell the dangerous gleam was back in his eyes without being able to see it, and he always had been able to read her mind.

"I really think I was a little crazy. You were right to be scared of me. I was scared of myself. You know, the thought of jumping in the lake went through my mind more than once." Gaela clutched him, and he patted her hands comfortingly. "But there was you. I watched your hands on your flowers, and I felt something. Maybe it was God. Maybe he was using you to call me."

"I hope so," she whispered.

"Anyway, you know most of the rest. Except my reaction on the day Ivy came here saying they were dead. I had almost brought myself to the decision that the next time they came I would stay." He gave a long, shaky sigh. "Might-have-beens. God forgive me. So anyway, I ran. I couldn't help myself. I had no idea the place had any possibility of coming to me. I don't care about that, but I assure you, I have no intention of allowing my Aunt Vivian to get her hands on it. My memories of her are early, but they're vivid." He thought for a minute and amended, "Maybe I do care about it, at that. I love this place. More now than I ever did before."

Adam turned her face up to his, running his fingers lightly down her cheek. With their faces inches apart, she could tell that his eyes and mouth were still a little swollen from crying. She thought he looked dearer than ever, but her eyes drifted closed as he began to touch his lips to her hair, her eyes, her cheeks, and finally, her mouth.

It was different, this kiss. A kiss not just of two bodies, but of two souls, two souls who had come home, who stood at the gates of paradise regained.

Chapter Twenty

Adam's lips and beard and the tip of his tongue trailed fire and electricity down Gaela's neck, spreading heavy lassitude through her limbs. His fingers had progressed through the second button of her work shirt by the time conscious thought intruded enough to remind her that paradise couldn't be explored, not just yet. She put her arms around his neck and pulled herself hard against him for a moment, then stood. He put his hands at her waist and pressed his face into her stomach with a long sigh, and she held him like that for a few minutes.

"Where are you staying, by the way?" She ran her fingers through his tangled, wet hair.

"Nowhere." His voice was muffled against her ribs. "I jumped off the bus and ran all the way here." He finally lifted his head and looked up at her. "Don't worry about me. I can sleep somewhere."

"No, not in the rain you don't. Maybe I could put you in the workshop—" Gaela stopped herself and laughed. "You're the lord of the manor, for heaven's sake! You can sleep in the master bedroom."

Adam pushed her back a little and stood. "No! I don't want to!" His voice sounded panicky.

"Why not? It's yours!"

"I don't—I don't know. It's one thing sitting here in the dark and the rain and spilling my guts to you, but the reality of popping up and claiming my inheritance—an inheritance I should never have had and don't deserve . . . Listen, don't tell anyone yet, will you?"

He was pulling away, backing off, and Gaela hadn't known him for six months without learning to recognize a disappearing act in the making. She acquired a firm hold on one arm. "Oh, no, you don't! You are not running away this time!"

"I'm not leaving, I swear. I just don't—"

"C—Adam. *Adam!*" Gaela got one fist in his beard and made him face her. "Stop it. I'm going to unlock the security alarm and let you in your house. You can sleep on the floor of the kitchen, for all I care. But you will be there when I wake up and come looking for you in the morning! Got it?"

He put his hand over hers. "You don't have to pull my beard out."

"I will, I warn you."

"All right, all right. Unlike your creepy Archie friend I know when I'm defeated. But I won't be in the house when you get up." She opened her mouth, and he covered it with his. After reducing her brain to mush again, and before she could get her wits back to argue, he murmured against her lips, "I'll be in the Secret Garden, waiting for you." Then he raised his head, grabbed her hand, and turned toward the gazebo steps. "Let's get going before I forget I'm trying to learn to be a gentleman."

The rain had let up a little, but they still hurried to the door of the big house. Gaela unlocked it, and they shared another kiss, steamy in more ways than one. Adam pulled back, laughing. "This is ridiculous. We're both so waterlogged we squelch when we move. Get out of here. And take a hot bath!"

"I will if you will," said Gaela, and then had to flee before the look in his black eyes.

"Wait!" he called, starting after her. "I should walk you to the cottage."

"Oh, no, don't you dare. You're not coming anywhere near my house tonight."

"Afraid of me?"

"No, of me!"

His laughter followed her. She wondered if his laughter would warm her soul quite so much if it hadn't been so rare.

When she got inside her own door, locked it, and fell against it, her heart was pounding, and it wasn't only from running. She soaked in a bubble bath, trying to get her mind around what seemed like a whole new world. She had to go back and rethink practically every conversation they'd ever had. Adam Sullivan! That was going to be hard to get used to. Calling himself Caine and telling her he'd been cast out of Eden. And to think he'd been here before the Sullivans' last visit. She remembered Mr. S's sadness, and wept a little for what might have been. Should have been.

If only she'd known. Maybe she could have convinced him there was nothing to fear in talking to his parents. But no, they hadn't both been his parents. What had Mrs. S been crying about in the garden? Her husband's unhappiness? Or was there more? Well, they'd never know now.

She couldn't wait to see Ms. Crandall's face. And Vivian's! Oh, how she'd love to be a mouse in the corner when Vivian learned that one of Gaela's good-for-nothing, deadbeat crew was the heir! Gaela laughed out loud at the thought. Now Ivy wouldn't get the estate, though. Gaela wondered if she'd be upset. Somehow, she didn't think so. Relieved, maybe.

At least Eden wouldn't be cut up by developers. Despite Ms. Crandall's assurances, Gaela had continued to fear that. Belatedly, she realized she had a sure job and a home. Adam would never kick her out. "Thank God!"

A thought startled her. Would she—could she—was it possible that someday she herself might be the lady of the manor? She couldn't decide if the thrill that ran right up the back of her neck was excitement or terror.

Or maybe it was just the water getting cold. Gaela got out, dried off, and went to bed. But it was a long time before she slept.

ॐ   ॐ   ॐ

Adam prowled around the building that had once been his home. It was the same in some places, totally different in others. It was certainly true that no one who saw these rooms would ever know there had once been children here. There were no pictures, except for a formal portrait of Sam and Georgiana in the front parlor. He looked at it for a long time, hoping and praying that his dad had been happy in the end, wishing he'd known Georgiana. She looked like a kind, strong person. He thought over the stories he'd heard from the crew about the gazebo and grotto, and smiled, but sadly. If only he'd got his courage up a little sooner. "You tried to tell me, didn't you? I wish I'd listened."

His old room was now a den, with comfortable chairs and a big screen TV. Had Dad sat in here and watched TV and thought of him? It had nearly killed Adam to learn from Gaela that Sam Sullivan had sat and sorrowed over his lost son. Maybe, if he'd known that sooner . . . No sense looking back. Nothing could be changed now.

Adam went to Eden's old room and stood in the hallway for a long time, trying to find the courage to open the door. When he finally did, he saw it was a sewing room. That seemed strange. Georgiana didn't sound like the kind of woman who'd like to do needlework. Or had this been here since before Grandmother Eden's death? Adam remembered she had been teaching Eden to embroider, or something, before she— He turned and left the room, looking for one of the guest rooms. No way was he sleeping in his dad's bed.

He found a tasteful, but sterile, bedroom with a bath, dropped his filthy clothes on the floor, and took a shower hot enough to warm his bones back up. He tried not to think of Gaela in the clawfoot bathtub he'd seen the one time he visited her house. Tomorrow he'd find a laundry room somewhere in this pile.

Lying in a bed ten times as comfortable as any he'd slept in for years, Adam tried to pray, but didn't know what to say. He let his mind drift to Gaela in the gazebo, Gaela in the grotto, Gaela working with her flowers, Gaela forcing him to face up to life. Anything to think of yesterday, and keep from having to think about tomorrow. Gaela in the Secret Garden, tomorrow morning. He refused to think further ahead than that.

ଔ   ଔ   ଔ

Gaela awoke feeling an undercurrent of intense excitement. Something wonderful was going to happen today--what was it? Returning memory yanked her straight up in bed, gasping. She washed and dressed hurriedly, caroling a praise song she'd learned from Lillian.

It was hardly light when she arrived in the Secret Garden, and she'd beat Adam there. She dried the swing seat with a towel she'd brought for the purpose and sat down, glad she'd put on a sweater. After the rain, it was chilly this morning. Looked like fall was beginning after all. She swung a little, still humming the praise song.

Gaela looked at her watch. No, she would not believe he had run this time. She swung some more, prayed a while, looked at her watch again. "So help me, if he's absconded again, I'll—"

"You'll what?"

Gaela jumped up and ran to him. "I'm sorry! I just expected you earlier, that's all."

"I don't blame you a bit. I'm the one who's made running into a way of life. I just overslept. I had every intention of being here before you, watching you walk in that gate. But I didn't sleep all that well." His eyes glinted at her. "You?"

She smiled. "Not that well."

He drew her to him. "Thinking about me?"

"Maybe a little," she admitted, toying with the buttons on his shirt. To her disappointment, Adam only kissed her forehead before stepping back. "Did you practice while I was gone?" He pulled two recorders out of the pockets of his jacket.

"No. A couple of times, but mostly I didn't have the heart."

"Well, this is the moment of truth, then."

Adam handed her the little sopranino, and she regarded it with alarm. "I don't know how to play this!"

"It's the same. Or you can pretend it is. Play *Mary Had a Little Lamb* the same way you played it on your soprano. You'll be playing it in F, that's all."

"Is that how it works?"

"No, you're supposed to learn how to make the same notes on this recorder. For instance, this—" He showed her a fingering she knew as G— "is C on this recorder. But you can wait to learn all that. You are allowed to cheat and play the same fingerings you're used to, as long as your duet partner knows you're going to do that. I'm going to play with you on the alto, in F also. Unless you'd like to find out what our piece sounds like in C and F at the same time?"

"Sounds like a delightful idea," laughed Gaela, loving this more playful Adam.

"Well, run through it once without me, since you admit you have neglected your practice." He scowled mightily at her.

So she did. It wasn't too bad, considering she hadn't played it since—heavens, it seemed like another lifetime!

Then they played together, and playing it on high and low-voiced recorders gave the piece a completely different attitude. Gaela was disappointed to realize it was almost time for her to go to work.

"Come with me. You didn't get to say hello to anyone last night."

"No, not this time."

"No?"

"Gaela, listen. I don't want you to tell anyone yet. No, hear me out. It's my story to tell, in my way and my time. Isn't it?"

She had to admit it was, but he scared her. "You will tell, though?"

"When and if I'm ready. Promise me."

She sighed and nodded. "What am I supposed to say when they ask about you? They all saw you here."

"Tell them the truth—you told me what's been happening, and that I don't have a job—not that I expected one after cutting out, by the way—and I've gone away again. I swear I'll come back. I've got to go and do some thinking before I make any decision. Did you say you have weekends off now? Good. I'll meet you at the gazebo Sunday morning. Okay?"

No, it was not okay. "Okay," she said reluctantly. "But you'd better—"

"I will. I will be here, Gaela. Trust me."

He didn't kiss her good-bye, either. Back to his old disappearing acts. Gaela frowned after him, annoyed and alarmed. What did he mean, before he could make a decision? Surely he knew there was only one decision to make!

She possessed her soul in what patience she could muster. The crew accepted her explanation, only asking how Caine was. She told them he seemed fine.

"Looks like I don't have to wreak vengeance on that Archie slimeball for you, after all," Ted observed.

"No—in fact, I think Archie's in for the surprise of his life." Gaela couldn't quite hold back that much of a hint.

She knew that Ted and Lillian, at least, were concerned about her. She was clearly falling for some kind of vagrant. They couldn't know anything had changed. Maybe nothing had. Anyway, she'd fallen for him while he was still a vagrant. It was nothing but the truth.

Why did she trust him? *He'll be here,* she whispered to herself.

The days were a little cooler now. Gaela tried to decide how she should plan for fall. Would the gardens be opened again this year, or not? If not, there was probably a lot less to do. Empty spots in beds mattered less, and there weren't enough hands to fill them in with potted mums or gaillardia, buried in mulch to their rims so they looked as if they were growing there. The pumpkins, gourds, and ornamental Indian corn were nearly ready for the October fall festival that might not even happen.

Why did Adam have to be so aggravating? With him at the helm things could go on just as they had been. Only better! Trying to be fair, Gaela did her best to put herself in his shoes. Suppose she had just learned all this was to be hers. It would be overwhelming. Frightening, she had to admit.

First he had to prove he was really Adam Sullivan. Would he have to go to court? Vivian and Archie would certainly oppose him. And even once they knew he was who he said he was, which she didn't think could be doubted for long, they would probably try to prove him unfit or something. They would have some real ammunition, too. Her heart sank as she realized what a grand time the papers would have this time! And just when she had thought all the problems were over.

Still, it wasn't as if Adam hadn't been raised in this environment. Despite his recent vagabondage, he had once been the son of Eden's Gate. He had known all his early life that it would one day be his. Then he had been gone for fourteen years. Almost half his life. And what had he done during those years?

So her thoughts whirled round and round the same subject. That afternoon, she spilled powdered lime all over the shed floor. On Friday, she knocked over a stand of lilies with her wheelbarrow. On Saturday, she cut herself on a pair of pruning shears.

Sunday morning couldn't dawn early enough. She had practiced "Alleluia" and "Amazing Grace" on her recorder each evening, and planned to surprise Adam. She just prayed he wouldn't surprise her by not showing.

Chapter Twenty-one

Gaela didn't own many dresses. It wasn't that she didn't like them, but her life wasn't conducive to dresses. Sunday, she put on an old favorite, a peach-colored linen with simple lines whose color brought a glow to her tanned cheeks. Brushing her short curls, she wished for the first time that she knew something to "do" with her hair. It was lightened almost blonde by the summer in the sun. Did Cai—Adam like blondes?

She was at the gazebo by eight o'clock, reading her Bible. She used to be too shy to take it outside except at her own cottage, but that was one of the new leaves she was turning over. There were so many leaves turning lately, it was as if the book of her life had been dropped in front of a fan. She read for a while, then stood on the top step of the gazebo and looked out over the lake. The young Canada geese looked just like their parents now, and were practicing for the long flight south.

When she saw Adam coming, she caught her breath. He, too, had dressed up for the occasion, wearing new black jeans and a red shirt that made him look like a particularly beautiful Indian. She grinned at the thought of what he would probably say to that, as he bounded up the steps and stopped one step below her. His face was only a little above her own, a novel perspective. His eyes were much too opaque.

"Good morning, Pixie," he said, and proceeded to kiss her until her knees gave way and his embrace was the only thing holding her up.

As the world righted itself again, Gaela told herself it was her own uncertainty that made him seem desperate, as if he were kissing her good-bye. "Is that how you greet all the girls when you go to church?" she asked in what she hoped was a light voice.

"Only this girl. Have you missed me?" He wasn't smiling.

"Not a bit. Were you gone?"

He wasn't even hearing her. Letting go of her, he climbed the rest of the gazebo steps to lean on a railing and look out toward the lake.

Gaela followed him, laying her hand over his tense one on the gleaming white rail. She followed his gaze to the red- and gold-edged maples and dark green pines tiptoeing their reflections in the still water. With a strange sense of déjà vu, she knew Adam wasn't seeing the trees or the water or the geese.

"I don't think I'm up to this," he blurted.

"Adam—"

He pulled his hand from under hers and silenced her with a sharp gesture. "I've been doing a lot of thinking, and I can't help wondering if I ought to let Ivy have it. You said Aunt Vivian couldn't really do anything, that other woman—what's her name?—would be there to look out for things."

Gaela felt like yelling at him, but something made her hold her tongue. He looked so distraught. She put her head on his shoulder. "I can only imagine how overwhelming this is. I have enough trouble getting used to the new Adam Sullivan. You have to *be* the new Adam Sullivan! I've been thinking too. I've been wondering what my reaction would be if I suddenly learned all this was to be mine."

"You'd do a better job than I would."

"Oh, Adam!"

"I mean it. You've already been managing Eden for years! You know more about it than anyone. I'm not trying to put myself down, I'm really not. Although I should be the very last person in the world this place comes to. Even you,

198

prejudiced as you are, have to admit that. It's not *right* for me to get it!"

Gaela put her arms around his stiff waist. "Yes, I'm prejudiced, and yes, God does know why. He's prejudiced in your favor, too. Haven't you learned that by now? When you think of it, you're a living picture of heaven," she told him, and watched the look of disbelief spread over his face.

"I'm a picture of *what*?"

"Heaven. Think about it. We're all prodigals. None of us deserves to go home again. But we get to anyway. Why? Because we reform, and walk the straight and narrow really, really well?"

He half laughed. "I keep hoping."

"Not a chance," said Gaela. "You, Adam Sullivan, have inherited this estate for one reason and one reason only. Your dad wanted you to have it. If he had cut you out of his will, you would have felt you deserved that, and wouldn't have tried to overturn it. But if you had tried, and the probate court looked at your past, do you think you'd succeed?"

Adam shook his head slowly.

"But he didn't. He loved you, and he forgave you, and he spent a lot of money and time looking for you so you would know that. And even though he's not here to tell you himself, his will tells you. You are my beloved son, in whom I am well-pleased. Enter into the joy of your father. It's all yours, Adam. All you have to do is have the courage to say yes."

"And give up my whole life. Learn to live a completely different life that I know nothing about. I don't know if I can do it."

"But you don't have to do it by yourself. Ms. Crandall will help you. I'll help you. God will help you. You're his son, too. He already knows what you've done and not done. He's been calling you. You told me that. He wants to throw his arms around you, welcome you home, and give you the signet ring and the keys to the mansion." They didn't seem to be talking about Eden's Gate anymore.

With a start, Gaela remembered what she had been reading before Adam arrived. "Wait! Look what I found." She turned away and picked up her Bible, abandoned on the gazebo bench. The breeze had ruffled the pages, and she had to find Galatians again, with fingers that trembled. "Here it is. Listen." After a moment, Adam joined her on the bench and leaned close, looking over her shoulder and reading with her.

> "Now I say, as long as the heir is a child, he does not differ at all from a slave although he is owner of everything, but he is under guardians and managers until the date set by the father. So also we, while we were children, were held in bondage under the elemental things of the world. But when the fullness of the time came, God sent forth His Son, born of a woman, born under the Law, so that He might redeem those who were under the Law, that we might receive the adoption as sons. Because you are sons, God has sent forth the Spirit of His Son into our hearts, crying, 'Abba! Father!' Therefore you are no longer a slave, but a son; and if a son, then an heir through God."

Gaela stopped reading and looked at Adam. He took the Bible from her and silently read the passage again. She watched thoughts and questions chase themselves across his face. After a minute, he lifted his eyes and gazed unseeingly across the lake again. Gaela watched the ripples and prayed. A breeze ruffled their hair.

A long sigh seemed to come from the depths of Adam's soul, and suddenly Gaela did something she had never dreamed of having the nerve to do. She took Adam's hand and prayed out loud.

"God—you are our Father and our Mother, our Maker and our Restorer. You are everything to us. You love us and forgive us and lead us and never lose patience. You've taught us—" *oh, please, don't let me choke up—* "so much! You made us in a garden, and you still come to us in gardens. Now you've given Adam back his garden. How can we thank you enough?" Clinging to Adam's hand, she waited until she had regained command of her voice. Then she concluded, "You know what we should do, and we know you'll show us."

It seemed that long a time had passed when Adam closed the small book and stood.

She looked up into his haunted face and some instinct made her ask, "Should I go away for a while?"

He nodded his head. Gaela understood—she was a private person herself.

Taking her recorder, but leaving the Bible, she went to the Secret Garden to wait and pray. While she was at it, she prayed for an accepting attitude for herself. "You have a plan, and you know what it is," she said aloud. "All I want is what you want."

Peace stole over her. It would be well. The September breeze sighed around her.

ૅ૨   ૅ૨   ૅ૨

Adam stared unseeingly out into the bright sunshine. "Well, God," he said aloud, "it seems you and I have some talking to do. You've been whispering at me, and I've been yelling at you, but I couldn't really say we've had a sensible conversation yet. Gaela and David, and I guess lots of other people, too, seem to think you hear and not only that, you answer." It didn't seem as strange as it once would have, talking out loud to the empty air. "Here's the thing. Apparently my dad really wanted me to have this place. You and I both know I don't for one minute deserve it, but he seems to have wanted me to have it anyway. I don't know why I'm so scared of the idea. I always knew when I was a kid that it would be mine someday."

His voice quit on him as he looked out over the garden and saw the kids that ran there yesterday. Bratty little Eden, as unlike her name as it was possible to be, and Adam, the royal pain in the neck. How they'd fought, and how they'd loved each other! He had hated himself so much over her senseless death that he'd never really faced the loss itself. His eyes blurred.

"Can you really forgive me?" he whispered. Somehow, his decision over this house seemed to be all bound up with a bigger, deeper one.

Yes.

This time, he knew the voice.

ଔ   ଔ   ଔ

Gaela looked up when the gate squeaked. A completely different person stood there. He was as gorgeous as ever, and his black hair against the red shirt still made her pulse speed up. There was still danger for her in his eyes. But there was something else. Peace.

They moved together like magnets. When his arms closed around her, they felt different, too. The desperation was gone. They stood in each other's arms a long time.

Finally, she backed up and said, "You know, I practiced diligently for today."

Adam seated himself with a flourish. "Well? Play for me, maestra!"

So she performed her two hymn tunes to unanimous acclaim from her appreciative audience of one. He begged her to play them again, and improvised harmonies that were so lovely they played them a third time.

They decided to keep the story to themselves for the day.

"I want to practice it on the crew first," Adam told her. "We can tell them first thing in the morning, and see if I survive that. Then, presuming I'm still conscious, we can call Ms. Whatsername."

Gaela laughed. "You really have to learn her name. She is going to be very important to you. Crandall. Elizabeth Crandall. Repeat after me: E-liz-a-beth Cran-dall. By jove, I think he's got it!"

They explored the gardens, went out on the lake, and then went into town and found a church that had an evening service. Gaela was ashamed of herself for being so apprehensive. It was lovely. Of course, it didn't hurt to have a man who looked like a New Testament apostle on your arm.

The next morning, they waited nervously for the staff to assemble. As each one came in, he or she had a surprised look for Adam, quickly covered, and then a cheerful welcome. Gaela could hardly contain herself until Randy finally showed up.

After a brief staff meeting, Gaela said, "Okay, boys and girls, there's someone I need to introduce to you. Now, this is going to be pretty shocking, so prepare yourselves." She looked nervously at Adam. Now that the moment had come, it really did seem like a lame story. How would they take it? Only one way to find out. She took a deep breath. "This is Adam Sullivan, only son of Sam Sullivan and his deceased first wife." Like herself, the others didn't get it at first. They just looked blankly from her to Adam.

"Deceased first wife?" said Lillian.

"It's true," said Adam. "I don't blame you if you can't believe me. I never met his second wife. My fault, not theirs. When I came back here this past spring, I was trying to get up enough courage to contact my dad again."

Ted frowned. "What do you mean, contact them? They came. He was right here."

Adam met his gaze. "I know. I chickened out." His mouth twisted and he looked away.

The faces watching him were beginning to show signs of horrified or sympathetic comprehension, according to the individual. Ivy appeared to be in shock.

Lillian spoke up. "But you came back."

Adam shrugged sadly. "I couldn't quite stay away. I had just come to the point where I thought maybe I could talk to him when . . . you know. Of course I ran again. In case you haven't figured it out yet, I've made quite a practice of that."

There was silence. Adam looked around at the circle of faces. Then he visibly squared his shoulders. "Like I said, I don't blame you if you don't believe me. To tell you the truth, I really hit bottom the last time I ran. I never would have come back if I hadn't seen a tabloid with some horrible story of Gaela getting beat up." He looked at her, and she tried to telegraph love and support. "But I did, and now it seems that I'm the heir." He shook his head. "I still can't believe that. It almost made me run again!"

There was a slight stir of amusement or disbelief. Chuck was looking at the floor, and Ted was still frowning, and looking at Ivy, who seemed to have turned to stone.

"I was certain that I had been cut out of the will years ago. I should have been, believe me."

"Pretty convenient," observed Chuck.

"Not for me," replied Adam evenly.

"He can prove it, you know!" Gaela moved closer to Adam's side.

"I hate to say this, Gaela, but are you sure you're being objective about this?" Randy asked.

"If all he wanted was the inheritance, why did he come back this past spring?" asked Lillian. "If he was just showing up now, it would be one thing. Are you trying to accuse him of knowing about their accident in advance? Arranging it, maybe?"

"That's a point," conceded Ted. "I was as suspicious of Hunter—or whoever he is—as anybody, I guess. But I don't suppose he killed them. He was here with us, for one thing."

"Not accusing anybody, all I'm sayin' is—" Chuck stopped when all eyes turned to Ivy, who had suddenly moved to stand in front of Adam, looking searchingly into his face.

"Why don't I know you, if you're my cousin? I hardly even knew my aunt and uncle had ever had a son, although I remembered it when the lawyer mentioned it."

"Well, I am a lot older than you are. And don't forget, Georgiana wasn't my mother."

"That's right. I guess I knew it was a second marriage. I just never thought about it. Still, it seems you'd have been mentioned."

Adam's feet shifted. "I've always been something of a black sheep."

"Why?"

He looked away from her. "I. . ." He visibly straightened and met her eyes. "I was involved in the accidental death of my sister. Among other things."

"Your sister! I never even knew you had a sister!"

"You moved to California when you were, what, three? We were already in our teens. I only remember seeing you once or twice even before that. Eden died when you were, let's see, five. They certainly wouldn't have talked about it to you, or even in front of you. I ran away two years later, and I wouldn't be surprised if my name became anathema and was never spoken again."

Gaela watched Adam look around the circle of intent faces, and could almost feel him drawing in on himself. She opened her mouth, but couldn't think of anything to say or do.

"Truthfully, Ivy, I don't deserve to receive this inheritance. Not at all. If you want it, I'm sure there's some way I can sign it over, or something."

Ivy searched his face. "You'd really do that?"

"In a heartbeat."

Gaela held her breath. She was surprised when Ivy's eyes turned thoughtfully to her for a moment.

"No, I don't want it," said Ivy. "I just want someone to have it who will really care for it. Do you?"

"Yes."

Ivy nodded. "Well, then. I always knew there was some skeleton in the closet. If you can prove your identity, then welcome home. I'm sorry you didn't get to make up with your dad. But I knew him pretty well, and I can tell you he would have forgiven you. . . anything."

Gaela looked around. The atmosphere seemed lighter than it had been a few minutes ago. She spoke brightly. "So you see, we're about to get a new boss."

"Does this mean we get to keep our jobs?" asked Randy.

"Well, I definitely want to keep the garden open. But you know, I still have to jump through all the legal hoops and whatever." Adam looked around. "I don't expect you to just jump in and believe me. But I was less afraid to talk to you than to my Aunt Vivian, whom I *do* remember from the old days."

Ted raised his eyebrows. "I'll bet. Well, I always thought there was more to you than met the eye. Adam, huh? Adam Sullivan. This'll be interesting."

Chuck moved. "Even if it's true, that don't mean it ain't awfully convenient," he said stubbornly. "I'll be out on the lake."

And he left.

Adam shrugged. "He's right. Who can blame him?"

"Well, I believe you, boy," announced Lillian. She thumped Adam's shoulder encouragingly.

"I hate to say it, but I think I do, too," said Ted unexpectedly. He looked at Gaela. "Mainly, I guess, because I trust Gaela's judgment."

Gaela blinked. "Ted! I think that's the nicest thing you've ever said to me!"

"Well, you don't always make the smartest choices, but you know Caine — I mean — whoever this guy is! And I don't think you'd stick by a liar. I trust Lillian's judgment, too. So I guess, until proven wrong, I'll accept it."

"Thanks." Adam smiled, then looked around, his eyes ending on Gaela. "Even if I can satisfy all the legal experts, I'll still have one question."

They waited expectantly.

"Can I still work with you sometimes?" he asked plaintively.

Everyone laughed.

"Tote that barge, lift that bale!" chanted Ivy.

Ted finally smiled. "If you think you can stand our chief, that is. We have an awful mean boss!"

"My cue, obviously," said Gaela. "Get to work! Noses to the grindstone! March! March!"

There were groans, but nobody moved.

"Better watch it," Adam warned, his eyes glinting. "I'm about to become your lord and master."

The atmosphere lightened further with hoots, catcalls, and cheers.

"Okay, lord and master," Gaela hollered over the rabble, "next hurdle." The crew settled down expectantly. "I'll make the call." She had the business card ready. Everyone hovered while she thumbed in the number, hoping to be able to hear the unflappable Ms. Crandall yelp over the phone.

They were all disappointed when Gaela hissed, "Answering machine! What do I say?"

The machine beeped imperatively, so Gaela simply said that she had important news for the executrix, and asked her to call at her earliest convenience. She left her cell number.

"Well. That's that for now, I guess. Off we go, cave trolls." And brandishing an imaginary whip, she drove her minions to the salt mines.

She herself hardly noticed what she did that day. The sun shone down on an enchanted garden. The hero of the story had become a prince, the worthy peasant girl was going to keep her home, and might even possibly enchant the prince—a fairy tale ending all around.

She pulled out her phone and looked at its unresponsive face every so often, then jumped when it finally rang sometime later.

"Ms. Clancy? How strange that you should call. I was going to call you today. We need to meet. What is a good time for you?"

"Anytime," said Gaela happily. "Wait till you hear my news!" She couldn't contain herself. "I've found the heir!"

There was a long silence.
"Ms. Crandall?"
"Are you quite sure of this, Ms. Clancy?"
"Oh, yes, Ms. Crandall. Adam Sullivan is here on the estate, and will be delighted to meet with you anytime. Don't worry, he'll be able to prove his identity easily."

"Well. Good heavens. Shall we say two o'clock this afternoon, at the house?"

"Great! We'll be here."

"Ms. Clancy? Perhaps you should prepare yourself. And Mr. Sullivan, if he is indeed the heir. I am afraid my news is not nearly so pleasant." Gaela felt her smile dissolve and slide off her face. "In fact, if this is a false heir, called forth by the hope of a windfall, I fear we shall soon be rid of him. Are you there, Ms. Clancy?"

"I—I'm here. I don't understand."

"I shall explain it all this after—well. No, I shall have to hold the news, I fear, until this man's identity is proven or disproven. Two o'clock, then. Good-bye."

Gaela was left staring at a silent phone again.

Chapter Twenty-two

Gaela ran outside to tell Adam, then remembered he and Ted had gone into town to pick up some supplies. Disconcerted, she wandered to the greenhouse, where Lillian was working with young Christmas poinsettias. Nobody knew what they would do with the hundreds of flowers this year.

Lillian saw her face and straightened. "Whose ghost did you see?"

"Ms. Crandall called back. She said she was going to call me already. She says to prepare ourselves, that she has bad news, and if this is a false heir, he won't get a windfall."

Lillian deciphered this. "You mean the money's gone?"

"That's what it sounds like. She's coming here at two. Oh, I can't stand it! Adam finally comes home, everything looks like it's going to be all right, and now this!"

"Well, now, honey, maybe we should wait until we hear what Ms. Crandall has to say before panicking."

Gaela was in no mood to be philosophical. "I *can't* wait! I just—I wish—oh, I feel like I'm on a roller coaster!" She went back outside and paced distractedly for a while, then tried to remember what she'd been doing.

She was on her knees in a bed she had discovered with weeds poking through the mulch, jerking weeds out and flinging them into a wheelbarrow when she felt someone watching her. She whirled. Adam was looking at her. "Oh, you scared me!" She jumped up and ran into his arms, fighting tears and losing. "Oh, Adam!"

"Now, what's this, my pixie?" he asked, holding her close.

"Ms. Crandall called and I think you've lost your fortune!" wept Gaela.

"Really! Well, that's funny."

"Funny!"

"I didn't even have it yet. It hardly seems real anyway. I wonder if I should be relieved."

Gaela pulled back and took a punch at his shoulder. "You're being deliberately obtuse!"

"No, I'm being deliberately calm, hoping thereby to calm you. Not working, huh?" He wiped her tears with his thumb. "Did you know that's the exact same place I saw you first? You were transplanting those crabapples, only they were just little bare sprigs then, and I didn't have any idea what they were. All I saw was your little brown hands tucking them into their mulch like babies. I wished you would comfort me like that. You made me think of my nanny."

She let him distract her momentarily. "You mentioned a nanny before."

"Yes. She was the most loving thing in my early childhood. She lived in your house."

"She did?" Gaela was amazed. Would he never stop surprising her? She hoped not.

"But at the time, I didn't want to remember her. I wanted to believe I was unloved and unlovable. I was so angry, and so empty. Don't you understand, Gaela? I have my fortune right here. If there's no money, how is that different from the way I've lived my whole adult life?"

"I love you." She didn't mean to say it. It just came out. But she forgot her embarrassment at the slow smile that spread across his face and warmed her right to her toes. "I love you, too," said Adam, kissing her tear-streaked cheeks and then her mouth.

"All right, you two, knock it off!" bellowed Ted, coming toward them with a wheelbarrow. "Somebody's got to get some work done around here!"

"That's your lord and master you're talking to," Adam reminded him. "And Gaela says all the money's gone, so you just might be out of a job if you're not properly respectful."

Ted put down the wheelbarrow and came nearer. "What did you say?"

Calmer now, Gaela told them both about the message. "And now she can't even explain herself until Adam proves who he is!" she wailed.

"Well, I guess we'll find out eventually. Two o'clock, huh?" Ted looked at his watch "You two better clean up. Let us know if we still have jobs. This is getting to be more exciting than a soap opera."

When Ms. Crandall arrived, she walked up to Adam and held out her hand, holding on to the one he gave her and looking at him searchingly. "You will have to go through all the proper channels," she told him, "but you don't have to prove yourself to me. You are the image of your mother. Physically. I had dealings with her on a few occasions." It was clear she hoped he would not be the image of his mother in more than form and feature.

Another piece of the puzzle clicked into place in Gaela's mind. She had wondered why he was so different from his father. She keyed in the security code to let them into the house.

"We must, however, follow the proper processes of making your legal standing secure," continued Ms. Crandall. "What proofs of identity have you?"

"Well, at the moment, that will be difficult," Adam admitted. "I've been living—I hate to say this, but I've been living on the streets, and under an assumed name. I don't have any ID right now." His voice trailed off.

They had reached the office where they had met before, and Ms. Crandall opened her briefcase and took the reins of the situation with her usual briskness. "It will not be difficult to identify you. We will take you to be fingerprinted. A copy of your birth certificate and social security card are easily obtained. You don't happen to know your number by heart?"

Adam thought, and produced a number, which Ms. Crandall wrote down. "Should this be correct, it will be a convincing piece of evidence in itself. Are there pictures of you in your youth somewhere here in the house? A baby book?"

"Probably. I'll look. But actually," Adam hesitated, then gave a rueful shrug. "The easiest way to prove my identity would probably be through the local police department. I was involved with the law on two or three occasions when I was seventeen, the last year before I left home. They should still have my fingerprints in some archive somewhere, shouldn't they?"

"No doubt they do." Ms. Crandall took more notes. "You have not been involved with the police more recently?"

"No."

"Good." She nodded her gray head.

Gaela trailed them as they searched likely places for memorabilia of Adam's childhood. They didn't find anything. As they walked, Adam related his story.

A nerve-racking two days later, Gaela and Adam sat in Ms. Crandall's office in town. It was monastically neat. No photograph or plant disturbed the geometric regularity of her desk blotter, in- and out-boxes, and telephone. A thick file reposed precisely in the center of the blotter. On one corner of the massive desk sat a small tray containing a pitcher of water and three glasses, each filled to precisely three-quarters.

Adam had survived interrogations, paperwork, and several meetings with police and lawyers. His mother's relatives had been located, and had promised to send a photo album they had in their possession, which was now in transit. Everyone whose opinion mattered was convinced of the identity of the heir. Finally, Ms. Crandall was to "explain everything" as she had promised to do

Ms. Crandall nodded with a satisfied air. "I am happy for you, Mr. Sullivan. I wish I had better news. The truth is," and they had the unusual and most unsettling experience of seeing the unflappable Ms. Crandall decidedly flapped. She cleared her throat, settled her glasses, and said firmly, "The truth is, disaster has struck on several fronts at once. First, the stock market. Do you pay any attention to the stock market? I thought not. You ought to now, but your father never did. They left all such things to their accountant and their broker. With the result that practically impregnable blue chip stocks have been traded for exceedingly chancy internet ventures." She made the phrase sound like something no lady should say.

"I was unaware of how matters stood until I took over as executrix of the will. I was not impressed with the order of their affairs; however, I believed they were merely messy. I was wrong. To put it quite bluntly, the income on which your parents have lived quite lavishly for some years is reduced to a trickle. Apparently, they have been existing on credit cards for a while. Add to that the fact that other creditors, previously unknown to us, having heard of the Sullivans' untimely demise, have been coming out of the woodwork like vultures, one might say."

Gaela expected the firm nod, and managed to keep her face unmoved. She heard a small choke from Adam, but didn't dare look.

"It appears the Sullivans have been running up quite scandalous debts. Add to *that* the expense they have laid out recently in an attempt—" Ms. Crandall hesitated, and went on in an apologetic tone— "in an attempt to locate their son. They hired several private investigators, none worthy of the name, I fear. Some of these individuals have presented shocking expense bills. All of this means, Mr. Sullivan, that you have practically no income. The damage, however, is not wholly unsalvageable. I can direct you to much more suitable stockbrokers and accountants, and I am not unhopeful that, if you are careful, you may be able to regroup in a few years. I assume you are accustomed to living on slender means."

Adam laughed. "You could say that. It was the large means I was afraid of!"

Ms. Crandall looked politely disbelieving. "Yes. Well. I am happy you are able to be so sanguine. You have not had the upkeep of a large home heretofore. In any case, I am sorry to say, that is not the worst of it." Here, she definitely faltered. "The only thing left, other than the house itself, is the trust fund set up to care for the house and gardens. This is the scene of the final disaster."

Ms. Crandall reached for one of the water glasses and sipped from it. Gaela stole a look at Adam, feeling that they had already been asked to swallow quite sufficient disasters for one day.

Fortified, Ms. Crandall visibly forced herself to go on to what appeared to be, in her eyes at least, the worst catastrophe of all. "The trust fund should be inviolate, Mr. Sullivan. It was managed by these law offices. We have been the lawyers of the Sullivan family for nearly a century. I am deeply pained to inform you that one of our number has been guilty of embezzlement. He has been at it for some time, it appears, covering his tracks with some of the fanciest paperwork I hope I ever have to witness. You are not the only victim. In fact, some dozens of clients have lost money in the sum of tens of millions of dollars."

Gaela felt faint. She looked at Adam again, and saw that he was looking sympathetic, but not especially worried.

Ms. Crandall continued. "All of this, of course, is under investigation. There will be legal proceedings. There will be some recovery, as well as insurance settlements, but I do not know if we can save your home, Mr. Sullivan. I do not know if we can even save our legal firm."

Before their horrified eyes, a tear ran right down Ms. Crandall's businesslike cheek and landed on the front of her suit.

Adam leaned forward. "I'm so sorry to hear that, Ms. Crandall."

"Thank you." Ms. Crandall fished in her purse for a tissue and blew her nose. "I beg your pardon! It is your own affairs which concern us today. I must admit, I am unable to understand your sangfroid."

"So am I!" declared Gaela. "How can you be so calm?"

"Well, I'm not sure how to explain it," said Adam. "All I can say is, I wasn't even sure I wanted this inheritance in the first place, but. . ."

After a moment of silence, Gaela prodded, "But?"

"Well, this may sound strange, but God seemed to want me to take it."

She blinked. Was this Adam?

"He told you so?" Ms. Crandall looked dubious.

"Sort of. I mean, well, I've always believed in God, in a vague sort of way, but in recent months, he has made himself known to me in an unmistakable way that I've never experienced before. So when this all came up, I decided to ask him what to do. He seemed to say 'take it,' so I have to assume he has some plan." Adam shrugged as if that explained everything.

Ms. Crandall was regarding him fixedly. "It would seem so. Yet God does work in unarguably mysterious ways."

Adam laughed. "I can vouch for that!"

Gaela looked from him to Ms. Crandall. "Well, I believe in God, too, but—"

"So do I," Ms. Crandall put in, looking a little unnerved by the spiritual turn the conversation had taken. "I just don't think it's quite so simple as you may think it is.

Perhaps it is because you are new to—to—" She seemed to search for a term.

"To faith?" Adam scooted forward to the edge of his chair. "But that's just it. It *is* simple. We're the ones who make it so complicated. It seems to me that if I've given myself to God and told him I would trust him, then I have to put my actions where my mouth is, so to speak, and *trust* him. I don't know whether that means he'll work it out for me to keep Eden's Gate. Maybe he has some other plan I can't fathom. But I think I have two choices. One is to trust him, do what I can, and await developments. The other is to get all upset and give myself high blood pressure and heart disease and who knows what else, and still have to take whatever happens in the end. Right?"

"Very likely," agreed Ms. Crandall, looking thoughtful.

"I've tried that way," said Adam. "I didn't like it. I believe I'll try the other." Watching him hesitate again, Gaela could only be amazed at his courage when he continued, "Forgive me, Ms. Crandall, but it seems to me that you're in more trouble than I am, right now. The firm you believe in, to which you've dedicated your life, is in trouble. Clients who depend on you are in trouble. So...doesn't that mean you have the same two choices?"

Chapter Twenty-three

Gaela discovered her mouth was open and shut it.
Ms. Crandall lifted her chin.
Then Adam smiled his engaging smile, and the executrix was not proof against it. With an abrupt return to her businesslike manner, she said, "Mr. Sullivan, I am relieved that you are able to take it that way. There is much in what you say. I must consider. Meanwhile, I am afraid you must let the remaining staff go, at least until we know more. There is enough for you to live on, if you are frugal. Miss Clancy's fate is up to you."

"Miss Clancy stays," said Adam decidedly.

Gaela started to speak, but Adam stopped her with a look. "Miss Clancy stays, or I go," he said.

Gaela raised her brows. "Blackmail, right here in a lawyer's office!"

Ms. Crandall almost smiled. When they left, she wrung both their hands in a very speaking way.

In the estate truck, on the way back to Eden's Gate, Gaela took her eyes off the road long enough to look at Adam. "You amaze me."

He preened. "Do I? But then, I'm a pretty amazing guy."

She wasn't to be put off. "How could you just talk to her like that?"

Adam lifted a shoulder. "I wasn't the one to open the subject. I was a little embarrassed, but she—and you, too—asked questions. So I just told the truth. How hard is that?"

Gaela flipped on her left turn signal and shook her head. "It's hard enough for me to talk to close friends about God, or spiritual things. I've been working for years trying to build a faith like you've found in two days!"

He looked at her soberly. "This didn't begin two days ago. It began in gutters and alleys years ago. It led to this place six and a half months ago." He gestured to the sign as they passed it. " 'Peace for the weary soul.' I was a weary soul all right. You were the first to offer me rest."

"Me?"

"You. I've fought it and argued with it at every turn, as you, thank God, never have. It finally led me right to the *brink* of reconciliation with my father, but I was still fighting, and lost the chance forever." His voice wavered slightly and he paused, then continued, "Well, not forever, but for the rest of my life. I'm a stubborn person, Gaela, and I decided last night that I'm going to be as stubborn for God as I was against him. Might as well use it for some good purpose. It's caused enough destruction for enough years. Don't envy me, Pixie. Just help me stand."

Gaela pulled into the space by the workshop and turned off the engine, turning to face Adam. "How can I help?"

"Be your sweet self."

"Come on, be more specific. I think this whole situation is terrifying. I can see developers getting Eden after all, just when I thought everything was safe. I really want to be a help and a support to you. I think that would help me too."

Adam got out, looking thoughtful. Gaela slid down from the high seat of the truck and went around the hood to meet him.

"Okay, specifically, here's what you can do. Nurture me as you do your plants. You've planted me, God rooted me, now what do you think I need next?"

Gaela smiled with delight. Here was language she could understand. "Water," she said without hesitation. "In John, Jesus says that's the Holy Spirit and promised He would come and live in anyone who asked. You know, it would be a good idea if you and I started going to church more regularly, don't you think?"

He kissed her. "I do think."

Ted caught them again. "Good grief, you two never quit!"

"Jealous?" Adam let go of Gaela unwillingly.

"You bet. Well? What did you learn?"

Gaela made a face.

"Uh-oh," said Ted.

"Yeah. We have to call the staff together. We have bad news."

When they informed the crew that they were dismissed until further notice, Randy's round face lost the cheerful look it had managed to maintain throughout the crisis so far. "I don't really want to work anywhere else," he said. "I have some savings. I think I'll find some odd jobs and see if I can't get along for a while until you know what's what. Maybe you'll be able to hire us again."

"My daughter has been after me to go stay with them for a while," said Chuck gloomily. "I could wait, too. Just so you call me back before she drives me clean outa the rest of my brains."

"I hope so," Adam told them. "But you'd better be prepared for the worst. Ms. Crandall sounded pretty hopeless."

"I hereby officially retire," Lillian announced. "Been meaning to for a long time. That way," she winked at Gaela, "I can still come in as much as I want to."

"I can spend some spare time here," Randy offered.

Chuck cleared his throat. "Fair's fair. I said my piece in public, I better apologize in public." He met Adam's eyes and held out his hand. "If you're still stayin' now, with the money all gone, I guess I was wrong. No hard feelings, I hope."

Adam shook his hand firmly. "None at all. I said all along you were right. I don't deserve anything, and I know it."

Ted looked the saddest of all. "I've got to have a regular job," he said.

"Of course you do!" said Gaela.

"I didn't expect otherwise," Adam assured him.

"I'll see if I can't get on at the landscaping company with Ivy. The two of us can probably drop over in the evenings sometimes and see if you need a hand."

Adam had to clear his throat before he could say, "Bless you all. I never thought when I came back here that I'd find the best friends I'd ever had."

Gaela and Adam met every morning in the Secret Garden. They formed the habit of sitting quietly for a while, in the presence of God and the garden. Then they practiced their recorders. Adam was of the opinion that music had been the only thing keeping him alive for years, and that it ought to get him through the present crisis as well. And of course they gardened. Gaela was equally certain that no crisis could be got through without a garden.

The great unveiling of Eden's Lost Prodigal caused a media frenzy. For the third time in as many months, they found themselves in papers of varying repute. Reporters found Eden's security just as easy to breach as Adam had.

Archie and Vivian descended on them "like vultures out of the woodwork," giggled Gaela, when she was telling Adam about their visit.

He was away the first time they came, and Gaela simply reminded them of the restraining order and invited them to leave before she called the sheriff. Vivian shrieked and wailed and threatened lawsuits and DNA testing. When she found out bankruptcy hung over Eden's head, she lost interest momentarily.

Then Archie realized that if the estate was bankrupt, they could get it for a song, and develop it for even more dizzying profits than they had imagined. He began silkily making insulting offers, telling Gaela with great sympathy that he would not offer so much money to anyone else, but she and Adam were practically family, and where else could they turn? Archie could, and would, get them out of this mess. No hard feelings. She could trust him. Did she have the authority to schedule a time when he could meet with Adam?

Gaela was tempted, she really was. A meeting with Adam would be just what Archie Williamson needed. But she steadfastly told Archie no, and to leave now.

He left, but he came back, this time when Adam was there. Archie left Vivian at home this time, and brought a regular, written-up offer for the house and the fifty-seven acres. Gaela laughed at it. Adam didn't laugh. He invited Archie into his office to discuss the matter.

Gaela thought fast. How would you nurture a plant that was going to reach out and strangle another plant? You'd lop off its branches, that's how. She grabbed Adam's hand, but he squeezed hers reassuringly and winked at her, so she let him go with a warning look.

She never did find out exactly what happened at that meeting, but Archie left and didn't come back.

October began to flaunt its rubies and topazes against a sapphire sky. The creaking legal machinery of a class action suit against the embezzler ground its slow way along.

The news from Ms. Crandall, however, was increasingly grim. It didn't look as though there would be any stock left, whether impregnable or chancy, to take to those "more suitable stockbrokers" she had mentioned. Everything that wasn't nailed down was going to have to go to the debts. The trust fund, even after legal recourse, would not pay for a tenth of the house's upkeep.

"If Eden could somehow bring in some of its own income . . ." said Ms. Crandall hopefully.

"The garden's always been free to the public," Gaela said. "We've talked about charging, but even if we did, we'd have to have ready money to cover staff and upkeep. I don't think it could possibly pay its own way."

She and Adam turned over various wild ideas. A bed and breakfast. A conference center of some kind. Everything they could think of required money, and lots of it. They looked into donating it to the state historical society, and into agricultural easements.

The thought of selling began to loom more insistently over their heads. "Do you think we could sell it with conditions?" asked Gaela. "That they keep the house and the ten acres or so of developed gardens as is and only sell lots on the other side of the lake?"

They walked out together to look at the lake and try to determine how close to Eden they could stand to see high-dollar fake Colonials springing up.

"We could sell some of the land."

They wouldn't raise enough to cover a fraction of the debts, though.

They sold some of the more valuable furnishings and *objet d'arts* from the house.

Adam started teaching music lessons at the local high school and a nearby college. He drove to work in the remaining Eden's Gate truck.

With deep reluctance, Gaela started looking for a job, too. When Adam found out, he told her to cut it out.

Gaela stared at him. "Surely you're not going to go all over-protective like Ted?"

"I'm not being protective of you, but of Eden. I need you here. And you're the one worker I can afford. Your house is there, and your expenses are few."

"The gardens can take care of themselves for now. They don't really need me. Legalities aside, these are my gardens as much as they're anyone's. I want a chance to help save them."

"Pixie, the amount of money one person can bring in won't make much more than a pennyworth's difference."

Gaela gave him a searching look. "There's more to it than you're telling me."

"Truth?"

"Please."

"I can't stand the thought of Eden sitting here empty, all by itself. I somehow think as long as my garden pixie is here, things will come out all right."

So she stayed. She worked alone in the garden as she used to do, and remembered why she'd loved those days so much. The crisp fall days gave her plenty of time to think. Would she really have to see Eden in the hands of strangers? Worse yet, would her years of work and love be bulldozed for a mall, or something? She got out all the gourds and pumpkins and cornstalks and decorated the place as if they were going to have the fall festival anyway.

Secretly, Gaela was both relieved and ashamed not to have to get a Real Job. She had a deep reluctance to go outside the garden, to even think of working or living anywhere else. But surely she had grown up more than that? It was beginning to look inevitable, anyway. Why not face facts? Neither prayer, nor her renewed Bible study, nor her relationship with Adam was going to magically fix all her neuroses.

"You know what else I think we should do?" she told Adam one day. "I think we should get counseling, both of us."

Adam looked alarmed.

"Really. Think about it. If we'd had poor physical health for years, we wouldn't expect God to just heal us, without our looking for medical assistance, would we?"

"I guess not."

"So we should get help for our chronic spiritual illness, shouldn't we?" She couldn't even believe she was suggesting this.

"You're probably right," Adam admitted, " but I can't believe you're suggesting it. I thought you were so certain all the help anybody needed could be found in this garden." An arrested look came into his face.

"What?"

He didn't answer. She could swear his face actually began to glow with excitement.

"Adam? Come on, you're killing me with suspense!"

He grabbed her by the waist, picked her up over his head, and swung her around three times, while she screeched. Then he brought her down, though not far enough for her feet to touch the ground, and kissed her until she forgot her question.

Finally, he set her down. "I have to think!" he exclaimed, and disappeared into the woods.

Gaela looked after him with her hands on her hips. She was too dizzy to run after him. In fact, she was just a little offended that he could run like that after a kiss like *that*. But he'd hear from her later. Of all the nerve! She thought he'd gotten over pulling those disappearing acts.

She puttered around in the garden, waiting for Adam to appear and explain himself, but he didn't. When she found him later at the house, he was distracted and absent-minded.

Finally he said, "Listen, I have to go somewhere. I may be gone for a few days, so don't go getting scared. I'll be back."

And he kissed her and disappeared *again*.

Chapter Twenty-four

The day after Adam left, Gaela climbed to the top of the boulder that pushed out into the lake. She missed him with an ache that was frightening. She had known the man seven months. And for half that time, she'd been afraid of him! Now it seemed she couldn't live without him. She wondered if he felt the same way. She knew he had strong feelings for her. He had even said he loved her, although she'd said it first. But in all this confusion and uncertainty, romance was taking a back seat, and she couldn't help wondering where, in fact, it was going. She and Adam had been through so much, and, honestly, she had to admit they were both damaged people. Was she crazy to think they could find true happiness together? Did he even want to? Or was he just attached to her because she came with the territory, so to speak? The garden pixie.

No, she knew it was more than that. She sighed and asked God for patience. Again. Right away, she added with a smile. For someone who valued security more than almost anything else in life, it was terrifying to live with an axe hanging over her head, never knowing what the future held.

"My Father/Mother God has a plan, and it's a good one. He/she knows what's going on," she reminded herself for the hundredth time. Funny, these days it was Adam who helped her keep the faith. He was so calmly able to accept whatever was dished out next. He had told her not to envy him, but she did.

The next day she happened to be in the house when the phone rang, so she picked it up. "Eden's Gate, Gaela Clancy speaking."

"Ms. Clancy, hello. My name is LuEllen Meade. Is Mr. Sullivan in?"

"No, I'm sorry, he's away just now."

"Am I correct in thinking you are the head caretaker at Eden's Gate?"

These days, she was the only caretaker, but she answered politely, "Yes. May I help you?"

"I am hoping I may be able to help *you*, Ms. Clancy. I understand there is trouble in paradise, so to speak." And the woman laughed lightly at her own joke. Gaela wasn't sure whether to laugh or not. "Let me get right to the point. I have been told that the new owner of Eden's Gate and that young man who plays the recorder so delightfully are one and the same."

"Yes," Gaela said hesitantly. What on earth was this woman getting at?

"I would like to suggest a benefit concert for Eden's Gate. I believe I could easily promise a hundred people, at one hundred dollars a head. There may well be more."

Gaela couldn't speak.

"I was there on several occasions this summer, and I heard Mr. Sullivan. I assure you, he is a world class musician. And I have contacts, Ms. Clancy. What do you say?"

"Well, uh, I don't know what to say, quite honestly! Mr. Sullivan, as I said, is not here to ask, but I think he might be interested. What exactly did you have in mind?"

"Quite simple. We set a date, have a short reception in the house, bring in a caterer with some *hors d'ouvres* and drinks, and then Mr. Sullivan delights us all with a concert of music of his choice. All proceeds go to benefit Eden's Gate."

Gaela was breathless. "We don't have the money for a caterer . . ."

"Oh, you leave all that to me. I believe I know a service who would donate their time if we pay for the food. We'll take care of everything."

"Well, I think it's a wonderful idea, Ms. Meade. But I can't say with certainty, of course, until I speak with Mr. Sullivan. May I have a number at which you may be reached?"

Gaela had hardly put down the phone when it rang again. "Eden's Gate? This is the post office. We have a whole bag of mail here for you. Will someone be there if we bring it out now?"

"Uh, yes, sure."

What on earth was going on?

She met the truck in the parking lot, and brought in, not a whole bag of mail, but a sturdy stack, too much to fit in the oversize box. She hauled it into the office and began to open it. Then she began to cry.

For the past several weeks, it had seemed as if troubles were pouring down on Eden from a never ending supply. Now, blessings seemed to be pouring nearly as thick and fast. If only Adam were here!

The stack of mail was all from supporters of Eden's Gate They were mostly local, but there were some from other states as well. All expressed appreciation and concern, and most sent money. Not much, it was true, five to twenty dollars, mostly. It was the thought behind it that made Gaela cry. When she had come to Eden, it was because she needed what it had to offer. Over the years, her goal had grown to include a desire to share what it had to offer with others. Piled on her desk was the evidence that that goal had succeeded.

Ted and Ivy came that evening, and Gaela hurried them inside to see. "Four hundred and seventy-five dollars! Ms. Crandall says we ought to open a special bank account, and call it a benefit fund, or something. There may be more." Then she told them about the call from Ms. Meade. Ivy cried, too.

"But will it be enough?" asked Ted.

"I have no idea. I just think it's wonderful, either way. I wish Adam would get back. He didn't give me the slightest idea where he went or why."

A whole week passed before Adam finally returned. In that time, almost $2,000 had come into the Eden's Gate Benefit Fund. Lillian and Gaela were taking turns staying in the house to answer the phone.

They kept meticulous records, because Gaela was afraid the place would still have to be sold, and all the money would have to go back where it came from. It was a very minor drop in the ocean of their need. As soon as Adam returned, she was going to suggest he give an interview to the paper, thanking everyone.

She was cleaning leaves out of the beds near the woods when she heard a car pull into the small lot by the workshop. She looked up to see which of her volunteer crew had shown up this time, and saw two men. One came running toward her, and she dropped her rake and flew across the grass to meet him. They crashed together with a shock that knocked the breath out of both of them, but they didn't notice. Breathing wasn't necessary at the moment anyway. When they finally pulled apart, Gaela was laughing and crying at the same time.

"How could you just leave me like that? Where have you been? What took you so long?"

"It wasn't easy, I've been in Philadelphia, and it took me a while to track David down."

She remembered the presence of a second person and turned in embarrassment to see a large black man with the kindest eyes she'd ever seen, beaming on them as if their reunion had been all his idea.

"David Curtis, ma'am." He held out a large hand, and she took it. "Mm-mm," he added, shaking his head. "You weren't exaggerating, brother!"

Adam grinned, while Gaela looked an inquiry, but the only explanation he offered was, "This is my friend that I told you about, who fed me that night on the streets, and warned me that God wasn't going to give up. Let me tell you about our wonderful idea!"

"I have some pretty wonderful news myself," she informed them, "but you can go first."

So they all went to the gazebo, and Adam began excitedly explaining. "I got the idea when you talked about us getting counseling. Which I think is a good idea, by the way. I thought about how you always say all the healing anyone needs is in this garden, and how it's certainly been true for me, and all the ideas we've had to save this place, and all of a sudden, it all came together!" He had to stop for breath. "Wouldn't it be great if we had a retreat center here? A place where people could come for peace and healing in a more formal way than to just visit the garden. There could be church retreats, group retreats, women's retreats, family retreats, individual retreats . . ."

"Whoa, slow down!" said Gaela. "Yes, it would be great, but how do we afford it?"

"We—David and I—think if we start small, it could pay for itself. We wouldn't do anything fancy right away. We could cook and clean ourselves, as long as the groups were small. Eventually, I'd like to have counselors here, and seminars with maybe some big name speakers, and everything, but in the beginning, it could be really simple. And another thing. For every ten paying people, we'd let one person who couldn't afford it come without charge. That's David's idea. We want to bring out inner city kids, and have parenting seminars, maybe, oh, all kinds of things."

Gaela had never seen Adam so excited. She turned to David. "And how do you fit in?"

"Well, to tell you the truth, I don't know what made Adam come haring off to get me. But I'm glad he did. I suppose the Lord told him to. I had told Adam I was waiting to see what my ministry was to be. This could be it. I used to be a psychiatrist. I can't practice anymore, and truthfully, I don't think I want to. I have better counsel now than I ever had then. But I know how things should be set up, and I still have a few contacts in the field, too. I can cook and wash dishes," he laughed, and Gaela remembered Adam telling her how comforting his rich chuckle was. "And I even know a little about gardening. I could use some more healing, myself." David took in a deep breath of fall air and looked around happily. "Mm-mm. It's a garden of Eden, all right!"

"Well, I love the idea, if we can make it work. I even know how we can get part of the money." And she told them her news, which made Adam whoop with joy and drag them inside to look at letters right away.

"Look here, some of these say they don't have money, and ask if there's any other way they could help. Couldn't we maybe get some volunteers, or something?"

"Maybe. You'd have to talk to the lawyers about the whole thing, to be sure it's done right and all bases are covered."

"And this woman, whatsername, thinks she can get $10,000 just for hearing me play the recorder?"

Gaela laughed. "Meade! LuEllen Meade! You really have to start learning the names of the benefactors in your life, Mr. Lord and Master Sullivan. That reminds me—I think music has to come into your dream retreat center somehow."

"Well, of course, that goes without saying—"

Just then the phone rang, and Gaela answered, expecting it to be another offer of money or encouragement, but it was Ms. Crandall, fairly vibrating with the first good news she'd been able to give them. Gaela hurriedly motioned to Adam to pick up another phone. "The embezzler has broken down and confessed. He's given investigators numbers to some of the bank accounts he had squirreled away, and I will be able to recover some of your money. Not a lot, mind you. And none until the trial is complete. But I think we can get the bank to carry you once we have definite numbers that will be reimbursed. Eventually, we should be able to rebuild a trust account that will take care of the bare minimum necessities of the house, if you are extremely economical."

This was cause for another whoop of joy, and then they had to tell her their plans. She was cautiously optimistic. "Come in and we'll see about the legalities, and draw up a business plan. You might get some churches to sponsor you. But I cannot overemphasize, Mr. Sullivan, that you will still be deeply in debt for some years to come. You must be exceedingly careful."

"Oh, we will, Ms. Crandall. I really think this is the plan God wanted us to find," said Adam. "And by the way, if those law offices go under, you can always be sure of a job with us. I don't know how much money you'll get, but you'll have the satisfaction of knowing you're truly needed."

Ms. Crandall gave what sounded suspiciously like a sniffle. "Thank you very much for the kind thought, Mr. Sullivan. I may just take you up on it."

"No, thank *you*, Ms. Crandall. I can't possibly express what it means to us to have you in our court."

They had hardly hung up when the phone rang again, causing a general laugh.

It was LuEllen Meade, and she not only set a date with Adam, she said she thought they could do such a thing twice a year for as long as it was needed. "And Ms. Clancy? Are you by any chance having your annual fall festival?"

"Well, we hadn't planned on it . . ."

"Plan on it, then. Put an article in the paper saying this year it will cost five dollars per person, fifteen dollars per family, and will include a recorder concert by Mr. Sullivan. Have a Christmas festival, too. Everyone in the area is on your side, Ms. Clancy."

Gaela had tears in her eyes. "Ms. Meade, may I ask how you came to know about our need and decide to help us in this unbelievably kind way?"

"Archie Williamson!"

"I beg your pardon?"

"Archie Williamson has been raising a stink, and talking about Eden and how it's going under, and he's going to make a killing—not to mention some rather unsavory comments about you and Mr. Sullivan, I regret to say. Some of us decided we were not going to stand by and see that toad get away with it."

They managed to thank her and say good-bye in a civilized way before collapsing into overwrought laughter. They laughed until tears rolled down their faces, with David looking on benevolently. "Best medicine of all," he observed. "Lot cheaper than psychotherapy, too."

Later, the whole ex-crew showed up at once, so they all had to be regaled with the new plans, offer help and suggestions, and meet David.

"Our church would back this. I'd bet on it," said Ted.

Lillian led an impromptu rendition of Amazing Grace, and they discovered David possessed a bass that could sing with the angels.

That evening, after the others had gone home and David had been installed in one of the guest rooms at the big house, Adam disappeared again.

Gaela found him sitting on a bench by the lake, staring at the water. As she watched, he put his head in his hands, and she saw his shoulders shake. She went and knelt in front of him and wrapped her arms around him so that his head was on her shoulder.

"If only," he choked.

"I know."

"All of them, all gone. My sister, my mom, my dad. My own child. A stepmother I never knew. And I had the chance. I had the chance!" He sighed heavily. "I know I'm forgiven, but that doesn't stop it hurting, does it?"

"No."

"It's not fair! So I'm forgiven. Great! But others paid the consequences, not me. Were *they* healed? I stand before God as if I'd never sinned. Do *they* stand before him as if they'd never been sinned against?"

"I don't know. But I do know that a dear friend of mine says we just have to trust him."

Suddenly, Adam grabbed Gaela in a hold so tight she thought her ribs would crack. "Gaela," he said into her hair. "Gaela. My pixie. Don't ever leave me."

She ran her hands through his hair. "I'm not going anywhere. I come with the garden, remember?"

He stood, taking her with him. "You'll mash your knees, kneeling on these stones."

She leaned back in his embrace, looking up at him. "Did I ever tell you you're the most gorgeous man it has ever been my pleasure to behold?"

He gave a startled laugh. "No, but you're welcome to your illusions. Have I ever told you you're the most adorable little pixie ever to come my way?"

She grinned and took his arm, and they walked together. "I'm the only pixie to come your way. I'll have you know all the other pixies are much more beautiful to behold than I am, but I've warned them all off. I promised dire consequences if they so much as look at you!"

"I don't believe a word of it. Oh, Gaela. I shouldn't. I can't."

His voice failed him, and she looked at him nervously. He shouldn't couldn't what? If he thought she'd let him get away now . . .!

"We've only known each other a short time. I'm so messed up. You really shouldn't even consider this. I've been fighting it for weeks, but—"

"Yes."

"What?"

"Whatever you're saying I shouldn't consider, too late. I already considered it. The answer is yes."

"Gaela—"

"You're messed up, I'm messed up. We're going to get counseling, we live in a garden. How much better odds can you get?"

"It's going to be hard."

"What is?"

"Eden. The retreat center, the money, the debts— It'll be hard for a long time." He kicked a pebble toward the water.

"Then it's a good thing we'll have each other, isn't it? And God. Did you ask him?"

"Well, I've mostly been asking him for the strength not to ask you."

Her heart was deafening her. Ask her what? It had to be what she hoped it was. It had to be. She laughed breathlessly. "His answer is no. Mine's yes."

"We couldn't get married right away. There are a lot of things to work out."

Gaela closed her eyes. Married. He'd said the word. "I know. How about spring?" At the gazebo, when the yellow roses were in bloom, or maybe at the grotto, barefoot.

"We'll have to live in your little house."

Maybe in her own tiny garden; it wouldn't be a big wedding. "You didn't think I was going to move into that great mausoleum with you, did you?"

They both spoke at the same time, but it was okay, because they both said the same thing. "I love you." Gaela discovered her fingers were digging into his arm, and relaxed them.

They realized they had reached the grotto. It was too chilly to sit inside with the waterfall anymore, but they smiled at each other in the moonlight, remembering.

Adam turned Gaela to face him. "Past time I refreshed your memories of this place, isn't it?"

His teeth gleamed in a wolfish grin, and the danger was strong in his black eyes. The softness in his voice could still give her the shivers. With one finger, he traced the outline of her lips, and then tilted her chin. He bent at the knees, and she stood on her tiptoes. For a moment, their lips, the tip of his finger on her chin, and her hands on his arms were the only things touching. Then Gaela swayed, and Adam caught her around the waist and picked her up, slanting his head and deepening the kiss. His hair blew around her face in a breeze that touched them both with blessing. He tasted of moonlight and starlight and the swish of water, happiness and home and paradise found.

Dear Reader,

I've been writing since I could hold a pencil, but I always thought I had to Grow Up and Get a Real Job. So it was quite a few years before I got to really spend any time doing what I was really created to do. Over the years I had quite a few books and lots of stories and articles published, but my heart was still longing to write novels. You've just read the first one I completed. Thank you!

The story of this book is an interesting one (to me, at least). I was going stir-crazy one late winter/early spring, and ran away to a camping cabin on the TN-GA state line, where I fulfilled a longtime dream. It started out as a challenge to myself: could I write a complete novel in a week? I could, and I did, and it was just about the most fun I'd ever had, but the surprise was how deep the issues and emotions grew over those 5 ½ days.

Reconciliation and forgiveness are over-arching themes of my whole life, it seems, and sooner or later, everything I write touches on them. I hope the pain and the healing of these two wounded souls touched your heart, especially if you, too, need some healing. It's there, I promise. Never stop reaching for it. It's not easy, but what is, that's worth having?

May the blessings of the Earthmaker be upon you.

Debbonnaire Kovacs

Discussion Group Questions

What touched you most about this story? In what ways did you or did you not relate to the characters?

Do you think there is a difference between forgiving and excusing? If yes, can you explain it?

Does forgiveness lead to worse or better behavior? Why?

When was a time you needed to be forgiven?

When was a time you needed to forgive?

Do you think there are things that cannot be forgiven? Why or why not?

Do you agree or disagree with Gaela that all forgiveness comes ultimately from God?

How do you hear the voice of the Creator?

Do you talk to flowers?

Do they talk back?

If you would like me to come and speak to your group or organization, please contact me from my website at www.debbonnaire.com. Thank you!

Made in the USA
Charleston, SC
23 October 2012